A Period of
*un*Certainty

About the Author

Sheryn Munir is a big fan of romances. After reading countless lesbian romance novels based in the West, she craved a lesfic set in her home in India. Realizing that she'd have to wait forever for that wish to come true, she decided to have a crack at writing some herself. *A Period of unCertainty* is her second novel.

Though she has been writing since the age of seven, Sheryn was only recently inspired to write an entire book in a genre close to her heart that is about her own people. When she's not cooking up fictional romances, she is a writer, editor and web developer.

She likes visiting new places, though the journeys are a tad unpleasant. She has a weakness for chocolates, Indian street foods and British television dramas. She lives in Delhi, with three laptops and an e-reader.

A Period of *un*Certainty

SHERYN MUNIR

BELLA
BOOKS
2021

Bella Books, Inc.
P.O. Box 10543
Tallahassee, FL 32302

Printed in the United States of America on acid-free paper.

First Edition - 2021

Editor: Heather Flournoy
Cover Designer: Shweta Vachani

ISBN: 978-1-64247-264-6

PUBLISHER'S NOTE

To my old roomie, and midnight chai and cheese toast companion. I wish you could've read this.

PART I

SEPTEMBER–OCTOBER 2017

CHAPTER ONE

If Leela Saldana hadn't been only half asleep, the black leather bag would have most certainly fallen on her head. Fortunately, she spotted it losing its fight with gravity from the corner of her eye and put her hands up in reflex just in time.

The elderly Sikh man sitting in the seat across the aisle from her gasped loudly. He sprang from his seat as Leela caught the bag. It was neither heavy nor as big as it had seemed when it had been bound for Leela's head. In fact, she managed a very neat catch, and held it out to its owner, who leaned across from the seat right in front of Leela, a horrified expression on her face.

"Oh, I am so very sorry," she said, grasping the bag with both hands and taking it away. "I hope you're not hurt."

"No harm done." Leela looked up, a smile on the ready to emphasise her statement.

"You okay, madam?" the man from across the aisle called out.

With the train only minutes from pulling into its final station, the chair car compartment was empty except for Leela, the manhandler of the bag, and the old gent.

"Perfectly fine," Leela assured him. He sat down, giving the other woman a disapproving look.

"I am really, really, so very sorry," the woman continued. "I just...I don't know what happened, it just slipped."

"Really, it's fine." Leela flashed her most reassuring smile. "It wasn't heavy."

"Still. It's not done, dropping your luggage on fellow passengers."

There was a disarming charm about her—Leela could acknowledge that despite the fact that she had almost dropped a bag on her head.

"I'm sure you don't make a habit of it."

Her eyes were bottomless pits that regarded Leela in relief, and there was a part of Leela that struggled to look away.

"Well, then, you're too kind," she said. Her shoulder-length hair was tied back into a ponytail with just enough strands escaping to make it appealing rather than untidy.

Though Leela appreciated a good-looking woman just as much as the next person, it wasn't just the easy charisma that made her want to continue the conversation. Something else drew her towards this one. A stirring of familiarity nudged Leela as she studied the woman looking down at her. That slight tilt of the head and the curve of the mouth... In fact, if she were perfectly honest, they reminded her of—

"Nandini?" The name escaped Leela's mouth even before she realised it.

The woman's eyes widened. Leela pulled back a bit. Had she made a mistake?

Then the woman's face cleared and her mouth fell open. "Leela?"

"Oh my God." Leela's face broke into a smile. "It really is you."

The grin was mirrored in Nandini's face, and in an instant Leela was thrown back about two decades in time. Apart from the beginnings of crow's feet at the corners of her eyes and the filled-out face, this was indeed the same Nandini she had known so well.

"Well, I'll be damned. All these years, and I drop a bag on your head."

"Almost drop a bag," Leela corrected. "You're still a klutz, I see."

"And your reflexes are still top-notch, I see."

"You trained me well. Fancy meeting you here, all the way in the back of beyond. It's good to see you."

"Likewise." Nandini's smile seemed genuine. "I thought you looked so very familiar."

Leela grew a bit warm under Nandini's probing gaze. But then, she couldn't help studying Nandini back herself. It was all rather surreal, running into an old ex—that too the only woman she had ever been involved with—in an almost empty train headed to a remote mountain town.

A throat cleared, making Leela jump. "Madam?" Leela tore her eyes away from Nandini to find the elderly gent staring at her, a bewildered expression on his face. He glanced towards Nandini and back. "Are you…Is everything all right?"

Leela flushed, feeling inexplicably like a seven-year-old caught with an empty box of chocolates. "Er, yes, thank you. I'm fine."

"Okay, then." The man turned away, back to attending to his own luggage, and Leela took a moment to gather herself.

"So, how long has it been?" she asked Nandini.

"Let's see." Nandini scrunched her face in reminiscence. "We graduated in ninety-seven, right? So, twenty years. Wow."

"Wow," Leela echoed. She gave Nandini another once-over. "You look…good." She had been going for "fantastic."

"And you…" Nandini's penetrating eyes took Leela in one more time. "You look great."

Leela was saved from blushing by the train's staticky PA system announcing their imminent arrival at their final destination, Amrudpur. She stood up, thankful of something to do, and lifted her bag from the overhead luggage rack.

"There, that's how you do it without knocking your fellow passengers out," she said with a grin.

"Ouch." Nandini winced. "Guess I deserved that."

The train stopped with a slight lurch. As they gathered their things, a handful of porters peeped into the coach, but, seeing there were less than half a dozen passengers, most of them disappeared in search of greener pastures.

"You take care, madam," the Sikh gent called as he made his way out.

"I will, thank you." Leela smiled at his retreating back.

"He doesn't trust me," Nandini whispered.

"No, I don't think he does."

She followed Nandini down the aisle, into the vestibule, and onto the platform. Out of the air-conditioned carriage, the nip of a Himalayan autumn engulfed her, the smell of clean air filling her nose. A pleasant change from inhaling the fumes of Bangalore. She pulled her hand-knit cardigan around herself. Hopefully, the warm clothes she'd brought would be enough.

Amrudpur was a sleepy little hill station, a population of under 3,500, as her cursory Google research had told her. It did have some pretensions as a tourist destination, but that was mainly due to the presence of a famous residential school called Woodfern on the outskirts of town, which drew parents during the start and end of terms, and sometimes during weekends. Woodfern was in fact what had brought Leela here: to attend a weekend conference on digital innovation in education.

As the principal of a small but exclusive school in Bangalore, Leela had minions she could pack off to gatherings like this one. But with the Dussehra holidays on, there hadn't been anyone else available this time. Anyhow, the idea of an all-expenses-paid trip to a cosy mountain town had sounded appealing enough for her to volunteer.

She cast about on the tiny two-platform station of Amrudpur trying to figure out which way to go. It didn't need much brainwork. The main road was visible just beyond the tiny hall that served as the town's railway hall.

Given the way the smattering of people who had just disembarked were looking around, trying to orientate themselves, Leela wondered if they were all conference attendees as well. She turned to Nandini.

"You wouldn't by any chance be here for the Woodfern conference tomorrow, would you?"

"I was just going to ask you that," Nandini replied. She surveyed their surroundings as well. The place was sleepy enough that even the taxi drivers seemed disinterested in the newly arrived passengers. "I would be very surprised if there were *two* exciting happenings in this town this weekend."

Leela laughed. Nandini had always had a dry sense of humour. "Where are you staying?"

"The Glen. It's supposed to be a three-hundred-metre walk from the station. The question is, in which direction?"

Leela waved her mobile phone at Nandini. "Should I check on my GPS?"

"Oh, well, I can do that too." She reached for the pocket of her jeans. Leela couldn't help noticing the excellent fit— definitely designer jeans. They were tucked into ankle-length leather boots. The grey woollen jacket that Nandini had on also fell in delicious soft pleats around her. Also noteworthy were the additional curves that Nandini had acquired since their college days.

"Where are you staying?" Nandini asked, tapping away on her phone.

Leela looked away hurriedly. "A place called Himalayan Nest. Also supposedly walking distance from the station."

"Ah, there it is," Nandini said, squinting at her phone. "And it seems to be very close to my hotel. I think we go"— she pointed over Leela's shoulder—"that way."

"Madam, taxi?" a man in a thin cotton T-shirt called out.

"No, thank you," Leela said as they stepped out onto Amrudpur's main street, pulling her little bag on wheels behind her.

Shops selling everything from kitchenware to underclothing lined both sides of the street, which was barely wide enough for two large cars to pass. The traffic, fortunately, mainly comprised two-wheelers and a throng of pedestrians. For all one knew, all of Amrudpur's 3,500 residents were outside and this was what rush hour was all about here.

"If you don't have any other plans," Nandini said as they walked through the street, dodging enthusiastic Friday-evening shoppers. "Would you like to have dinner with me? It would be great to catch up."

"Yes, I'd love that too."

Her eagerness surprised her. Never in a million years had she imagined she would run into Nandini Mirchandani again, at least not this way. Despite all the excitement between them in college, Nandini had eventually become just a footnote in Leela's otherwise quite eventful past. She didn't mean that in a mean-spirited way—just that she had always considered her Nandini chapter to have been well and truly closed.

CHAPTER TWO

"I suppose this is what passes for fancy around here," Nandini murmured as they were shown to their seats in a more ostentatious manner than the empty restaurant warranted.

The Colonial Durbar was rather quaint, even though Leela did roll her eyes at the name. But then, the faded carpet, threadbare in places, the faux colonial furniture, the dusty portraits, and the dim yellow lighting did give it an air of a room rather stuck in time. Bulky old fans on extra-long down rods lumbered round and round, purposeless in the comfortably air-conditioned space. Even the waiters, dressed in an approximation of what someone imagined to be red-and-white livery—complete with a turban—of a gentlemen's club during the Raj, appeared to be remnants from history. If she squinted, Leela could imagine British officers from a hundred years ago, ensconced in clouds of smoke, gossiping around the tables over their gin and tonics, or whatever it was they preferred to drink.

"But rumour has it," Nandini continued, "that the food here is fantastic."

Her arm brushed Leela's as they navigated the narrow spaces between tables. Leela's nose filled with her perfume— something subtle and soft, something that reminded her of blue skies and a cool breeze.

"You seem well acquainted with this town," Leela said as she settled herself in her chair.

"I know everything that Google knows about this place," Nandini replied, reaching for the menu. "Which, I admit, is not a whole lot." Tucking a strand of hair behind her ear, she opened the menu.

The waiter returned and they ordered their drinks, rum and Coke for Leela and a sauvignon blanc for Nandini.

Leela reached into her bag for her reading glasses and picked up the menu before her, though she continued her study of Nandini from the corner of her eye. Nandini's hair now hung loose in waves, just short of shoulder length, pushed behind her right ear and falling forward to frame her face on the left. She had changed from her travel clothes to a grey calf-length skirt and a pale blue blouse, worn with the same grey jacket and boots.

Leela shifted in her chair, changing her position so the curves of Nandini's calves were no longer in her field of vision. Instead, she amused herself at how Nandini had to hold the menu at arm's length and squint to read. She hadn't changed much outwardly, apart from getting a little thicker around the middle and acquiring a few lines on her face. Leela had expected a few more grey hairs, though she could wager that that reddish-brown tinge had come out of a bottle. And, yes, she was still attractive.

Yet there was something else that Leela couldn't pin down, something different about Nandini. Perhaps it was the poise with which she held herself, the confidence. Leela didn't remember that from their younger days. Perhaps it came with being older—not that she imagined herself to be poised at all. True, she had no illusions that she was the same gawky twenty-one-year-old she had been, but could she imagine herself to exude the dignified, urbane elegance that Nandini did? No way.

Leela followed the movement of Nandini's hand as she tucked another lock of hair back behind her ear. It fell back out immediately, and Nandini reached up and ran her fingers through her hair, holding it back against the back of her head, away from her eyes. Leela studied her other hand, the one turning the pages of the menu. She had small, delicate hands with slender fingers, her nails cut short but expertly shaped and polished.

"You look exactly the same and totally different," Leela said.

Nandini looked up, her eyebrows arched. Neat, slim eyebrows, clean as a pencil line. That was new too. "And you haven't changed at all. Totally random." She smiled, a smile that was more in the eyes than the mouth. Leela's pulse quickened.

"Random? Now you sound like one of my teenagers."

"One of? How many do you have?"

"Oh, about three hundred."

The waiter came back with their drinks. They ordered their food and sat back after clinking glasses.

"So," said Nandini. "What have you been doing these past twenty years?"

Leela took a sip of her drink. The Coke was flat. She made a face. "First of all, please stop saying 'twenty years.' It makes me feel old."

"Pfft, we're not old."

"There was a time we used to think forty was unbelievably past it."

"We did, didn't we?" Nandini squinted into the distance. "The forties were for the aunties and uncles."

"But it's not so bad, though, is it?"

"Oh, no. The idea of being in my twenties again is terrifying now."

That made Leela laugh. "Who would have thought back then, huh?" She ran her finger down her glass, leaving a trail between the condensation beads. *Twenty years. Where had they gone?*

"So, you are the principal of a school?" Nandini broke into her thoughts.

"Yes, it's a small private school in Bangalore."

"What's it called?"

"Hanssen Academy. Owned by a Swedish trust."

"Is it one of those alternative schools?"

"No, not at all. Just a run-of-the-mill private school for rich brats. What about you? Tell me about your start-up. What kind of software company is it?"

Nandini spread her hands. "I'm here, aren't I? I'll give you three guesses."

"Um, let's see…" Leela narrowed her eyes, turning her head up towards the ceiling. "Totally wild guess, but…educational software?"

Nandini pointed a finger at her in a got-it-in-one gesture. "Two of my friends and I set up Discover-E about five years ago after we all quit Google together. The edu software scene is so tediously boring. We wanted to shake things up."

"You do know 'tedious' and 'boring' mean the same thing, right?" Leela ribbed.

"Nah, grammar was never my thing, you know that."

"But you always did like to take things apart and put them together in a different way. Is that what you do at Discover-E?"

"Something like that." Nandini tilted her head, seeming to accept the compliment between the lines. "So, um, you got married, right?"

Leela looked at her rum and Coke. Ah, there it was, that question. It was good that it had made an appearance so early in the evening. Now they could talk about it, get it out of the way, and enjoy the rest of their time together. "Yes, I did."

"Sorry I couldn't make it—I did get the invite."

Leela had to smile. "I wasn't really expecting you to show up, Nandini." She looked up and her stomach did a flip as she caught Nandini smiling too, though she was looking at her drink, not at Leela.

"I was quite heartbroken when I got the card. I know we had split up, but still. It was…" She shook her head and her recalcitrant hair fell over her ear again. She tucked it back one more time. "I can't quite recall what it was." She gave a little laugh. "It doesn't seem that dramatic anymore."

"I know."

"How did you two meet?"

"Kiran and I? We didn't, our parents did."

Nandini's eyebrows rose. "Oh, so you weren't swept off your feet?" There was a twinkle in her eye.

"Oh, come off it. I told you it was an arranged match."

"You said something quite odd, I still remember. That you couldn't find a reason to say no."

Leela nodded. "That's exactly how it was. My parents had been parading all these men before me, and then demanding to know why I was rejecting all of them, what was wrong with them. I ran out of reasons in the end, and also it was exhausting arguing with them all the time."

"And so you married Kiran Robinson because you were tired of arguing with your parents?"

"We-ell." Leela scratched an eyebrow. "It helped that he looked like Tom Cruise from one angle. That is, if you made him take off his glasses and put up one hand to block his receding hairline."

Nandini threw her head back and laughed. "If he looked like Tom Cruise, that's fine then." She looked at Leela, suddenly serious. "Did he make you happy? Are you happy?"

Leela nodded. She smiled, though her heart clenched. She swallowed. "He did. We were very happy."

Nandini's eyes narrowed. "Were?"

"Kiran passed away—it's been almost ten years."

"Oh my goodness, Leela. I had no idea. I'm so sorry."

"Thanks, it's okay. I mean, it's been a long time."

"Wow." Nandini exhaled. "And…heck, I'm not even sure what to ask. Did you have any kids?"

"One. Neil. He's sixteen."

"Wow," Nandini said again. "You, a mother, a single mother? Oh, sorry, I shouldn't assume—are you?"

Leela sighed. "Single? Yeah. Neil was quite small when Kiran died. Somehow, I never had time for anything apart from making sure we didn't fall to pieces. It's hard to imagine that it's been such a long time."

Nandini sipped her drink faster than she had been so far. Leela knew how it went. Chances were she was struggling to find something to say. The script never changed. When people found out Leela was a widow, they seemed to need to say something appropriate, something soothing and not inconsiderate. Something just right. It made her impatient. Everyone had their histories. This was hers, but it didn't make her a freak.

Their food arrived—naan and butter chicken for Leela, and a vegetarian sizzler steak for Nandini. Google had been right; it was very good, so she was happy to tuck in. They ate in silence.

"I suppose you never stop missing them, do you?" Nandini said.

"Pardon?"

"Sorry, it's just that…I mean, I can't imagine what it's like when your partner dies."

Leela put the piece of naan she was holding back on her plate. Maybe she had been a bit hasty in judging Nandini. "The missing just becomes a part of you. It's not so bad."

Nandini nodded, not attempting to respond. Then, partly to change the subject, though more because she was genuinely curious, Leela asked, "What about you? Are you…Is there anyone?"

Nandini shook her head as she swallowed her mouthful. She took a drink from her glass of water. "There was someone. It was a long time ago. We were together for three years, but"— she shrugged—"we wanted different things. I guess footloose and fancy-free is how I like it. There have been a few women now and again, but nothing long term."

"Never men, huh?"

"No, never."

"No pressure from parents to get hitched?"

"I think they've given up. They're too old and infirm now to worry about anything other than their own health. My brother has his, well, let's say, his suspicions. He studiously avoids talking to me about personal stuff."

Leela made a face. "So nothing's changed since we were young, then?"

"Oh, I wouldn't say that. Twenty years ago, a single woman in her forties would have stuck out like a sore thumb. Not so anymore."

"You think so?" Leela picked up a slice of cucumber. "My parents have never forgiven me for not marrying again."

"Really?"

"Mm-hmm. They feel I've cheated Neil out of a father figure, plus I don't have anyone to look after me in my old age."

Nandini shook her head. "Your parents don't seem to have changed a bit either."

"Yes, well, they have always been a bit conventional. But they've also been very supportive. After Kiran's death." Her defensiveness surprised her considering her parents drove her up the proverbial wall at the best of times.

"I'm glad they were there for you. Are they still in Bangalore?"

"Still in the same house, if you remember it." Leela grinned. "They were always so suspicious of you. They thought you were *such* a bad influence on me."

"If only they knew," Nandini said, a gleam in her eye, "what a terrible influence you were on *me*."

"I was, wasn't I?"

"Oh absolutely."

A warmth crept up Leela's body. Nandini's gaze was turned down to her own plate, though a small smile played at her lips. Leela smiled herself, giving her eyes permission to graze along Nandini's shoulders and the rise of her breasts against the pale blue cotton blouse. For a fleeting moment, she wondered what she might look like underneath.

The stirring deep and low in her stomach made her heart race. She looked down at the piece of chicken leg on her plate.

"What were the chances, do you think," Nandini began, the pitch of her voice a notch lower, "that we'd meet again here, like this?"

Leela's throat was dry. "You mean, twenty years later, both of us single, in a little town so far removed from our lives?"

The alcohol hummed in Leela's veins. She looked up to meet that mesmerising gaze, those eyes so deep that she was afraid she'd fall in.

"How is the food, ma'am?"

Leela jumped at their waiter's raspy voice, as good as a dash of cold water.

"Um…lovely, it's great," she managed.

Her ears burning, Leela turned back to her food. The tender, spiced chicken leg tasted like cardboard now. It caught in her throat when she swallowed. She had an uncanny sense that Nandini was looking at her but didn't dare check right away. Finally, she pulled her eyes up across the table, to Nandini's hand, along her wrist and arm, her shoulder, and finally reached her face.

Nandini's gaze skimmed up Leela's torso, lingering somewhere in the region of her throat, then slowly progressing to her chin, her mouth, and finally resting on her eyes.

Their eyes locked—and held. Nandini's unabashed acknowledgement of scrutinising Leela's body sent currents of thrill down her. Leela felt like it had been set alight from the inside.

"So…you were saying." Nandini's voice came out hoarse. She cleared her throat. "About the chances…of being here."

"I think…" Leela paused. "I think that anything could happen." Another pause. Her heart was in her mouth as she added, "Don't you?"

CHAPTER THREE

Unlocking the door to her room, Leela stepped aside to let Nandini enter first. Her heart fluttered like a panic-stricken bird in a cage too small. She turned around and shut the door much more slowly than she needed to.

Yet slowing down, allowing time to talk herself out of what she was doing was the last thing she wanted. They had history, her brain said. But the far more overpowering desire pulsing between her legs couldn't care less.

She turned. Nandini was—once again—watching her. Moments passed as they silently gazed at each other. Nandini's eyes were like two pieces of brilliant, black coal that seemed ready to ignite at any moment. All at once, Leela's throat felt very dry.

Without breaking the simmering connection between their eyes, Nandini slowly walked towards Leela. She stopped when she was just a hair's breadth away. Leela's heart beat a furious tattoo, like an endless parade of soldiers on Republic Day.

Nandini reached out her hand and gently touched the side of Leela's forehead with the back of her fingers, trailing them down to linger under Leela's chin. Heat rose up Leela's body and she met the blaze in Nandini's eyes with her own. All rational thought banished from her mind, she gripped the back of Nandini's head and pressed her lips to hers. The soft urgency of Nandini's mouth and her hands circling Leela's waist drew her in. Leela's arms moved down to wrap themselves around the warmth of Nandini's back. She leaned into Nandini. She had missed this, all that yielding softness and smooth skin of being with a woman.

"Is this okay?" Nandini pulled back just slightly so her whispered words were spoken against Leela's lips. It sent tingles along Leela's nerve endings. She closed the distance between them to feel the crush of those lips against hers again.

Nandini seemed to have got the message, as Leela felt a tug on her kurta. She obliged, letting Nandini pull off the garment. The brush of Nandini's knuckles on bare skin made Leela shiver. She unbuttoned Nandini's shirt with fumbling, urgent fingers and pushed it off her shoulders. Short work was made of Nandini's skirt and her own jeans, along with the rest of their clothing.

Leela took a step back and regarded Nandini. She did not know this body or the person it belonged to. If her memory served her right, young Nandini had been lankier than the deliciously curvaceous woman who stood before her now. Age had been more than kind to Nandini. Her breasts were fuller and sagged a bit, just like Leela's; there was more muscle on her thighs and arms; and she had a slight paunch. Leela's stomach did a flip at the prospect of tracing the contours of Nandini's figure with her tongue. As she let her gaze travel slowly up to Nandini's face, she found that almost-black, all-consuming gaze scanning her just as hungrily. Waves of desire thrummed down her body, threatening to sweep her away.

With a silent consent the women moved towards the bed, Leela letting Nandini guide her till she felt the back of her legs hit the bed. She lay down on the bed, pulling Nandini with her.

"You're stunning," Nandini whispered as she nibbled on Leela's ear, her hot breath tickling Leela.

"You're not too bad yourself." Leela ran her fingers down the side of Nandini's breast, her thumb flicking over the hardened nipple.

Nandini grazed her tongue up Leela's throat. She shifted on top of Leela, her hands meandering slowly over Leela's body. Every one of Leela's cells quivered at the touch. Parts of her she hadn't even known were asleep woke up, ravenous for more of that tormenting touch. Oh how she'd missed this. Touching someone. Being touched by them. Sex. She wanted more. So much more.

Leela shifted down under Nandini and took one breast in her mouth, causing Nandini to arch her back in pleasure. She rolled her tongue around Nandini's nipple, feeling its paradoxically soft and rough texture at once. She sucked and licked each breast in turn, harder and deeper, again and again, feeling like she would never get enough.

Then Nandini cupped her face in her hands and brought their mouths together for another sensual dance that reacquainted Leela with a long-forgotten sea of sensations.

Nandini broke away and started her journey downwards, dropping butterfly kisses on Leela's torso along the way. Moments later, Leela felt Nandini's breath teasing its way around her sex. She moaned and lifted her hips to give Nandini better access.

As Nandini's mouth pressed on her clit, Leela pulled in a quick breath. The movement of the tongue against her, slow and languorous at first, skillfully nudged Leela towards the edge of insensibility. Just when Leela thought she couldn't handle the exquisite torment anymore, it picked up speed. And Leela was lost. She grasped the bed sheet as Nandini's masterful tongue led her to a crescendo of brilliant tremors.

When she caught her breath again, Leela pulled Nandini up on top of her. "You're still good at that," she managed to gasp, her body still humming from the remnants of her orgasm.

"Ah, so you remember," Nandini responded.

Leela laughed. They lay side by side in silence for a few moments, so close that she felt each breath of Nandini's whispering across her face. Then Leela tipped Nandini on to her back and straddled her, sitting on her thighs, hands on Nandini's shoulders.

"My turn now to take you to the moon and back," Leela whispered and slipped down between Nandini's legs.

Nandini inhaled loudly as Leela dipped her hand into Nandini's wet folds and arched her head back.

"I remember what you like," Leela murmured as her two fingers slipped smoothly inside Nandini, making her moan. "Do you still like it?"

"Mmm," Nandini whimpered.

Leela took that as assent and slid down between Nandini's legs again.

Nandini gasped as Leela's tongue hit her clit. The duet of mouth and fingers brought Nandini's orgasm within moments. Leela stayed with her till it was over.

* * *

Leela unbraided her hair and shook it out. Picking up her comb, she began her daily morning ritual of brushing it down. The mirror caught a small smile at the corner of her mouth. Her hand, the one holding the comb, dropped as she studied her face. The person who looked back at her was almost a stranger. When was the last time she'd seen herself look so carefree?

She pulled out the slightly wobbly, antique padded stool that nestled in the recess under the dressing table and sat on it, leaning forward to take a closer look at herself.

She had actually done it. Had a one-night stand with Nandini Mirchandani, blast from the past. Unthinkable.

Forget the impromptu—and fantastic—sex; how long had it been since she'd spent an entire evening in the company of a friend, laughing and reminiscing without a care in the world? With no thought about needing to call home to check in on Neil or worry about the recriminations from her parents if she was late?

At one time, she had been quite the party girl, though after having Neil she'd had to seriously curtail her socialising. But it was Kiran's death that had made her completely withdraw into herself, and she had lost touch with quite a few of her old friends. It was only in the last few years that Leela had started entertaining again, but now they were mainly people she knew from work—unless it was family, of course, but that was different. Except for Davi, one of her closest friends, there was no one else who had known her in her breezy, happy-go-lucky days.

But running into Nandini, even leaving aside their instant attraction, had brought back memories of a different life, a different time. It didn't mean that Leela yearned to turn the clock back, just that it had been refreshing to meet someone who hadn't been involved with the dark bits of her life. Being able to tell her own story to Nandini, who hadn't been witness to the last ten years, had not only been liberating for Leela but also given her control over what had been the most difficult time of her life.

A light flashed on her bed. Her phone half hidden under her pillow was blinking—the missed-call indicator. She reached across and picked it up. Three missed calls, all from her parents' landline number, and all from the previous night. Her shoulders tensed, the knots in the back of her neck re-forming and tightening. It almost felt like the frown lines on her forehead were etching themselves deeper.

A tight knob of irritation rose in her chest, warring against the tremulous film of worry that welled each time she saw her parents' number flash at night on her mobile.

Just one night. Can't you leave me alone for just one night?

But what if something is wrong? What if something had gone wrong and I wasn't there? I didn't even check my phone.

But surely they would have called the hotel if she wasn't answering her phone.

What if it was about Neil?

Leela sighed. She wasn't going to win this argument with herself. Though this wasn't going to add to her joy, she had no option but to call back. Her thumb pressed the dial button.

"Hello, Ma. You called?"

"Hello? Oh, Leelu. Where were you?" her mother wailed up at her across the airwaves. "I called and called."

"I'm at a conference. I told you I had a dinner." Her ears burned. But she wasn't lying, was she? In any case, it wasn't as though she could tell her mother the whole truth.

"I am always amazed how you can go away without a care in the world."

Leela steeled herself to keep from snapping back. "Ma, is there a problem?" she asked. She imagined a red-skinned little version of herself with a pointy tail and horns sitting on her shoulder singing "I told you so" in an irritating sing-song voice.

"You didn't tell me that Neil has a test on Monday. Your father is so worried—that boy hasn't studied at all. He was on the computer all evening yesterday."

"Neil is sixteen years old, he can take care of his tests himself."

"This is not right, Leelu, going away at a time like this—"

"Is there anything else?"

"No, I…your father—"

"All right, Ma, I have to go now."

"You are coming back tomorrow, no?"

The little devil on her shoulder must have poked her with her pitchfork, for instead of confirming that she was, Leela said, "Let's see. I might decide to stay an extra day. I'll let you know. Bye."

She disconnected the call and threw the phone back on the bed. She squeezed her eyes tight, wishing she could be a teenager again, when it had been so easy to be blisteringly rude to one's parents. She shook her head. At least Neil wasn't like that. Which meant, whatever her parents thought, she hadn't done a bad job raising him.

She reached for the phone again, and this time she messaged Neil:

All ok?

Her phone pinged in under thirty seconds. These millennials—it was like their fingers were manufactured especially for texting.

All ok but grnma drving me nuts
A second text followed:
U bk tm?
Leela sighed. Of course she was going to be back. She was about to text back in the affirmative when the phone pinged again.
I have 2 go 2 chrch alone w her tmrw :'-(
She smiled.
When you go, don't forget to ask to be blessed with some vowels.
Neil's response was an emoji of a face with a wink and a tongue sticking out.

CHAPTER FOUR

As a teenager, Leela thought the acid test of the ultimate romance was the meeting of eyes from afar: two lovers finding each other in an instant across a room full of other people, and when those inconsequential others melted away into oblivion, the starstruck twosome was left in their own private universe.

The blame for her impressionable mind to have been filled with such thoughts could be laid squarely at the door of her Lesley Aunty, her mother's older sister. By day, Professor Lesley Prabhu peddled the intricacies of metre and rhythm in the works of the great poets of yore to her Bangalore University students. But when night fell, you were likely to find her curled up on her sofa with a romance novel in her hands and a glass by her side holding what young Leela had imagined was a tiny amount of apple juice with a lot of ice in it. Single malt whiskey was Lesley Aunty's second love, but Leela wasn't to know that till much later.

Anyhow, her aunt had an enviable collection of Mills and Boons, a library big enough to cover one entire wall of her bedroom. It was also arranged according to colour, giving the wall a vibrant rainbow effect. She was well into her twenties when Leela had comprehended the irony of that.

Be that as it may, she had spent many happy afternoons and weekends at Lesley Aunty's place, devouring her Mills and Boons systematically from the top left corner to the bottom right. Her favourites had been those in which she could immerse herself, imagining that she was in the story. Strangely enough, she had found that in quite a few instances she replaced the man in her mental playacting so she could pursue the woman. The significance of this switching of sides had also taken her a few more years to appreciate.

That morning in Amrudpur, when Leela took a deep breath outside the door of the auditorium at Woodfern School, she was reminded of her teenage obsession, which did nothing to dilute her nervousness at having to face Nandini. Not that she expected any such instantaneous meeting of eyes over strangers—or that a one-night stand equated with true love or any of that nonsense. She did, however, wonder what she would feel when she saw Nandini or came face-to-face with her the first time.

Would the attraction that had taken hold of her last night still be there, or would it have disappeared after having its call answered? Leela had a strong suspicion it was the former, if the butterflies in her stomach were anything to go by. She took a few extra moments to straighten her starched cotton sari and hitched her bag higher on her shoulder. *Be professional,* she told herself. Then, with a deep breath, she reached for the handle that instructed her to push.

The small lobby milled with people. There were tables covered in spotless white cloths on which tea, coffee, and a selection of biscuits, cakes, and savoury snacks were laid out. If she had expected her radar to zone in on Nandini automatically, it didn't happen, of course. Instead, she scanned the room to see if she could spot Nandini, but there were far too many people packed into it. The twinge of disappointment that touched her was proof that she was, indeed, looking forward to seeing Nandini again.

She got her name tag lanyard from the registration table by the door, a blue ribbon with a laminated plastic card with her name written in fancy calligraphy. She hated wearing name tags, so she stuffed it into her bag and went to get herself some coffee and a slice of cake. To her relief, she saw a few familiar faces at the coffee line and soon found herself drawn into the inevitable conversation about how long it had been since they had last met, and which conference it had been, and where.

* * *

Leela spotted Nandini the moment she stepped into the auditorium, not because of any magical meeting of eyes, but because the speakers were all gathered together in front of the stage, being addressed by one of the organisers.

She stopped in her tracks. Her old friend exuded the same elegant composure of the previous day. The only difference was, today she had the effect of taking Leela's heartbeat up a notch.

Nandini wasn't looking in her direction, which gave Leela all the time in the world to study her and appreciate how breathtaking she looked in her black trousers and flowy, silky, off-white blouse. A small, dark pendant, the details of which she was too far away to make out, lay in the hollow below Nandini's throat. Low-heeled boots completed her ensemble. Everything was simple and understated, but taken together, Nandini seemed to have been put together by a master artist.

Hanging from her shoulder was a laptop bag, definitely one of those high-end types. Her fingers grasped the strap near her shoulder, light glinting off the ring she wore. Leela had a flashback of those fingers trailing down her body, exploring every tiny bit of her last night, the images so lucid and real that for a moment she almost reeled. *Yep. Definitely attraction, alive and present.*

Someone touched her arm. "Leela, shall we sit there?"

She jumped. Ripping her eyes away from Nandini, her face flushed and her body feeling like it was aflame, she followed Sudha Kumar, one of the old acquaintances she had just met, to a seat deep in the middle of a row well back from the front. She set her things on the floor and concentrated fiercely on memorising the brochure the registration desk had provided her. *Time to focus on work, Saldana.*

Soon, there was a crackle of microphone. Leela looked up. The speakers had settled in the first two rows of the auditorium—Nandini was in the front—and someone from the host school was at the podium.

"Ladies and gentlemen," she began, prompting Leela to note that there were a grand total of three men out of the forty or so educators gathered for the event. "Welcome to our first Transmedia in Education conference. This year's theme is 'The Future is Digital.' I would now like to ask our principal, Ms. Sunaina Bakshi, to say a few words."

After the principal's welcome speech, an inconsequential one filled with predictable platitudes about the changing face of education, came the keynote speaker, a shiny-headed man of indeterminate age who professed to be a transmedia expert and had been in education for decades. But after five minutes of listening to him go on about how textbooks would be redundant in five years, Leela dismissed him as a blithering idiot and went back to rereading the brochure.

The presentations weren't bad, though. Leela knew that Nandini was going to present too, and while she had mentioned in passing the kind of work they did with schools, Leela was keen to know details. The first three speakers were all peddling various kinds of apps to aid learning. They were intriguing— Leela was always being newly fascinated by what technology could do—but nothing that she hadn't heard of before.

"I could have googled this," she murmured to Sudha.

"We tried that app in our school in Chennai," her companion said. "But it's too expensive and we couldn't scale up."

A break was announced, and Leela sighed with relief.

"You want something to drink? I'll pop out and get it while you keep our seats," she told Sudha.

"Yes, please. A black tea with no sugar."

"Coming up."

Leela followed the crowd out into the lobby. Her antennae were out for Nandini, but she seemed to have disappeared again.

She headed towards the hot beverages table and poured a cup of coffee for herself. She turned when she felt a tap on her shoulder, which brought her face-to-face with Nandini.

"Just stopping by to say a quick hello," said Nandini.

"Er…hello," mumbled Leela as her traitorous pulse quickened.

"Listen." Nandini touched her elbow lightly. She leaned in closer. "Just wanted to check that we're okay."

Nandini was close enough that Leela could feel the heat from her body. Her heart took on a raging beat of several bass drums. She did a quick sweep of the room to see if anyone was watching. Of course, nobody was—they were all too busy getting their own beverages.

"Okay? Of course. Why wouldn't we be?" She turned towards Nandini, her eyes alighting almost immediately on her lips. Warmth rose in her face, and she glanced down quickly. Which was a bit of a mistake, because now she was looking at that place below Nandini's throat, just under the dark crimson pendant, where the edges of her blouse came together at the top of the rise of her breasts.

"Careful," Nandini said.

Leela jumped, mortified. Then she was startled anew as fingers brushed against her hand and the coffee cup was taken away from her and put on the table. She averted her gaze as she took half a step back and composed herself, some amount of relief washing over her that it had been the teetering coffee cup Nandini had been referring to.

Nandini, meanwhile, continued to speak, her voice low. "After last night…I mean, I don't want things to be awkward between us."

"Awkward? Of course not." Leela attempted a laugh, but it came off a bit off-kilter.

"Are you sure?"

"Absolutely."

"Good, good." Nandini glanced behind, where people were filing back inside the auditorium. "I have to go now. I'm the next presenter." She started to walk away, then turned towards Leela. "See you later."

Nandini stood there waiting for an answer. It took Leela a moment to grasp that she had meant those three words as a question.

"Yes, of course," Leela replied, a slight tingle racing down her spine.

Nandini smiled and nodded, then headed off in the direction of the auditorium.

CHAPTER FIVE

"You didn't get anything for yourself?" Sudha asked.

"No, I didn't feel like it." It was a lie; she had forgotten her coffee on the table, and the reason for that was now on stage, setting up her presentation.

If Leela had thought she would struggle to concentrate during Nandini's session, she had been right and wrong. At first, her head seemed to be at sixes and sevens, but not for long. Despite herself, the presentation soon drew Leela in.

"The trouble with our education system," Nandini said, "is that the right hand doesn't talk to the left. So children are learning algebra and geometry on the one hand and Ancient Egypt and pyramids on the other, with no clue about the connection that exists between them."

She paused and let the audience titter. She was a good speaker, Leela noted, the kind who could engage the audience rather than make them feel they were being talked down to.

"The problem is, the education programme is designed to see each subject as a separate entity. So, as kids, when we closed our English textbook and opened our geography textbook, we were inadvertently being trained to shut one part of our minds and open another. Of course, we survived, passed our board exams, went to college, and today we manage to keep the world running. Just about." More laughter. "But what we were taught was to pass exams, not to understand the world.

"Fortunately, today, we are beginning to realise the importance of holistic education, the importance of seeing what children study not as disparate units, but as a whole. Though, from a practical perspective, what does that mean? How can we design a comprehensive education programme without overhauling the entire system? Is it even feasible? How are teachers expected to implement a brand-new education programme they may have no part in creating?

"I don't have all the answers, but I do know one thing—technology can help. And that is exactly what we at Discover-E are attempting to do. We won't offer you a fully developed app, with X, Y, or Z learning outcomes that you just have to load onto your school's computer network and click an icon to start. In fact, we take it one step back. What we offer, instead, is a shell that you—teachers—use to *design* your own programme. So *you* decide the outcomes, *you* decide the subject matter, *you* decide how you want to adapt it to your own curriculum.

"I will take you through a simulation in a moment, which will give you a clearer idea of how it works. Before I do that, I want to reiterate that this isn't an out-of-the-box solution. In fact, you have to do most of the hard work yourself, tailor the system to give you what you want. Whether you want your students to learn from worksheets or augmented reality—that's up to you. The process of setting up the programme for each particular school and the training of teachers is a simultaneous process. Actually, I lie. We don't even set anything up for you, we make you do it all instead—and bill you for it." A pause for the laughter to die down. "It's a comprehensive programme. It can be six months or longer, where learning outcomes and lesson plans are drawn up and integrated into the system. And even after that, there are continuous follow-ups. Most of the schools we've worked with have taken years to figure out exactly what they want, and they are still tweaking their systems. And that's fine, because that's how this is set up—to help you teach in the way that you want to, and in a way that can change and adapt even as we adjust and refine the software from our end too.

"I think all this will become clearer once I show you the simulation. Can you get the lights, please?"

When Nandini's presentation finished, the auditorium was agog with questions, so much so that the organisers had to finally request that Nandini speak to people individually offstage as there were other presenters and little time.

"That was quite interesting, don't you think?" Sudha asked.

"Definitely."

"I'm sure I can convince my school to cough up for a trial run."

"Yes, I think it might be worth it." Leela, too, would talk to her colleagues back in Bangalore to see what they thought and then take it to the school board.

They broke for lunch soon after, and Leela was drawn into an animated discussion about how to keep school libraries relevant in the digital age. On the other side of the room, Nandini chatted with a bunch of people. She caught Leela's eye once and they smiled at each other. There were more presentations, a tea break, and then a panel discussion. When the final session ended, it was almost 7:30 p.m. A dinner had been scheduled for all the speakers and participants, but Leela was exhausted. She was saturated with conversations on the sad state of the education system and the pat solutions that self-proclaimed experts had to offer.

People were filing out of the auditorium, and in front of the stage Nandini was still surrounded by people.

Turning to Sudha, Leela said, "You go ahead, I'll catch up."

"Okay."

Allowing herself the pleasure of checking out Nandini unobserved once again, she sat down and waited for her to finish. Why was it so hard to look away from her? When Nandini was finally alone, except for a nervous young volunteer from the organising team, Leela went up to her.

"There you are," Nandini said, glancing at Leela as she approached. She picked up her bag from the floor. "I wondered if you'd already left."

"You were quite in demand," Leela said. "It was a great presentation."

"Was it? Thank you."

"You're welcome. Think you'll get much business?"

Nandini shrugged. "These kind of events are hard to call. Lots of interest, but few people follow up."

"I might be able to scrounge up a budget. Do you think you could draw up some figures for me?"

"Glad to." Nandini smiled at her.

Leela held her gaze for a moment and smiled back. "Listen, do you want to skip out on the dinner?"

"Ooh, still as rebellious as ever, I see."

Leela could feel the colour rising in her cheeks. She was very glad that her dark skin made her immune to public blushing. "Is that a yes?"

"Back to the Colonial Durbar, or room service?"

Leela paused. "I think I'll take my chances with room service." Her heart leapt into overdrive. She wasn't unaware of the possible implication of what she had just suggested.

From the slight hesitation on Nandini's part, it was clear she knew it too. But she smiled and nodded. "Let's go back to mine." She lowered her voice. "But first we'll have to ditch my fan club."

"I hope I'm not taking you away from potential clients."

"You're not. If I have to explain Discover-E to one more person all over again, I'm going to scream."

* * *

The volunteer seemed rather miffed that Leela and Nandini had decided to go back into town, almost as though it was a personal snub. However, she insisted on seeing them off to one of the Jeeps provided by the school to ferry them to and from the town.

As they rolled down the winding mountain roads in the direction of Amrudpur town, conversation died down and the heaviness of anticipation filled the air. By the time Nandini was unlocking her door, Leela wasn't even sure if dinner was still on the agenda. To be perfectly honest, it was the last thing she was interested in herself.

Nandini's hotel was a four star, the fanciest this town had. The room contained a king-size bed and a sitting area. It was all spick and span, and looked very modern—nothing like the heritage guest house Leela was staying in.

"Make yourself at home." Nandini waved towards the sofa. "Do you want something? Water, drink?"

"Some water, please." Leela's throat was dry. She removed the pashmina shawl draped around her shoulders. How could she be feeling hot in this weather?

"Sure."

Nandini poured a glass of water and brought it across, sitting next to Leela as she handed it over. Leela took a sip, but suddenly, she couldn't swallow. She set the glass down, well aware that Nandini's eyes had never left her. It was as unnerving as it was thrilling.

"Leela…" Nandini's voice was quiet. From the corner of her vision, Leela could tell that she had turned away and was looking at the table in front of them. Nandini cleared her throat. "What we're doing—"

"I lied," Leela interrupted. "It was a bit awkward."

Nandini gave a soft, almost embarrassed laugh. "Yes, well, that it was."

"It's just that…" Leela hesitated. "I don't make it a habit of doing…this."

"Do you regret it, Leela?"

That was the second time Nandini had said her name in this short conversation, and the second time it had made her shiver. She turned towards Nandini.

"Oh my God, no," she said. And she didn't. In fact, she couldn't remember the last time she had felt so alive. Just the memory of Nandini's hand on her skin, even now, was enough to make her senseless if she would let it.

"Last night was…It…"

"I know," Leela said. "It just happened."

"And when you say you don't make a habit of this…" The question hung in the air.

"What I meant was, it took me by surprise. That's all."

"So, is it safe to say what happens in Amrudpur stays in Amrudpur?"

"Something like that."

She hadn't realised how or when their faces had moved so close together. Nandini's eyes were unblinking and focused only on her. Leela's gaze dropped to her mouth, as if drawn there on its own. The lips were slightly parted, and Nandini ran her tongue over them, making them glisten. She knew in that instant that she wasn't stepping back, and neither was Nandini.

It wasn't clear who moved. The kiss was hard and crushing at first, then eased into a gentle exploration. Leela held Nandini by her waist, her hands slipping over the soft material that promised the warmth of skin underneath. She could feel Nandini's hand by the side of her neck, pushing her sari off her shoulder, fingers dipping a few centimetres into the material of the blouse on her shoulder. Her other hand lay on her waist, cool against her warm, bare skin.

Leela shifted back slightly on the sofa, intending to get the sari that was bunched up between them out of the way, but Nandini caught hold of her hand and pulled her up, letting the sari fall to the floor. Then she picked up the trailing end and tugged. Leela turned obligingly, allowing the garment to unravel till it came right off, leaving her standing before Nandini in just a blouse and petticoat.

Nandini's eyes roamed Leela's body, demanding and hungry even without touching her, taking in every bit of her. She watched Nandini's hand as it inched forward to the drawstring of her petticoat, caught hold of one end, and pulled. It came loose and the garment dropped from Leela's hips, pooling lifelessly around her feet. Nandini edged forward and reached for the row of hooks that held the blouse closed. She parted the edges of the fabric, her fingers so close to her breasts that Leela could feel the warmth from them, yet not touching her.

Then, Nandini's arm curved around her back, snapping her bra undone.

Nandini pulled the blouse off and then pushed the bra straps over her shoulders, her eyes following each inch of skin as it was exposed to the cool air and goose-pimpled instantly. When the blouse and bra had joined the rest of the clothes on the floor, Nandini's hands trailed lightly down Leela's sides to the waistband of her panties, the ghost-touch making Leela shiver. As Nandini knelt in front of her to get that last item of clothing off, Leela closed her eyes, an involuntary low moan escaping her throat. She could feel her dampness coat the inside of her thighs and wondered if Nandini could smell her arousal from there. A thrill ran down her body.

She was completely naked and Nandini was fully clothed, and Leela couldn't remember feeling so inflamed in her life.

She let Nandini guide her towards the bed, and she lay back, giving herself over to those talented fingers and mouth.

CHAPTER SIX

Leela sat back as Neil fussed around her, taking her bag and getting her water and then coffee. She suspected the grandparents had started to get a bit overbearing. She wasn't complaining about his unrestrained happiness to see her, though, considering it went a long way in soothing her travel-weary nerves, and she was happy to sink into the sofa and put her feet up.

"I'm making a surprise for dinner," he announced.

"Bless you," Leela said. The last thing she needed after a whole day of travelling—a train ride to Delhi and then the flight back to Bangalore—was to figure out dinner.

"Was it a good trip?"

Leela suppressed a smile. "Oh yes, it was."

Neil studied her, a watchful expression on his face.

"What is it?" Leela asked.

"I don't know. You seem…"

"Tired?" Leela finished for him.

"Yeah, but also, I don't know—you're in a good mood."

The doorbell pealed. And pealed and pealed. It had to be her mother. Elsie Saldana had the propensity to ring doorbells like they were going out of fashion.

"Well, there goes my good mood," Leela muttered under her breath.

She dropped her head back on the sofa and closed her eyes as Neil went to answer the door.

"Leelu?" her mother's voice assailed her as soon as the door was opened. "There you are. Your father said he saw you getting out of the taxi. Neil, here put this in the kitchen, it's some fish curry for your dinner. Leelu, you can make the rice, no? Your cook did not come today."

"I know, Ma," Leela called from her seat. *It is my house after all.*

"Aw," said Neil, taking the dish from his grandmother. "I was going to make pasta…oops, it was going to be a surprise."

Leela raised her eyebrows at him, and he looked sheepish. "But thanks, Grandma."

"Pasta?" his grandmother said. "Why are you wasting your time cooking? You should be studying."

"I can't study *all* the time."

Leela stood up and stretched, already starting to tune out of a conversation she had been party to many times in the past.

"But you have a test tomorrow," Elsie persisted.

"I'm happy to see you too, Ma," she interrupted. "And I had a good trip, thanks for asking."

Elsie turned to her. "What?"

"Never mind. I'm going for a bath and then I'm going to take a nap."

"But it's almost dinnertime. And there's the rice to make."

"Neil can make the rice. Can't you, Neil?"

"Sure." He turned away, muttering something about it not being the same as making pasta, but who was asking him anyway.

Elsie followed Leela into the bedroom. "You shouldn't make him do all that."

"Do what?" asked Leela, pretending she hadn't a clue.

"Your father just doesn't like it, the way you treat the boy… Oh, speaking of your father, his blood pressure medicine is over. You forgot to get more."

"I didn't forget. I left the pharmacist's number on your fridge. I told you to call him on Saturday morning—you know he drops it off every month." She looked at her mother in exasperation. "I'm guessing you didn't call and now someone has to go and pick it up from the shop." *And guess who that someone is going to have to be?*

"If you didn't drop everything and run off—"

"Ma, don't be dramatic. You knew for a month that I was going to be away this weekend. It doesn't help if you keep disrupting the systems I put in." She sighed. She might as well make a quick run to the pharmacy right away. She reached for her purse on the side table but paused midway. "Wait a minute, he should have enough medicine to cover the first week of the month."

Elsie waved a hand. "Yes, he has enough for a few days. But it's running low."

Leela pulled her hand back. "You could have not made it sound like an emergency, you know." Her head was beginning to pound. Why had she expected to have a quiet evening to herself?

"I never said it was an emergency."

"Guess who I met in Amrudpur?" Leela said, veering from the pointless direction the conversation would have headed otherwise. "You remember Nandini? My friend in college?"

"Nandini?" Her mother's brow furrowed. Then her eyes became wide. "That north Indian girl?"

"She was Sindhi, actually, and her family were from Calcutta." Not that that made any difference; to Elsie, everything north of Bangalore was "north India."

"Yes, whatever. She was too confident. There was something bold about her." The way Elsie said it made clear these were not good things to be.

"She was fun. She was my…best friend."

Her mother shuddered. "Your father thought you were getting spoilt in her company."

"Well, I was heartbroken when she left." There was more truth to that statement than she would ever tell her mother.

"You know how childhood friendships are. You get over them. You got married soon after that and forgot all about her."

"Oh, I never forgot about her, Ma."

"How come you met all the way in Amrudpur?"

"She was attending the same conference I'd gone for. She is doing very well. She and two friends run a software company in Delhi. They make educational software."

"That's nice." Elsie's tone was dismissive. "What does her husband do?"

Leela almost laughed. Of course, *that* would be more important to Elsie. "She doesn't have a husband. Not everyone does."

Her mother's hand flew to her mouth. "Aiyo, she is also a widow?"

"No, no. I meant, she isn't married." And just to rile her mother, she added, "And before you ask, she doesn't have any kids either."

Her mother pursed her lips. "Why does that not surprise me? One of those modern women, I suppose."

Leela sighed to herself. In what universe had she imagined Elsie would have been happy to hear about Nandini? She should have come up with a better change of subject—God knew she had enough practice.

"Oh, *much* more modern than you could even begin to suppose," Leela called, stepping away towards the bathroom. She wished she had a more cutting repartee.

She could ignore her mother's less palatable comments at the best of times, but there were instances, like now, when they could suck all the joy out of Leela. It was probably unfair to blame her mother for her spiralling mood, but she was tired and annoyed, and didn't really care.

As the shower washed away the travel grime from her body, Leela watched the water swirling into the drain. It seemed to her that the soapy runoff was washing Amrudpur, Nandini, and their two nights of unbridled passion away along with it into secret, unknown depths, almost like they were never there in the first place.

Only, they had been. And however surreal it felt right now, now that she was back in her real life with all its attendant annoyances, it couldn't take away from the fact that Amrudpur and her tryst with Nandini had been an unexpected but memorable adventure.

* * *

Elsie and Joseph Saldana had been one of the first people to buy a flat in Garden City Apartments on the edges of Bangalore's Sadashivanagar locality. This was back in the 1980s, when the area had been called Palace Orchards. Garden City Apartments was a modest four-storey building with eight flats, and at that time the subject of much controversy in an area that was otherwise filled with standalone homes. But it was just the beginning of the rampant urbanisation that was to take over— some would use stronger terms like "destroy"—Bangalore and make its Garden City moniker redundant. In the city's current landscape, this humble pink-and-white building with its peeling paint and overgrown lawn would struggle to call itself an apartment complex, but it had endured, amid two larger and shinier complexes, like a smug little hill that nestled between towering mountain peaks. The upscale Sadashivanagar, however, had remained a locality mostly populated with individual houses, so Garden City Apartments had eventually moulded into the landscape.

Leela had been about seven years old when they had moved here. She had fallen in love with the flat, the building, and the area around it. Her most abiding memories of her childhood involved running around the tree-lined neighbourhood and spending hours by Sankey Tank. Later on, she had been devastated as the lake had slowly been choked by pollution and a lack of maintenance, and had then rejoiced when it had been restored and turned into a beautiful park. She still went there for walks sometimes.

When Leela had married Kiran Robinson, by a happy coincidence one of the top-floor flats had come up for sale. Kiran's father, who had made a killing in Dubai during the dot-com boom, had been happy to buy it for his newlywed son and daughter-in-law. At that time, it had seemed like a great idea, being able to live so close to her parents. As the years went by, though, it turned out to be a bit of a mixed blessing.

After Kiran's accident and his death soon after, when Leela was left holding the threads of her and Neil's lives, she had been incredibly grateful for the support her parents had provided. Neil had barely been old enough to understand why his father would never come home. His grandparents had stepped in without question, without hesitation, and Leela had been happy to let go for a while, moving back in with them, drowning herself in work, and pretending everything was under control and that she was fine.

It had taken her years to work through her grief, most of it thanks to her friend Davi's insistence that she seek counselling. As the sessions progressed and Leela managed to get a hold on things, the realisation that she had probably let go of too much sank in. Turning her life around on her own terms was the next challenge she faced. And she knew that, however grateful she might be for her parents' unstinting support, she had to step away from their circle of control. Further, once she had herself in hand, she had to make time for Neil.

First, she had moved back to her own flat. Her parents had convinced her to rent it out for some extra cash and it had been a good solution for a while. But when Leela figured she needed her independence—and that meant physical independence too—she gave notice to the tenants. Her parents had been furious, but Leela was equally adamant, so Leela and Neil had moved back into their own home about seven years ago. The other change she made was to spend all the time she could spare with Neil. She started to cut back on work despite the financial hit that resulted and spent more time with her son. She had seen the change in Neil almost immediately. His schoolwork stabilised and he became happier, more outgoing, increasingly resembling the happy, friendly little boy she once remembered. It also had the unexpected bonus of bringing them closer together.

For the past few years, every morning she woke up, the first thing she saw was the damp patch in the corner of the bedroom ceiling. It was a seepage problem that never went away no matter what they did. Kiran had named it "Australia" because of its shape and used to call it their pet patch.

Leela smiled. She missed Kiran, but the loss wasn't debilitating any longer. He had been a quiet, unassuming man, preferring to stay in the background and letting Leela and Neil shine. Some part of Leela believed he was still watching over them from another dimension.

On this particular morning, Leela's thoughts turned to Nandini and what could be best described as their heady two-night stand. It had been so long since she'd indulged herself in that way. It wasn't that there hadn't been other opportunities, though it had to be said that most of them had been created by her parents. They had pushed several men onto her path hoping she'd marry one of them—sex outside marriage would be a taboo. While Leela herself didn't look at it that way, she hadn't been interested in any of those men either. The only exception had been a friend of a friend with whom she'd had a two-month fling. This short-lived dalliance with Alok had only proved that a relationship wasn't exactly a priority for her.

She also hadn't imagined herself to be the kind of person who felt the need to seek out meaningless sex. But the memory of those toe-curling nights with Nandini made it crystal clear that she had perhaps been wrong about that, at least.

CHAPTER SEVEN

"It's most inelegant that you should go on such trips yourself," Davi told Leela as they walked down the hall towards Leela's office. "You should have sent someone instead."

"Someone like you, you mean?"

"What? No, not me. You know computers and I don't get along."

"You do realise, Davi, that if we trial the software at the school, you will definitely be one of the teachers who are trained in using it."

"You wouldn't do that to me."

"I absolutely would."

"I am breaking up with you," Davi responded, making Leela laugh at her disgusted expression.

"Good morning, ma'am, good morning, ma'am," chorused a pair of thirteen-year-olds who crossed them in the corridor, their braids swinging from side to side as they whizzed past.

"Good morning," Leela and Davi replied in unison. Leela frowned at their retreating backs. "Why do I feel like they're up to something?"

"They're teenagers. Of course they're up to something," said Davi. She raised her hand to wave at someone.

Leela turned to see Anil Dikshit, her vice-principal, waiting for her outside her office. "Morning, Anil," she called. "Be with you in a minute." To Davi, she said, "See you at lunch, then."

"Good luck," mumbled Davi as she turned in the direction of the staff room. Leela watched her walk away. Davi was the senior school physics teacher and was no doubt off to concoct incomprehensible problems to torment students with, all about how fast bathtubs would fill or empty. Leela and Davi went back almost two decades, having met when they were training to be teachers. Even though work had taken them to different schools all over the city, they had always remained friends. Leela could definitely say that Davi was her closest friend and ally. She was the one who had been there with her during her darkest days.

A part of Leela was bursting to share details of her weekend, not only the gossip and work parts, but also what had happened with Nandini. But something was holding her back. The trouble was, she couldn't figure out what.

* * *

"I took a quick look at the link you sent this morning," Anil told her as they settled in to their usual Monday-morning meeting. "It looks promising. You should run it past the department heads."

"I intend to." Leela picked up her telephone receiver. "Coffee?" she asked Anil.

"Yes, please."

"Gulshan, could you please send coffee for Anil Sir and me?" Leela said into the phone. She put it down and looked across her desk. "But full disclosure—Nandini Mirchandani, one of the founders of Discover-E, is an old friend. We went to college together."

"Does it matter?"

"Probably not. But I thought I should be up-front about it."

"If we end up working with her, at least it's good someone knows her. She's reliable?"

"I have no idea." Which, come to think of it, was true. "I mean, it was a long time ago that I knew her. She has a brilliant mind, one of those mavericks who have ideas that nobody ever thought of. Could you do some background research on the company? Meanwhile, I'll have a word with the HoDs. Then we can discuss running it past the board."

The Margitte Hanssen Educational Trust that ran Leela's school—and three others in Pune, Delhi, and Chennai—was headed by Raza and Maia Hanssen-Hussain, a father-daughter duo. It was named after Raza's late wife and Maia's mother, who had been a path-breaking educator in the 1970s in Sweden. After her death, when Raza had returned to India with his infant daughter, he had decided to continue Margitte's legacy by setting up an educational trust and the Margitte Hanssen Memorial School in Bangalore in 1976. From that one school, at first a small, neighbourhood primary school, were born the Hanssen Academies, a set of premier schools across the country.

Since Leela had first joined Hanssen more than a decade ago—first as a history teacher, then a supervisor, vice-principal, and finally, two years ago, principal—she had been fascinated by both Raza and Maia's passion for embracing new ideas. It was one of the things that had inspired her to straddle both the admin and teaching sides of the job.

Being a small, exclusive school, the students that came in were often entitled brats, but Leela enjoyed the challenge of trying to turn them into empathetic citizens by the time they left. That and seeking out the best ways to impart knowledge were the two things that had always kept Leela fired up about her job. Discover-E was exactly the sort of innovation they needed at this point, and if she knew anything about how Raza Hussain thought, he was going to love it.

Bopanna, her peon, came in with their coffees. He placed them on the table and retreated after Leela expressed her gratitude. Then she opened her much-thumbed diary stuck with Post-its all over, and for the next forty-five minutes Leela and Anil continued their meeting without interruption.

After Anil left, Leela checked her schedule for the day. She had the next half hour to herself before she was due in class eight for history, one of just two lessons a week that she taught. Her mind wandered back to Amrudpur, as it was wont to do these days, but this time she cast it towards Nandini's onstage performance rather than the ones elsewhere.

She picked up her mobile phone and scrolled through the contacts list. Finding the number, she quickly typed out a text:

Hey, are you back in Delhi? That proposal you promised me, by when do you think you could send it across? My vice-princi is very impressed with your work.

The phone pinged back in under a minute, multiple times, each message popping in before Leela finished reading the previous one.

Hi Leela, good to hear from you.

Ya, back in Del. Glad to know your people are impressed!

Could we have a quick Skype when you're free?

Need to ask a few questions, quicker than emailing back & forth.

Just 5 mins, any time you're free.

When the flurry of messages stopped, Leela texted back:

I'm free now if you are.

It was surreal. Just thirty-six hours ago, they had been tearing each other's clothes off. And now she was about to come face-to-face with Nandini again, this time for purely professional reasons. And a few minutes later, when she found herself staring at a slightly pixelated Nandini through her webcam, the surreality only increased.

"Hi, can you hear me?" Nandini asked.

"Loud and clear. Can you hear me?"

"Hear and see you. Good morning. You get to work early, don't you?"

"It's nine thirty. Is that early for you?"

Nandini held up a red-and-black mug and a piece of toast. "I'm having my breakfast."

Leela shook her head. "Completely decadent."

Nandini laughed.

I've missed that laugh. The thought caught Leela by surprise. She brushed it away. "So what do you want to know?"

"Right." Nandini looked down, and from the tapping of keys Leela figured she was opening a document, readying herself to take notes. "I just need to...oh shit!"

"What happened?"

"My toast fell on the keyboard...hang on, hang on, ah, all right. Okay, so, I was saying, I just want to get some basic info so I have an idea of the scope of what you need."

Leela regarded Nandini as she waited for her questions. She had a few of her own. Ought they have done a better job of keeping in touch over the years? Was it too late now? Could they be friends? Or had sleeping together put paid to any possibility of that?

"Are you listening?"

Leela jumped, yanked out of her what-if rabbit hole. "Sorry, yes, I'm here."

Among all those lingering unknowns, there was one that she was almost too afraid to ask: What would happen if they ended up working together?

CHAPTER EIGHT

"Mama?" Neil's voice roused Leela out of the stupor that her book had sent her into. She uncurled her leg from underneath her on the sofa, pins and needles prickling it immediately.

"Yes?" Leela didn't turn towards Neil, though her bullshit meter went on high alert. That particular form of address by her son meant only one thing. "What do you want?"

He sat on the edge of the sofa. "What makes you think I want something? Why are you always so suspicious?"

Leela looked up. He wore a suitably pained expression. She held her laughter at bay. "Okay, then, sorry for jumping to conclusions. Nice to see you, too."

He shifted around. "Actually, I wanted to ask something."

Aha. "Go on."

"So, you know those sketches I've been making, the portraits?"

"Yes."

"I drew some of my classmates, sometime last week."

"All right."

"I made one for Rahul, and his little sister really liked it, so I made one for her as well, a really nice one with a cute border and all. She loved it."

"If you say so." Leela tapped her finger on her book. The narrator had finally been going to stand up to her controlling husband, and, while the ponderous narrative was boring Leela to death, she was still keen to find out why reviewers were calling that scene the most uplifting feminist moment in the history of modern literary fiction.

"And when I went to Rahul's house yesterday, Rahul's mother told me that she saw it too and it was really good, much better than those portrait artists you see in malls or those booths that have a machine that takes a picture of you and turns it into a sketch, and Preethi, Rahul's sister, was really excited about how I'd drawn her and she asked me if I would come and make sketches for her friends during her birthday party, and Prabha Aunty was upset she asked me like that, but I said it's okay, I can do it, so Prabha Aunty said fine then, she would pay me for them, she insisted she would, so can I please do sketches at Preethi's birthday party?"

Leela stared at her son, who was almost panting by the time he finished that sentence. "Let me get this straight. You would like to do portraits for the kids at Rahul's sister's birthday party, and their mother will pay you for it?"

Neil nodded. "Can I, please?"

"And when is this birthday?"

"Around the end of January."

"You realise that's more than three months away?"

"I know. But still, can I do it?"

"Sure. It's your decision. But if you're being paid, you have to do a really professional job of it, you know that, right?"

"Yes, of course. I'll get some nice paper and I may need new colours. Can I borrow some money? I'll pay you back."

"You want a loan?"

"Yes." He grinned what he surely imagined was a winning smile. It wasn't, it was just sickly sweet. He had loved to draw since he was little, and over the years he had developed an artist's eye and started noticing things Leela herself never did. Lately, he had started to get serious about it, to the extent of thinking about a career in art or design. Leela had always encouraged him, and now it had become more than just a hobby. He seemed to have a vocation for it and she was never going to do anything to discourage him from exploring it. But a healthy dose of pragmatism to go with talent didn't hurt anyone.

"I can give you a loan, but first I want to see some paperwork. How will you do your costing? What will you charge Prabha Aunty? And I want to see a budget too—what kind of paper you need, what sort of colours, and what your profit will be after you've paid me back."

"Yes, of course, of course. Thank you." Neil jumped up, his face shining. "I'll go and do a budget right away."

"Oh, Neil," Leela called to his retreating back. "It might be a good idea not to mention anything to the grandparents, okay?"

"Okay."

Leela leaned back against the headboard. Kiran would have been proud if he could see their son today. It was a pity her parents were so disapproving of Neil's interests. They were so much in denial that they couldn't see what was staring them right in the face: their grandson was going to pursue a career in some sort of artistic field and Leela was going to do everything in her power to make his dreams come true. As far as possible, she did all she could to shield him from their disapproval, though she didn't always succeed.

There was one thing, though. It niggled Leela more and more whenever Rahul came up, either in conversation or in thought.

She and Neil were quite close. His was a naturally friendly and open personality, so it wasn't hard. But Leela had always been careful to give him space because it would've been so easy to cross over from being close to being clingy. In the line of work she had been in for almost two decades, she had often seen this in children growing up in single-parent households, where both parent and offspring were often trapped in a cycle of codependency. She wanted Neil to have a life of his own, and she wanted him to be a typical teenager with the space to have his little secret world that teenagers seem to live in—as long as he wasn't doing anything dangerous, of course. She wanted him to explore and experiment (within reason, always!), and fail too. The advantage of her work was also that she had access to resources to make sure she always kept channels of conversation open. So from giving him the sex talk to discussing their financial issues, Leela had tried to let him know that no subject was taboo.

Which was why the Rahul thing bothered her so much. She could be wrong. After all, she knew better than most people to jump to conclusions. But it still gnawed at her.

Since he was about nine or ten, Neil's best friend had been his classmate Aadya. They had been reluctantly paired for a science project in class five and had been inseparable since. While it wasn't unusual for boys and girls to be close friends, in Leela's experience most of the time they either drifted apart once they hit adolescence, preferring to hang out with their own genders, or the relationship shifted to a romantic one.

For Neil and Aadya, neither of these happened—the reason Leela knew this was that Aadya had acquired a boyfriend around the time they were fifteen, and all three of them had been thick as thieves. But this trinity had been ripped apart when Aadya's family had moved away earlier that year. Neil had been gutted, and at first there had been a lot of Skyping and WhatsApping, but as was to be expected, that had become more and more infrequent.

Then Rahul had come into the picture. He had been among the new class-eleven intake at Hanssen Academy at the same time that Neil had started the eleventh. Rahul had performed brilliantly in the entrance examination and the school was falling over itself to take him. Leela had privately been thrilled when he and Neil started to become friends, first because Neil had been lonely since Aadya's departure, and second because she hoped some of Rahul's work ethic would rub off on Neil's rather indifferent academic performance.

There was a third reason. Leela had known since the first time she clapped eyes on Rahul Sridhar that she—and the school in general—would have to keep an eye out for him. And thus, Neil taking him under his wing had been the best thing that could have happened. She hated to think of him this way, but Rahul was the very personification of a stereotypical gay teenage boy. He was tall and willowy, and not in the gangly way that Neil was—there was something utterly graceful about him. He was given to exaggerated gestures, a manner of speaking that was always proper but bordering on the camp, and was incredibly well groomed at all times. The more Leela told herself that one should not slot people based on outward appearances, the more certain she became that he was gay.

Anyone else would have been singled out for bullying, but Rahul's academic brilliance kept the haters at bay. That and the fact that he was the principal's son's best friend. Leela wasn't complaining about either of these things.

What nagged her instead even now was a growing question in her mind, seeing Neil and Rahul's friendship developing, or if friendship was all it was. Yes, she was being a bit *Will and Grace* about it, but was it possible that was why Neil had a female bestie and hadn't seemed to be that close to any of the boys despite always being part of the crowd? He had never shown any interest in a particular girl either.

It wasn't Neil's sexuality that irked her—of course it didn't, that would be having double standards—it was the fact that he wasn't telling her. Leela tormented herself wondering how she could let Neil know that it was okay, and it didn't make *any* difference to her if Neil was gay, straight, or anything else as long as he was safe and happy. But Neil wasn't giving her the chance to be the super-cool mum she was, and that was driving her crazy.

CHAPTER NINE

Leela checked her laptop case one last time, making sure her cables and her USB 4G stick were in there. She lay the bag down on the sofa and went into the kitchen, where Eeshwaramma was noisily cooking their meals for the day.

"Your omelette is ready, Akka," she said to Leela. "You want toast?"

"Thank you, Eeshwaramma, but I don't think I can manage an omelette." Her stomach was doing cartwheels, as it had been off and on since last night. "I'll just have the toast." She popped some bread into the toaster, but before she could turn it on, Eeshwaramma batted her hands away.

"You go sit down. I'll get you toast." She followed Leela out, as if to make sure she did as she was told, carrying a piping-hot steel tumbler of fresh, frothy coffee. She set it down at the dining table, in front of Leela. "New dress?" she asked, looking pointedly at Leela's Rajasthani embroidered blouse. "Going somewhere special-aa?"

Leela squirmed under her scrutiny. "Meeting," she mumbled. "And the 'dress' is not new either." She shook the newspaper open in the hope that Eeshwaramma would take the hint. It wasn't like her cook not to have an opinion on what she was wearing, but Leela could do without the third degree today.

Eeshwaramma looked disappointed. "Only meeting? Tcha."

Leela took that to be a compliment, but nevertheless heaved a sigh of relief when Eeshwaramma retreated to the kitchen. She hoped everything would go off well today. Though it would help a *lot* if she could just relax a bit and not feel so nervous just because Nandini would be at the meeting.

She and Nandini had been in touch these past few weeks, on email and Skype, mostly about Leela's school's interest in Discover-E's application. Then Nandini had called last week to say that she'd be in Bangalore for a few days and had the Saturday morning free if the school's bigwigs would be interested in a first-hand demonstration of what the software could do. Raza and Maia Hanssen-Hussain also happened to be in town for a family event, so Leela had jumped at the chance to fix up a meeting between Nandini and the board.

But what exactly was it that she was so jumpy about? They were experienced professionals, and the fact that they'd had a weekend fling and agreed to keep it at that ought to have no bearing on their working together. Yet, whatever she told herself, Leela still had apprehensions about what it would be like to face each other, at least the first time. It was evident that until she got the moment over with, she wouldn't be able to relax. She gave herself a mental shake. *Get a grip. It will be fine.*

There was a shuffling noise and Neil appeared, rubbing his eyes, a general air of dishevelment about him.

"Good morning," Leela said.

"Morning," he mumbled back.

He slipped into a chair and lay his head down on the table, closing his eyes. Leela rubbed his head. It felt like a bristly brush, given the severe crew cut he preferred because he hated the tight curls that resulted if he grew his hair even a bit. "You know you can go back into bed, right? It's Saturday."

"Can I go to Rahul's place?" he said, eyes still closed. "We can do our homework together."

Leela raised an eyebrow. Was that a euphemism? She scuttled the thought. "If you want. When are you going? I can drop you if you can be ready"—she glanced at her watch—"in ten minutes."

Neil heaved himself off the table and sloped back into his room. He reappeared in under four minutes, fully awake, dressed in a pair of jeans and a T-shirt, and reeking of deodorant. Leela didn't ask any questions. He dashed into the kitchen and came back with an omelette and a pile of toast, which he then proceeded to demolish in the remaining six minutes.

The phone rang just as they were leaving, the single ring indicating it was a call on the building intercom and not an outside number. She considered ignoring it, but Neil reached across and picked it up. He handed it to her. "Grandma."

Of course it was. "Ma? What's wrong?"

"Nothing is wrong. Why would you assume something is wrong?"

"Because you know I have a meeting today. So I'm in a bit of a rush."

"Oh, is that today? You father was saying you haven't spent any time with us lately—"

"Ma, please, not now. I have to go."

"Everything is more important to you than us."

Leela pressed her eyes closed. She was certain Elsie had hidden a spycam somewhere in her house. She had the uncanny ability to choose those exact moments to make demands on her daughter when she knew Leela was going to be otherwise occupied. "Don't be dramatic, Ma. I'll drop by later. Maybe we can have dinner together."

"Your father has a Rotary Club dinner. What about lunch?"

Aaargh. "I don't know how long I'll be. I may not be back for lunch."

"What? What about Neil?"

"He's going to his friend's place."

"And his lunch?"

"He's not a child. There's food at home, he'll figure it out."

"Put him on the phone."

"There's no time. I'm dropping him off. I'll talk to you later."

She hung up before her mother could find any more fault in her parenting duties or in her commitment towards her own parents, and followed Neil down the stairs. As she had expected, the door to her parents' was open and her mother was standing on a stool, dusting the lintel with an innocent air about her.

"Neilu, you come and eat with us this afternoon, okay?"

"Um, okay, but I don't know when I'll be back, Grandma."

Leela smacked his shoulder lightly with the back of her hand. "You'll be back by lunchtime, that's when."

"Fine," Neil muttered. "See you, Grandma."

"Good boy," his grandmother said, giving Leela a triumphant look.

"Why are you going to school today?" Neil asked when they were in the car.

"Board meeting."

"What do grown-ups do in meetings anyway?"

"It's just an important word for sitting around and talking, sometimes with snacks and drinks."

"I see. Which means Rahul and I are going to have a meeting too."

Leela slowed down and stopped near the turning to Rahul's house. "Okay, that's as far as I'm taking you. Have a good meeting."

"You too," Neil replied with a grin, hauling himself out of the car along with his backpack.

Leela drove off, smiling. The silly interaction with Neil had left her much relaxed. But by the time she pulled into her reserved space in the school's car park, the butterflies in her stomach were at it again. She glanced at herself in the rearview mirror. The face that looked back was outwardly calm, though Leela couldn't be sure if there was a sheen of sweat on her forehead. She took a tissue and patted her face. Strands of hair were already escaping the tight bun she preferred—unruly hair was a family trait—and there was no point stressing about it. Without much ado, she brushed the loose hairs back and did a quick check of her makeup.

She looked at her watch. Five minutes early. Perfect. She took a few deep breaths and practised her cool, collected face. She stepped out of the car, retrieved her things, and walked into the school.

She stopped to take another deep breath before entering the board room. Six pair of eyes turned towards her—four school board members, plus Rina Pant, the senior school supervisor, and her vice-principal, Anil. She was just about to heave a sigh of relief when another figure unfolded itself from a chair in the corner. Leela turned around and all thought beat a hasty retreat from her mind.

"I was just telling Ms. Mirchandani that we are grateful she could make time for us." The deep voice of Raza Hussain, the head of the school board, cut through Leela's momentary fugue.

"Ah, yes," managed Leela. She pulled herself together and smiled back at Nandini, reaching for her outstretched hand. As their fingers touched, Leela flashed back to the last time those hands had been on her. Tearing her eyes and her hand away from Nandini, she went to take a seat. Her face was flushed and her heart was hammering.

Nandini was here in person, sitting across the table from her. Not a pixelated image at the end of a Skype call. All of a sudden it made what had happened at Amrudpur just a bit more real.

And that wasn't all. Her reaction on shaking Nandini's hand was not something she had anticipated at all. She had believed that sleeping with Nandini in Amrudpur had taken care of the attraction simmering between them. But now, her sweaty palms and racing pulse said otherwise.

Was this going to be A Complication?

She cleared her throat. "Are we all here? Should we begin?"

"Maia will be with us in a minute," Anil pointed out. Even before he finished his sentence, the door opened. A peon with tea, coffee, and biscuits came in, Maia right behind, holding the door for him.

"Great," Leela said when everyone had settled. "I gather you've all already introduced yourselves, so perhaps we could start. Nandini, once again, on behalf of the board and the school, thank you for being here." She gestured towards the head of the room, where Nandini's computer was set up and the projector whirring. "The stage is yours."

She leaned back in her chair and was soon drawn into Nandini's presentation, just like she had back in Amrudpur. The tension left her shoulders bit by bit.

* * *

The presentation was a success, as Leela had been certain it would be. Raza, Maia, and the others had all appeared keen and they'd had plenty of questions for Nandini. Almost an hour and a half later, when everyone was shaking hands, exchanging farewells, and making promises to be in touch, Leela was a hundred per cent sure that a long-term contract was coming Nandini's way. She hung back as the others exited the room.

"That went well, I think," Nandini said. They were alone now except for the two peons behind her who were taking down the screen and putting away the equipment.

"I think so." Leela perched on the edge of the table, watching Nandini pack up. "Thank you for doing this, by the way."

"Hey, it's what I do." Nandini gave a slight smile. "Much of my time is spent trying to charm people into writing me massive cheques."

"You seem pretty good at it."

"I aim to please."

Now there was a twinkle in Nandini's eye. Was she flirting? Leela wished she didn't find the thought so alluring.

Nandini might have been the first woman Leela had ever been attracted to, but she certainly hadn't been the last. The only difference in the other cases had been that she either hadn't been interested (when Kiran was still alive), or that the possibility of that attraction resulting in anything other than secret fantasies had been non-existent. With Nandini anything was possible, which was what made it so…exciting. And dangerous. Leela couldn't explain or even find a word for this roil of thrill, fear, and lust that proximity to Nandini seemed to conjure up.

"What are your plans after this?" she asked in her attempt to manoeuvre the conversation to safer grounds.

Nandini consulted her phone. "I guess I need to be on my way to the airport in about an hour or so."

"So, lunch?"

Nandini glanced up. That twinkle was definitely not Leela's overactive imagination. "And by 'lunch,' you mean…"

Leela laughed, as much to cover the flush that rose in her cheeks as in admiration of Nandini's audacity to openly flirt with her at her place of work. She was glad at least that they were alone now. "I mean *lunch* lunch. With food and all."

Nandini made a face. "I don't think I have that much time. I had thought I'd go on to the airport and grab something there."

"I know," Leela said. "There's a small restaurant almost next door. If you're okay with local grub, we could get us some dosas or something. Bopanna will run across and get it, won't take him ten minutes."

"Sounds good to me."

"Great." Leela went outside and found Bopanna, and sent him off with some money to get them two masala dosas. Then she led Nandini to her office.

"Drink?" Leela asked.

Her room was equipped with a seating area with comfortable sofas, coffee table, a minifridge, a water filter, and an electric kettle with tea and coffee things.

"Just some water, please."

Nandini took one end of the sofa, putting her laptop bag down beside her. Leela got her water and sat down in the seat perpendicular to the sofa.

"Thank you." Nandini took the glass. "Nice office. Our entire company operates out of a space as big as this, so this seems very fancy to me."

"It's not bad, is it?" Leela looked around, trying to see it with Nandini's eyes. The heavy mango wood furniture with the light printed cotton curtains rippling gently from the breeze outside, the walls covered with bookshelves, and a split air-conditioning unit high on the wall, rarely used. "I inherited it from my predecessor. Didn't have to change a thing. It was perfect."

Bopanna returned with their food and bustled about setting out plates and cutlery. The gusto with which Nandini attacked her food reminded Leela that she was hungry too.

"Mmm, this is good," mumbled Nandini between bites.

"Better get used to the taste. You might be spending some time in Bangalore over the next few months after all."

"Fingers crossed."

Leela swallowed. This was the perfect opportunity. "Listen, Nandini, there's something…I mean, I think we need to talk, clear the air. About us, I mean."

Nandini put down the spoonful of sambhar that had been travelling towards her mouth. "About us?"

"Yes, um." Leela looked down at her hands, her fingers oily. "The thing is that, I think—and this is a bit embarrassing if it's one-sided—but I think we have a…I don't know, a spark."

"We definitely have a spark." Nandini's voice was low. It produced a shiver deep inside Leela.

She caught Nandini regarding her, her expression neutral.

"So here's the thing. Looks like we'll end up working together, right?" She waited till Nandini nodded. "In that case, we need to keep things professional."

Nandini's face was still inscrutable. Then she moved her focus to her plate. "By professional, you mean…"

"You know what I mean, Nandini."

Nandini nodded as if considering something. "Okay, I hear you. But I have to ask. What happened in Amrudpur, we were both clear it was no strings attached, right?"

"Right."

"And it was"—she glanced up again—"good?"

Images from Amrudpur flashed in her mind. Leela almost blushed. "Yes, it was."

"So, then, why? The work and the sex, they have nothing to do with each other. You're not hiring me, the trust is. I probably won't even be doing all the work on the project. The tech team will handle quite a bit of it."

"Yes, I know, but still. It's just…I've always kept the personal and professional separate, and I think it's best to keep things simple." She paused. "Is that okay? I mean…I'm sorry."

Nandini gave her a crooked smile. "Don't be sorry. And of course it's okay. That's not to say I'm not disappointed, but that's just the way it is. All things considered, Leela, it has been fantastic meeting you again, and I…" She trailed off, like all of a sudden she'd forgotten what she was going to say. "Can we be friends, at least?"

Leela smiled back at her, relieved that the conversation had gone better than she had imagined. Whatever she'd seen of Nandini since they'd met in Amrudpur she had liked so far, her mind-boggling attraction for her notwithstanding. And friends were so difficult to come by as one got older. "Of course we can be friends. I'd like that too. We were so young when we last knew each other. I want to get to know the older you."

"Ditto," said Nandini.

Leela moved her hand back to her dosa. Her relief was tinged with a smidge of disappointment. Nandini was right, it had been good. More than good.

CHAPTER TEN

Rain pattered at the windscreen as Leela and Davi inched forward on the packed road in front of Palace Grounds. A faculty meeting had run late and they were caught in the early evening rush-hour traffic. This stretch of road was notorious for its jams anyway, but past five o'clock and any time it rained, it became almost impassable. Leela was glad she wasn't the one driving.

Ever since Davi and her family had moved to one of the apartments near Sankey Tank, the two of them carpooled whenever possible. Given the traffic situation in this city, did one car less make even a whit of difference? Little drops of water, little grains of sand, she thought as she reassured herself for the umpteenth time.

"So this Rahul Sridhar and Neil are good friends, right?" Davi's voice cut through the prattle of the annoying radio jockey talking about some inane new fad that Bollywood was currently responsible for.

"Hmm? Yes, they are. Why do you ask?"

Davi drummed her fingers on the steering wheel. The SUV in front of them moved and they rolled forward another two or three metres. "I've been wondering if there's something going on with him."

"What do you mean?"

"His work hasn't been up to the mark lately. He seems distracted."

Leela frowned. "Distracted how?"

"Inattentive in class, forgetting assignments, that sort of thing."

"That doesn't sound like him."

"Yes, it's completely out of character. I had a chat with him today, but he insisted everything was all right."

"Well, sixteen-year-olds are not best known for pouring their hearts out."

"No. That's why I'm asking if you know anything."

Leela looked out of the window, trying to remember when Rahul had last come over. "They usually do their homework together on weekends, Neil and Rahul. He came over last week and they were preparing for...oh wait, it couldn't have been last weekend because Neil was away at Kiran's parents'." Leela turned back to Davi. "Actually, I don't remember when I last saw him, except at school."

"He's been off school a couple of days last week too."

"Maybe he's been ill?" Leela ventured.

"I hope so. I mean, of course, I don't want him to be ill. But it would explain a lot."

"I'll talk to Neil, see if he can shed some light." She paused. "To be honest, I worry about Rahul a bit."

Davi caught her gaze. "I do too. There are a couple of thugs in that batch, and Rahul is...he's different, you know."

"Do you think he's gay?"

Davi narrowed her eyes. "What, just because he's a bit unconventional? You're the one who's always lecturing us about stereotyping the kids."

"True, but that doesn't stop the students from jumping to conclusions or bullying him."

"You think he's being bullied?"

"I don't know. But I do worry. Especially after the trouble we had with Krish a few years ago, and with Parul and Hema."

"Yes, but Krish also gave it back as good as he got. As for the girls, it sort of petered out."

"Only because Hema left Parul heartbroken. And we had to pick up the pieces." Leela shook her head. "Uff, teenage drama. Let's not get sidetracked. Thing is, Rahul seems vulnerable to me, I don't know why."

"It's an instinct, I suppose," Davi said. "Bound to happen, after almost twenty years hanging around with teenagers."

"Though I wouldn't mind being wrong about this one."

They managed to catch the green light at the crossing and sailed along for a full two hundred metres before coming to a halt once again just before the T-point where they had to turn towards Leela's house.

"I think I'll get out and walk," Leela said. "The rain has stopped, and it'll be quicker for you if you go straight."

"Are you sure?"

"Yes." She unbuckled her seat belt and reached for her bag on the back seat. "See you tomorrow."

"Bye. And don't forget to talk to Neil about Rahul."

"I won't."

PART II

NOVEMBER–DECEMBER 2017

CHAPTER ELEVEN

Leela straightened a doily on the side table and brushed an invisible speck of dust from it. She glanced around the room one last time. Everything seemed fine. The stray books had been put back into the shelf, Neil's art things were nowhere to be seen, there were no telltale coffee rings anywhere, and every surface was more or less dust free. Neither she nor Neil were terribly neat people, and they were both quite content to restrict the cleaning up to whenever they were entertaining, which, thankfully, was frequent enough to keep the house from turning into a tip.

She was looking forward to introducing Neil to Nandini and catching up some more. The only slightly annoying thing—all right, it was exceedingly annoying—was that Elsie and Joseph had muscled an invite as well. All Leela had wanted was a quiet evening, but quiet and her parents didn't really belong in the same sentence.

Catching up with old friends and classmates from school and college was rather fascinating, and Leela had had her fair share of it. It was always intriguing to see how much people had changed. She supposed she had changed too.

Back then, they had all been so starry-eyed and full of themselves. The funny thing was, there were those she had been friends with back in school and college who had turned out to be obnoxious people when she'd met them later, and then there were those she had barely interacted with that she now found were on a similar wavelength.

With Nandini, it was a bit complicated, of course, but she had a sense that they would get along. Platonically, that is. Now that the board had said yes to hiring Discover-E, they would be seeing more of each other. True, she was anxious about the attraction bit, but given the mature way they had handled their Amrudpur tryst, she was hoping that they'd be able to move past that.

Back in college, their friendship had progressed into something more very quickly. But as Nandini was always going to go abroad to study after three years of undergraduate college and Leela was always going to stay on, there had never been scope for anything long term. Knowing that, however, had not been enough to protect Leela from the heartbreak she encountered on Nandini's departure. They promised to keep in touch, but there had been no Skype or WhatsApp back then. Even Internet access hadn't been as ubiquitous as it was today. So letters had travelled back and forth at first, and sometimes emails, but they had slowly dried up as both moved on with their lives. Nandini did call one time, about a year later, when she was home for the holidays, which was when they had decided to call it off officially. As far as breakups went, it had been quite tame.

The doorbell rang, shaking Leela out of her trip down memory lane. She moved towards the door. That would be Nandini.

"I'm having déjà vu," Nandini said by way of greeting. "This place has not changed a bit, though everything around has. I almost rang the bell at your parents'. They're still there, right?"

"Yep." Leela stood aside. "Come on in. It's great to see you."

And it was. Nandini looked stunning as usual, this time in a navy-blue linen dress and dark brown sandals. Her shoulder-length hair was hanging loose about her face. "Thank you for inviting me." She stepped forward and gave Leela a kind of a half hug.

Leela was left a little nonplussed as she wound her arm lightly around Nandini's back, feeling somewhat gauche. *What a Delhi thing to do*. Not that it didn't make her stomach flutter.

She waited for Nandini to take off her footwear and then led the way into the living room. "Speaking of my parents, they have decided they are coming for dinner. I hope you don't mind."

"Mind? Of course not. I was wondering if I should go and say hello in any case." Nandini sat on the sofa and put the brown paper bag she was carrying on the table before her. "I brought some cake. Thought Neil would like it."

"I think he'll be your best friend, especially if it's chocolate." Leela sat down opposite Nandini. "Neil," she called. "Come on out."

Neil appeared at the door. He had scrubbed himself to shining—bless the boy—and instead of the bizarre T-shirts he was partial to—the ones that didn't have any other design except for the logo of the T-shirt company printed in a large size—he was actually wearing a shirt, tucked neatly into his ironed jeans, sleeves folded just under his elbow. Leela smiled to herself.

"Hello," Nandini said, holding out a hand.

"Hi." Neil shook her hand and darted a glance from Nandini to Leela and back to Nandini. "Is it true you knew my mother when you guys were in college?"

"Very true."

"Wow."

Leela shook her head. "Now, before you say something uncomplimentary and spoil the first impression, will you go and see what's keeping your grandparents?"

"There's cake," Nandini called to his retreating back.

He turned around, eyes shining. "Oh, thank you." He took the proffered bag and went away.

"You have an almost-grown-up son," Nandini said. "How weird is that?"

"About time he was almost grown up. It's been a very long two decades."

"I'm sorry, I didn't mean…"

Leela waved a hand. "I know, don't worry. It was a bit of a joke. He's a good boy, and believe me, I know some terrors." She stood. "Do you want something to drink? I have some nice local wine. A merlot."

"Sounds great."

Leela went into the kitchen to open the bottle of wine and pour herself and Nandini some. When she came back into the living room, Nandini was standing by the bookshelf, a photo frame in her hand. Leela couldn't remember who had taken the photograph in it, but the image was ingrained in her mind. The deep blue sea, white sandy beach, and windswept hair, Kiran holding Neil, who had been about six, and his other arm around Leela's shoulders. They all looked so happy. It was a rare photo of Kiran smiling—he always froze when a camera was pointed at him. It was their last holiday before the freak accident that had put Kiran in a coma from which he never woke up.

As Leela watched, Nandini brought up one hand and placed it over the top third of the photo. Leela frowned. What was she doing? Nandini squinted, and the penny dropped.

"Spitting image of Tom Cruise, wasn't he?"

Nandini jumped, and the frame slipped from her grasp. Leela's heart leapt into her mouth and she just about managed to keep herself from wincing as it clipped the edge of the shelf and fell to the floor.

Nandini gasped. "Shit! I'm so sorry!" She bent to pick it up and it was—miraculously—undamaged. "I'm so sorry!"

"It's all right." She put one of the wineglasses on the shelf and took the photo frame from Nandini to put it back. "Don't worry, no harm done."

She held out the other wineglass to Nandini. "Here you go. Or would you be more comfortable with a steel tumbler?" She batted her eyelids, her lips twitching.

"Oh, ha ha."

Neil came back right then to say that the grandparents were on their way up.

"You're an artist, your mother tells me," Nandini said to Neil.

He nodded, blushing. "I mostly like drawing people."

"Will you show me some of your work?"

"Sure."

"Nandini Aunty is an artist herself," Leela put in.

"Really?"

"It's more of a hobby, actually," Nandini replied. "Do you know what fractal art is?"

"Kind of. I looked it up online once, but it was too confusing. Isn't it computer-generated art?"

"It's mathematical art, representations of equations. It can result in some beautiful imagery. I'm not that good, but I like exploring it."

"That makes absolutely no sense to me," Leela said.

"I'll show you some day," Nandini promised.

"Me too," Neil piped in.

"Of course." Nandini nodded. "That goes without saying."

* * *

The bowl in the microwave went round and round in the kitchen. Leela couldn't exactly put a finger on her apprehensions about having her parents at dinner, but a full ten minutes after Elsie and Joseph Saldana had made an appearance, when the conversation had degenerated to a stilted exchange of pleasantries, she had forced herself to relax. It was one thing for her parents to be judgemental and opinionated with her, but usually with outsiders they were perfectly proper. And this evening they had been on their best behaviour. So far. They might be boring the pants off Nandini, but at least they had asked no needlessly personal questions. Leela crossed her fingers it would stay that way.

"The table is set," Neil announced, coming into the kitchen. "Shall I take the salad and chutney?"

"Yes, please."

Dinner was a simple affair—a spiced dal preparation, with a side dish of vegetables cooked with grated coconut, mustard seeds, and curry leaves, served with red rice, mango chutney, papad, and fresh salad. When they had been young, Nandini had loved the traditional Mangalorean Catholic cuisine in Leela's home, though, being a vegetarian, her choices had been restricted.

"I hope you still like this kind of food," Leela told her as they settled around the dining table.

"I love south Indian food," Nandini said. "Please don't kill me for generalising, I do know there are many types of food in the south, just that"—she sniffed deeply—"this smell of coconut and curry leaves and mustard…mmm."

Joseph appropriated the place at the head of the table. Leela gritted her teeth. That was *her* place and this was not the first time her father had usurped it when they'd had guests.

"You didn't make fish?" Elsie asked. "I thought you said you were making fish."

"Nandini is a vegetarian, Ma. I had forgotten for a moment."

"Neil loves fish, don't you, Neilu?"

Leela pursed her lips. "I'm sure he'll live without it for one meal."

"I'm fine, Grandma," Neil said.

"So, Nandini," Joseph began as soon as everyone finished serving themselves. "Leela tells us you didn't get married."

Leela groaned inwardly.

"That's right, I didn't," Nandini replied.

"Why not?"

"Dad, that's kind of personal, don't you think?" Leela asked.

"It's all right," Nandini said, her tone much calmer than it ought to be. "It was not possible to marry the person of my choice, Uncle. But the relationship didn't work out anyway, so it was okay."

"Tcha. Work out. What does that even mean? You modern women have all these fancy ideas. No husband, no children. Who is going to look after you people when you're old?"

"More like who *we* are going to end up looking after when we're old," Leela muttered, giving Nandini a sideways glance.

Nandini's mouth twitched in a smile, but she managed to keep a straight face. "I know that you worry, Uncle, but I respectfully disagree. I think people should get married or have children because they want to, not because they think they should."

"Everybody should, because that's the way society functions."

"It is for security and stability," Elsie put in. "You have to be rational and think of these things. For years we've been trying to convince our Leela that she should settle down again. And poor Neil, growing up without a father figure."

"Hey, leave me out of this, Grandma." Neil looked pained. "I'm growing up fine."

"Leela looks pretty settled to me," Nandini ventured.

"It's all work, work, work with Leela." Joseph never liked being left out of a conversation for too long.

"I don't get the feeling that Leela is all about work." Nandini's tone was mild.

Leela almost choked. She reached for her glass of water, looking up to see Nandini, whose eyebrows were slanted downwards in mischief. She shook her head slightly.

"It wasn't like this when Kiran was alive," Joseph went on like Nandini hadn't spoken.

"I wasn't the principal of a school when Kiran was alive, Dad," Leela said gently.

"I just realised something funny," Neil piped up. Everyone turned to him. "Grandpa, you're always boasting to DeSouza Uncle about how great Ma is at her job and how she is the youngest principal Hanssen has ever had and all, but in front of her you're always telling her that her job is crap."

"Language, Neil," Leela said, stifling a laugh, both at Neil's outrage and her father's gobsmacked expression. "Actually, can you go and get some more rice from the kitchen?"

"That boy," Joseph muttered. "Needs a firm hand, he does."

"But, Nandini, you are such a beautiful and successful woman." Elsie, clearly, wasn't prepared to let the subject lie. "I'm sure there are plenty of older men for you."

Leela cringed.

"I don't think a man is going to do me much good, Aunty," Nandini replied.

Leela caught Nandini's eye again. She was going to burst from the effort of clamping down on her laughter. This had to be both the most excruciatingly embarrassing and the most hilarious dinner she'd had in a long time.

* * *

"I am so sorry about my parents," Leela said as they waited by the pavement for Nandini's driver to bring the hired car around from the visitors' parking at the back of the building.

"Don't worry about it. Though it's been a while since I was given this sort of third degree."

"I will completely understand if you never want to see them again."

Nandini laughed. That same unrestrained laugh that Leela was beginning to get used to once again. "I hope that isn't code for *you* never wanting to see me again."

"Of course not. Though I can't say for the other way round."

"I had a good time. Even with your parents, believe it or not. The food was fantastic. Who'd have thought—Leela Saldana, dignified principal by day, outstanding chef when darkness falls."

"Why, thank you."

"What do you think would have happened if I'd told your parents I'm a lesbian?"

Leela considered it. "I think they would have spontaneously combusted. Or left the table."

"Seriously?"

It was Leela's turn to laugh. Then she paused. It was a good question. How would they have reacted? She shrugged. "I don't know. I think, perhaps, it wouldn't compute with them."

Nandini nodded. "Neil is lovely, though. Talented too."

"I agree, though I'm a bit biased."

"I noticed he has a sweet tooth just like his mum."

"I do not have a sweet tooth."

"Oh really? Would you like me to remind you of the time you single-handedly polished off two boxes of sandesh my parents had sent?"

"Mmm, sandesh…" Leela's mouth watered as she imagined that delicious Bengali sweet melting in her mouth. She tilted her chin up and looked at Nandini with half-hooded eyes. "That was a one-time thing. I was famished and you said there wasn't anything else, so I could help myself."

"Yeah? And what about when you would drag me to the Corner House every Saturday evening to feast on those sinful Brown Bombs?"

Leela scratched her head and tried to look dignified. "Well—"

"And that one time—"

"Okay, okay. Enough of that!"

Nandini smirked, and Leela scowled at her in mock anger.

They stood in silence. A cool breeze whipped around them, tugging at Leela's skirt. She hugged herself over the stole she had wrapped around her shoulders. Nandini didn't seem to feel it, though. In fact, she shut her eyes for a moment as if she were welcoming the wind that swept her hair away from her face. The gentle glow from the streetlamp across the street enhanced the reddish tinge in her hair, and shadows cast by the leaves of a nearby tree danced across her profile. A certain sublimity surrounded her. Leela stared at her, mesmerised. Nandini opened her eyes and Leela quickly averted her gaze.

"It feels surreal," Nandini said, looking away into the distance, "to be standing here with you again, so many years later. Remember, I used to wait for the bus right here to take me back to the hostel?"

Leela cleared her throat. "Oh, right. The bus stop used to be on this side, didn't it?" Leela sighed. "Funny how life takes you around and about, and then, suddenly, you're back at the same place half a lifetime later."

"Only we're not the same people anymore, are we?"

"No, we're not." Leela turned towards Nandini.

Nandini's gaze lingered on her for a few moments longer than was appropriate before turning away and peering down the road. "Where the hell is my car?"

A warmth had crept up Leela's face. It wasn't just the wine. "There is usually a lot of traffic on the road just behind the building. Give him a minute or two."

"The traffic here is crazy now. Bangalore used to be such a quaint, sleepy little place in the nineties."

"The weather is still good, though—mostly. What's Delhi like right now?"

"Beginning to get cold. Time was when early December used to be freezing. Not anymore."

"Is that your car?"

A grey Honda City drew up next to them and stopped. Nandini turned back to Leela. "Thank you once again for an entertaining evening. I had fun, really."

"I believe you," said Leela, grinning at her. "My father can be quite entertaining."

"See you." Nandini reached out and touched Leela's arm.

"Bye."

Leela waved as the car pulled away. She could feel the ghost of Nandini's fingers on her arm, and with it came the reminder of how great they had been together in Amrudpur. She felt a pang of disappointment at their current arrangement to be friends.

Maybe it was just the wine making her maudlin.

CHAPTER TWELVE

At lunch the next day, Davi asked, "Did you get a chance to talk to Neil?"

"About what?" Leela reached across the table to help herself to the lime pickle that Davi had brought. They had lunch together every day, usually in Leela's office.

Davi pursed her lips. "You forgot? About Rahul, of course."

"Oho. No, I didn't forget. Neil didn't have anything useful to say, so there was nothing to report. Is Rahul in today? How does he seem?"

"Yes, he's in. I can't really tell how he is. He's quiet anyway, so it's harder to figure out if he's withdrawn."

"Have you spoken to his class teacher? Asha, right?"

Davi clicked her tongue impatiently. "Asha Rao is more spaced-out than half the kids she teaches."

"Davi, honestly, I know there's no love lost between you and Asha, but you have to play nice to get to the bottom of this."

"Psh. I don't need to play nice with her as long as I have a direct line to Rahul through Neil. Could I come over and speak to him this evening, do you think?"

"You're not going to get anything out of him."

"Just because you didn't, you think I won't either?"

"All right, all right, you can go all Spanish Inquisition on him whenever you like, but I have to remind you that you are wanted for the after-school workshop with Discover-E today."

"Oh fu…I mean, oh hell. I'd forgotten about that."

"You can swear, there are no kids around," Leela pointed out.

"I don't know why you want me in this project," Davi grumbled. She packed up her multi-layered lunch box with a lot of extra banging and clanging, while Leela pretended to have suddenly developed an unusual interest in her phone.

"Come over on Sunday?" Leela asked by way of a peace offering. Not that she herself didn't want to know what was going on with Rahul, or if anything was. "We can tackle Neil together. Bring the kids. We'll go to Sankey Tank in the evening."

"Fine," Davi threw back as she stalked out of the room.

Leela returned to her desk and opened her diary. She was due to meet with Raza next and then preside over a senior-school prefects' meeting. She looked at her watch. Nandini and her people would've probably arrived. She had just enough time to go and say a quick hello.

* * *

Nandini's "people," it turned out, was one unsmiling, serious-faced young man with the contrary name of Amandeep Singh Jolly. A room right next to the school's computer lab, which had earlier been a storage space, had been cleared out and set up with half a dozen computers for Discover-E to commandeer. Five teachers, all teaching maths and science, had been selected to be part of the project, and once the software was installed, they would be trained to program it and then integrate it into their classroom teaching.

"Everything to your satisfaction?" Leela asked Nandini, who was sitting on a chair, one elegant trouser-clad leg crossed over another and an arm draped over the back as she watched Amandeep flit from one machine to the other with the air of a ruffled chicken. Only Nandini could make sitting on these hard plastic chairs with tablet arms look fetching. With a bit of effort, Leela schooled her eye to stay on Nandini's face.

Nandini turned around and smiled. "Oh yes, everything is just fine. We should be done with the installation in a couple of hours and then we'll be ready to start."

"Great."

Nandini stood up. "Aman, can you manage without me for a while?"

"Yes, sure," Aman replied without looking up.

Nandini gestured towards the corridor. "I'd love to stretch my legs," she said to Leela. "Do you have time for a little stroll?"

"Of course." Leela led the way out, down the hall, and out into the lawns. It was a pleasant afternoon. The sun was hidden behind clouds, hinting at the possibility of rain later. "Aren't CEOs a little senior to be doing the donkey work of installing software?" she asked.

"Not when they are CEOs of tiny companies," Nandini replied. "Don't laugh, but Aman is our entire IT department."

"It's amazing how you guys do such complicated work with just four or five people."

"It was developing the software that was the hard work. Now it's just a matter of training people to use it."

"Are you going to be handling the training bit?"

"Not the whole thing. Most likely Vikrant, one of my partners in Discover-E, will do most of the training. I'll just help out sometimes. Vikrant is the tech brains. Most of it."

"You're being modest, right?"

"Ha, not at all. The whole damn thing was my idea in the first place. That modest enough for you?"

Leela laughed. "So you never stopped having crazy ideas, then?"

"Looks like it. Just like you never stopped wanting to change the world."

"But I'm not changing the world."

Nandini gestured around her. "What do you call this, then?"

"What do you mean?"

"Learning—isn't that how the world changes?"

Leela shook her head at Nandini. "Really, you say the strangest things." Though it kind of did make sense, and it wasn't altogether bad thinking about her job like that.

"Madam, madam!"

Leela turned around at the sound of Bopanna's voice. He hurried towards her. "Madam, Raza Sir has arrived. He is waiting in your office."

"Okay, I'll be there right away. Thank you, Bopanna." To Nandini, she said, "I'm afraid duty calls. I'll look in on you later."

They walked back inside together. "By the way," Nandini said, "I saw in the papers this morning that there's a fractal art exhibition in town this weekend. It's supposed to be really good. Do you think you and Neil would like to come with me?"

"Oh, I'm sure Neil would love it. When is it?"

"Saturday and Sunday, I think. I'll send you the details. You let me know."

"Sure, thanks, Nandini."

"No problem. See you."

CHAPTER THIRTEEN

"Neil?"

Leela dropped her keys into the little bowl on top of the shoe cupboard in the hall. She set her bags of shopping down on the floor and slipped off her shoes. The house was unnaturally quiet and dark. Where was Neil? It was a weekday; he shouldn't be out at this time.

A piece of paper on the dining table caught her attention. It was torn out of a writing pad, weighted down by a water bottle. She picked it up and recognised her son's untidy scrawl. For an artist, he had appalling handwriting.

Going to grandparents place to help with rat emergency

Leela grimaced, equally at the mention of the rat as at Neil's lack of punctuation. Should she call her parents? Or go down to see if she could help? *Nah*. If they needed help, they would've been hounding her with calls. And if they didn't, she would rather not have to deal with rats after her long day battling a staff meeting, followed by grocery shopping.

She went into the kitchen to get herself some coffee and something to eat—there were leftover noodles from last night—

and walked through to the living room. She set her mug and plate down on the side table by her chair, and reached for the light switch with one hand and the TV remote with the other with the sort of ease that comes with years of doing the same thing every evening.

A fraction of a second before the tube light blinked on, a flickering green in the dark alcove of the room where the computer was caught her attention. She clucked her tongue— that boy had forgotten to turn off the PC again. She was getting tired of nagging him about leaving it on for days.

She went towards it and tapped the spacebar, waiting as the monitor came back on and the CPU whirred to life. She reached for the mouse to shut down the PC when her eyes fell on the window that lay open on the desktop.

It was a browser tab open at a search page showing results for the term "Section 377." Another tab open behind it showed search results for "arrested for being gay in India." There were numerous other tabs, presumably the search results he had clicked on.

Leela's heart was pounding. She sat down heavily on the chair in front of the computer. Why was he looking this up? Did it mean she had been right about Neil being gay? Or had he been looking up stuff for his friend?

Does it matter?

The question that popped into her head was just as much its own answer. Leela cycled through the open tabs, her heart sinking further and further as she skimmed over the contents of each page. Laid bare before her were all sorts of half-truths and half-explanations and sensationalisation that the media, and more so the Internet, were notorious for. If this was what he had been reading, he must be terrified, and none the wiser. Leela wanted to weep. Not just for Neil, but for every other teen and young person who must be petrified at this ocean of information available at their fingertips but no opportunity to discuss or understand it.

She pressed her fingertips to her forehead and sat still for a few minutes. Then she went back to her sofa chair and sank down on it. She had lost her appetite for the noodles, and the coffee was tepid and disgusting.

The key jangled in the lock and Neil appeared at the door. Leela had no clue how long she'd been sitting there, motionless.

"Hi, Ma," said Neil, breathless. "Did you see my note about the rat? It was so big"—he held his hands out in the approximation of a small dog—"and Grandma said it must have eaten the rat poison because it was moving across the house like it was drunk and it was so gross, so I said we should call the gardener to help and when he came, he just picked it up with a plastic bag—cool as anything—and took it away, but Grandma was disgusted and she called Vidya-Akka to come and move all the cupboards and clean up and all, and it took *ages*…Ma?" Neil moved further into the room, a frown etched on his animated face. "Are you all right?"

Leela roused herself and tried a smile. "Yes, I'm all right. Come here." She stood up, grabbed him by the shoulders, and pulled him into a hug. When had he become taller than her?

He struggled free. "Stop it!" He leaned back from Leela and stared at her. "What's the matter?"

"I need to talk to you about something." She pointed to the sofa, and he went and sat obediently, his eyes never leaving her, his expression now worried.

"There's nothing wrong," Leela assured him. "I only wanted to…" She hesitated. She hadn't really thought about how she would talk to him, but her intuition nudged her towards a direct approach. "The computer was on, I noticed you were looking up information on Section 377."

Neil's eyes went round for an instant. Then he looked away, back at Leela and away again. Leela could spot an evasive gaze from a mile off.

"You're not in any trouble, if that's what you're worrying about," she told him. "I just want you to know—I think you do know—that you can talk to me about anything, right?"

"Uh, yeah, sure."

He didn't elaborate, and she waited. Staying quiet was often a better way to get people to talk rather than hammering questions at them. Also, now that it was clear what they were talking about, she was afraid of preempting anything, of jumping to conclusions. It would be much better if he spoke first.

"It's just…someone was…I saw something in…in the papers, you know, about it. And I wanted to…find out." He twisted his hands in his lap as he spoke.

"What did you want to know?" Leela asked, trying to keep her tone neutral.

"About…it. What it means and…that's all."

"And? Did you find out?"

His shoulders rose and fell.

"It's okay to want to find out about things around you, Neil."

He looked puzzled. "It is?"

"Yes. Perfectly okay." She smiled slightly. "No need to look so shifty about it."

His smile was faint too.

"So, did you find what you wanted?"

"I…don't know. I read that it was de-…er, decriminalised…"

"Read down," Leela prompted. "The law was 'read down.' It means the court narrowed the interpretation of the law."

"Yes, that. But a few years later the Supreme Court made it, er, criminal again."

Leela sighed inwardly. This was what happened when there was no space to talk about sexuality. Even most adults she came across had a very skewed idea of what Section 377 really said.

"What was it the Supreme Court made illegal again?" she asked, wanting to be absolutely sure of what he knew, or thought he knew.

Neil looked up at her, surprised. "Being gay, of course."

Leela took a deep breath and exhaled slowly. "Remember how I keep telling you that while the Internet is great for finding information, sometimes it isn't the most reliable source?"

"Ye-ah. Something about context and filters, you said."

"Do you understand what that means?"

Neil screwed up his face, as if trying to recall something particularly tricky. "It's like, it doesn't know what you are looking for specifically and why, and sometimes that results in misleading information. Or something like that."

"Yes, something like that. And some things are trickier than others. Like Section 377. Neil, look at me." She waited till he complied. "Being gay is not a crime in India. That is not what the law means. Okay?"

"But"—he pointed at the computer—"it said…it is."

"If you read the news reports carefully, you'll find that's not what they necessarily say. The trouble is, they don't always say it in a way that most people can understand."

"So what does it really mean, this Section 377?"

"Section 377 criminalises…" Leela paused for the briefest fraction of a second, as this was one place where Neil was likely to bolt. "…certain sexual acts that it believes are unnatural. This can impact relationships, whether it is between two men or between a man and a woman." She paused, properly this time. "Do you understand?"

Neil's blank face was an answer in itself, but he shook his head and said, "No."

"In simple terms, the law assumes that certain kinds of sexual acts are 'natural' and others are not. It doesn't actually list what these 'unnatural' acts are."

Leela looked away for a few beats, trying to figure out how to explain this better to him. "You know how we've talked about the Bible being open to interpretation?"

"Yes, that different people find different meanings in it."

"Exactly. In a similar way, a law can also have more than one interpretation. In this case, the law is interpreted in a way that makes sex between two men a crime. In some cases between a man and a woman as well. This makes it possible for gay men and transgender people to be harassed.

"But, from what I know, in the recent past, in your lifetime at least, nobody has been sent to prison under Section 377 just because they are gay or because they have said they are—there is no law against that. But people *have* been bullied and mistreated by the police because of it."

"It's a stupid law. Why have it?" Neil asked.

"Yes, it is a stupid law. But the bigger problem is the way that it is understood. That's why in 2009 the High Court said that any relationship between adults, when both of them are agreed on it, should not be a part of this. But a few years later, the Supreme Court overturned this decision."

"Why?"

"Because, clearly, some people still believe homosexuality is unnatural. But you and I both know that isn't true." She paused. "Do you understand?"

"I think so. I don't know. So, being gay is not a crime?"

"No."

"But if gay people, you know, then it becomes a crime?"

"Um, it's a grey area. It *can* be interpreted to be a crime."

"So gay people cannot...you know?"

Leela wished heartily he would stop using "you know" as a euphemism, but at the moment it was more important to keep the conversation going, so she let it be. "If two adults decide to have sex," she said, "which one of them, do you think, is going to go to the police to report it?"

"Oh God, Ma! Geez." He pulled out the cushion from behind him and buried his face in it.

"Your grandma would tell you not to take the Lord's name in vain," Leela said, hoping it would lighten the atmosphere. "Anyway, to sum it up, there is a lot of hoo-haa around Section 377 but it doesn't actually say that being gay is criminal. It can, however, be misused by the police to harass the innocent, and gay people are one of the groups that are vulnerable to it. Got it?"

"Yeah. I think so." He put the cushion down on his lap and stared at it. "It's so unfair."

"Yes, it is. But there is still some hope. Remember the Right to Privacy judgement that came from the Supreme Court in August?"

"Yeah. That privacy is a fundamental right."

"Yes. It also specifically says that sexual orientation is part of that privacy, and no one should have to face discrimination because of their sexuality."

"So one thing says this and the other thing says something else."

"Yes. It's contradictory. But those who are against Section 377 are now using the privacy judgement to make the courts take another look at it."

"That's good, then."

"Yes, it is." Leela took in a deep breath and released it slowly. "But you know what's a bigger problem? Even if a law like Section 377 didn't exist, it would still be difficult to be gay in our country."

"Because people are so narrow-minded?"

Leela nodded. "And plenty of gay people live in shame and secret and even lose their lives because they have no support either from their families or friends or anywhere else. But we are not like that, you and me, right?"

"Right."

She waited, but he didn't speak.

"Neil, as I said before, you know you can tell me anything, right?"

"Yeah." He didn't say it with as much conviction as Leela would have liked.

"I know it's a terrible cliché, this you-can-tell-me-anything statement, but I want you to be safe and happy. So even if it's something you think I'm going to freak out about, I promise you, I will deal with it."

"I know. Your freak-out threshold is pretty high, Ma."

That was high praise indeed. "So, is there anything else you want to tell me or ask me?"

"No. Can I go?"

"Of course."

She watched him go into his room, still unsure if there was something he was hiding from her.

CHAPTER FOURTEEN

The Chitrakala Parishat complex, CKP for short, was teeming with weekend visitors, mostly because of the sari and handicrafts exhibition on its grounds. Temporary stalls had been set up, creating a labyrinthine network of narrow alleys for visitors to navigate. Snack vendors crowded outside the gates, selling everything from bottled water and ice cream to boiled peanuts and chaat.

"If you're going to see the sari exhibition, then I'm going to have both boiled peanuts and an ice gola," Neil said as they wove their way between the crowds towards the main building.

"You fell asleep in church—I don't think you can do any negotiations today," Leela reminded him.

Neil's face fell. Leela laughed. "I'm kidding. And anyway, so am I."

She checked her phone to see where Nandini had said she'd meet them.

"So are you what?" Neil asked.

"Have peanuts and ice gola," Leela replied, casting around for Nandini. She had said she'd meet them in front of "the gallery," but did she know there were more than a dozen galleries here? Leela looked at her phone again. Maybe she should call Nandini.

"There's Nandini Aunty," Neil said.

Leela turned to where he was looking, and there she was, indeed, coming towards them with a big smile. She was wearing a red sleeveless collared cotton shirt and tight blue jeans— designer again for sure. A cloth bag was swinging from her shoulder. "Hello. Sorry, I got distracted by the exhibition."

"Hi," Leela said, ignoring the quick shiver that rippled down her spine. "Did you buy anything?"

"A shirt for a friend." She opened the mouth of the bag to show them the rich blues and greens. "Shall we go in?"

There was a standee display in the lobby that told them where the fractal art exhibit was. Apparently, it was a travelling exhibition that had started in Germany and was going around the world, collaborating with local artists.

"I didn't know there was an Indian Association of Fractal Artists," Leela said when she read the pamphlet she had picked up at the door.

"To be honest, neither did I," Nandini replied.

Neil had gone ahead and was admiring the artworks mounted on the walls. The gallery was empty apart from a couple right at the other end.

"Whoa! Ma, come and look at this," he called.

Leela went over. He was gazing at a collection of images in black and white, and to her distinctly unartistic eye, it seemed just a mass of swirls.

Nandini clearly had a different opinion about it. "Lovely," she said.

Neil seemed enthralled. He had an animated discussion with Nandini about an artwork that was maybe a big eye surrounded by several smaller eyes. The two of them stayed together, pointing out and talking about other pieces they found interesting in the section, while Leela followed quietly behind.

The next section had images filled with vibrant colour. Neil's fascination was so absolute by now that he bounced from one collection to another leaving behind Nandini, who went at a more temperate pace.

Leela hung back, following Nandini as she moved through the display. She had agreed to come to the exhibition as Neil had been enthusiastic, but now she had to admit that some of the works were indeed eye-catching. Especially one that appeared to be an incredibly intricate snowflake, and another that could best be described as a series of magical flames in a mix of wispy colours. Despite herself, she was slowly drawn into the images. Soon she, too, was moving between the displayed frames and taking them in at her own pace.

The one that particularly resonated with her was a work with earthy tones of browns and yellows and reds in a vibrant interaction. The composition itself reminded Leela of a dense network of twisting staircases leading away into infinity—not that there were any actual staircases in the image, but she just had an impression of them.

Maybe that's what art is.

She moved on to the next image, which brought to mind a steampunk, clockwork worm. It was closer to the grotesque end of the scale, and it burst Leela's temporary bubble of being at one with art. Nandini, though, seemed quite transfixed by it, studying it with her head tilted to one side. Her hand clutched the strap of the cloth bag on her shoulder and her index finger reached out to brush her hair back behind her ear. Leela had a sudden flashback to their college days. That gesture, of brushing her hair back with a finger, her head tilted to one side, was definitely from back then.

Seemingly unaware that Leela was standing behind her, Nandini stepped backwards. Leela only had a split second to react. She caught Nandini by the arms before she could crush her sandal-clad feet.

"Careful. Right behind you," Leela said.

Nandini whipped around. "Oh…uh…" She stared back at Leela, stupefied.

Her gaze moved to her arm, which Leela was still holding. Leela jerked her hand away, moving back at the same moment that Nandini also stepped back. She cast a quick glance around to see where Neil was, but he was safely wrapped in his own world.

"I just, I mean, you were…" began Leela.

"Sorry, I, um, wasn't paying…" Nandini started at the same time.

Then they both laughed, the air a little awkward between them. "It's all right," Leela said. "No toes broken." She could still feel the warmth and softness of Nandini's skin and the smooth curve of her biceps tingling on her fingertips. The urge to run her thumb over her fingers was overpowering.

"Good, good." And after a moment's hesitation, Nandini pointed back towards the artworks. "So…back to the…uh?"

"Yeah, of course."

Leela went and joined Neil and remained stuck to his side for the rest of their circuit of the room.

"Thanks for bringing us here, Nandini Aunty. It was awesome," Neil said when they exited the gallery.

Leela winced at this catch-all term that youngsters seemed to use these days to mean anything from "okay" to "superlative." "I have to admit, that it was quite fascinating," she said to Nandini. "Though I can't quite imagine what this has to do with maths."

"I can try to explain, but I'm not sure if you're still allergic to maths."

"I am."

"Okay then, can we have the ice golas now?" Neil asked.

They trooped outside to the gates. The ice-gola seller was quite in demand and they had to wait a few minutes before they were each handed a crushed-ice lollipop dipped in a cup of their chosen flavour of syrup.

"Mmm, can't remember the last time I had one of these," Nandini said, leaning forward to keep the bright green pista-flavoured syrup she had chosen from dripping on her clothes.

"I have one every time I come here," Neil announced. "I try to take a different colour every time."

"So do I," Leela confessed.

Neil wanted more snacks afterwards, so they all got newspaper twists filled with warm and salted boiled peanuts. They walked along the footpath, towards the car park where Leela had left her car, Neil up ahead, she and Nandini following more slowly.

"When is your flight?" she asked.

"Seven o'clock. I think I should make a move towards the airport sooner rather than later."

"It shouldn't take you more than an hour from here, but"— Leela glanced up at the sky—"it might rain, and you know what happens to the traffic when it rains."

"What are you guys going to do after this?"

"My friend Davi is coming over with her kids. We had plans to go to the lake."

"Davi, that's Davinder Srinivasan, right?"

"The same. We go back a long way. In fact, we met very soon after you left Bangalore."

Nandini raised her eyebrows. "You mean, you two—"

"Oh no, no, no! Nothing like that."

"Ah, I see." Nandini had turned back to her paper cone, popping peanut shells with one hand.

Was that relief that Leela sensed in her tone? "Would you be jealous?" she teased. It wasn't an altogether unpleasant thought.

"What?" Nandini seemed to be studying her peanuts with great interest. "No, of course not. Why should I be?"

"No reason, just wondered."

"I was just curious."

"Right." Leela cleared her throat. "So, er, my car is parked here."

"Right, and my driver said he'd park down that road." They stopped and faced each other. "So that's goodbye for now, I guess."

"Yep." Before she could think too much about it, Leela leaned forward and gave Nandini a hug. A big mistake. Every part of her body that touched Nandini felt ablaze, and Leela quickly stepped back. "Neil," she called in a tone that sounded high-pitched to her own ears. "Come and say bye to Nandini Aunty."

Neil jogged back towards them, full of gratitude for having been introduced to fractal art. "You'll show me your work, won't you?" he said. "When will you come to Bangalore again?"

"Soon, I hope."

"We'll see you then," Leela put in, trying her best to forget her body's reaction to its proximity to Nandini. "Though I'll be in Delhi next month for Hanssen's annual principals' conference. Maybe we'll catch up there?"

"You bet." Nandini's smile was warm, and Leela couldn't help being consumed by a confusing mix of excitement and trepidation.

CHAPTER FIFTEEN

Leela hated appraisals season, not only because it was tedious and a waste of her time, but also because she detested standing judgement over her colleagues. She belonged to the school of thought where co-workers and bosses kept lines of communication open throughout the year and resolved any issues as and when they arose. She had suggested to the board to make the latter method official ages ago, but some of the older members hadn't been convinced. That of course hadn't stopped Leela from implementing her preferred method informally at least, and she hoped that one day she'd have enough case studies to convince the board.

For now, though, files covered the dining table and her laptop lay open before her. There were Post-its everywhere, a riot of colour to the ignorant but carefully coded as per Leela. So obviously, when the doorbell rang, she ignored it.

Neil came out of his room and went to see who it was. He glanced sideways at Leela from afar—he was banned from coming within five feet of the dining table.

"Hi, Leela Ma'am," Rahul said as he walked past with Neil.

Leela looked up to acknowledge his greeting just in time to notice Neil nudging Rahul. "Bad mood, don't push it," he muttered.

Leela ignored him. "Hello, Rahul, how are you?"

"I'm well, thank you."

He was always so polite. But he seemed haggard and drawn. True, he'd always been on the slender side, but he'd also had a healthy spring to his step. Today, his pleasant, angular face had none of the keen-eyed awareness that she'd hitherto associated with him. His cheeks seemed hollow and there was an unhealthy pallor about him. She had trouble reconciling this skin-and-bones stranger with the same Rahul she'd known for months. Davi had been right to be worried about him—and, come to think of it, she couldn't remember the last time he'd come over here. In fact, she had barely seen him in school as well.

"Ma, why are you staring?" Neil asked in his what-now voice.

Leela shook herself back to reality. "Was I? Sorry, miles away. Rahul, are you sure you're okay? You look a bit under the weather."

"I'm fine, ma'am," Rahul replied, his manner resolute. "I just came to pick up some homework."

Leela opened her mouth to cross-question him, but Neil caught his elbow and dragged him away. She stared after them. Davi was absolutely right; there was something going on with him.

Rahul left about half an hour later. Now she could buttonhole her son.

"Neil, come here," she called.

He came to the door, expression wary, his eyes tracking the empty space on the floor between him and the dining table.

"Stop the drama, come and sit down." Leela got up and gestured in the direction of the sofa as she moved towards it. Neil followed her, his gait dripping reluctance, and sat down on the chair perpendicular to the sofa. "Tell me what's going on with Rahul."

He went on high alert at once. Leela knew all the signs—not meeting her eyes, glancing everywhere but at her, and hands twisting in his lap.

"Nothing. Why are you so hell-bent on making out that something's wrong?"

"Don't mess about with me, Neil. I want to know. Now."

Leela expected him to resist some more, but his shoulders sagged and he dropped his head to his chest almost as soon as she finished speaking. His voice was so low that Leela almost didn't make out what he said. "I promised I wouldn't tell anyone."

"Did you see him just now?" Leela said. "He looks ill. Whatever is going on with him is taking a toll on his health. Is it something at home?"

Leela kicked herself for not having taken Davi's apprehensions more seriously and doing something about them sooner. And she was also annoyed with herself for failing to notice the deterioration in Rahul. She made a mental note to speak to Asha Rao, Rahul's class teacher. It was ridiculous that the other teachers hadn't noticed this change in him.

Neil shook his head.

"Then what? Is it school? Jesus Christ, this is like squeezing blood from a stone."

As the seconds passed, his misery increased. "But I promised," he said.

His hands twisted and worried each other faster and faster. Leela leaned forward and stilled them with her own hand. "Look at you, Neil," she said. "You're obviously worried about him too. If you tell me, maybe we can help him together."

"If I could help him…"

"Just tell me and let me figure out a way, okay?"

Neil exhaled. "Okay," he said. Then he paused. "You know, like, how he's…not like…I mean, he's a bit…he's not like—" His eyebrows bunched up in worry. "You get mad when I say things like this."

Leela tried not to grit her teeth. "Just say it. I'll take the circumstances into consideration."

"He's a bit girly, you know. Well, he's not like the other boys." Neil held up his hands in explication. "I don't care about it, I don't even think it's a big deal. But other people do. They make fun of him."

"I thought he was quite popular in school."

"He is, with most people, because he gets great marks and he's basically a nice guy. It's not like they mess with him or anything directly, just a few jokes here and there, saying things about chhakas and all. You know?"

Leela tried to keep her face still at the use of the derogatory term for transgender people, and nodded. "Is that what people call him?"

"No, no. Nobody calls *him* anything. It's nothing like that. It's just that they make jokes about things like that when he's around. Not everyone, some people."

"Who?"

Neil clucked his tongue in impatience. "You want me to tell you everything, but you keep interrupting me."

"Okay, sorry, sorry. Go on."

"So, a few months ago, he started getting emails and messages. They were horrible things, about…about…"

"Homophobic things?"

"Yes, that. And there were images and photos. Really terrible things, Ma, I can't even say them. And they said they would report him to the police and…and horrible things would happen to him in prison."

Leela clenched her fists to fight the horror and despair building up inside her. "And who's been sending these messages?"

"No idea. It comes from different email IDs, all made-up stuff. It's clear that the person is hiding his identity."

"Rahul has absolutely no idea who may be sending them?"

"No, but we think it has to be someone at school. He doesn't really go out or mix with people anywhere else."

"Is that why you were looking up information on Section 377 that day? For Rahul?"

Neil nodded. His woeful expression broke Leela's heart. He'd been doing his best for his friend—in his half-arsed, teenage way.

"This is cyberbullying, Neil. I don't know the specifics of the law, but as far as I know, posting harmful comments and images can be a crime. It can definitely be reported to the police. Does he have copies of the messages?"

Neil shook his head. "He deleted them. They were awful, Ma, nobody should have to read such things. It even made me feel so…" He shuddered. "Anyway, they came from anonymous accounts, I told you."

"Emails and other accounts can be traced. Very little is anonymous online. There are IP addresses and headers and things like that, which the police can use to find out which computer or mobile phone the messages came from. I thought you kids were the experts in these things."

"You don't understand, Ma. They're just too upsetting for him to hang on to."

Leela exhaled. "I'm sorry. I do understand. I'm just frustrated that all of this was happening under my nose and I was clueless."

"It's not your fault."

"It is." Leela pressed her lips together. "I'm responsible for keeping all of you safe." She reached across and grasped Neil's hand again. "Thank you for telling me. You did the right thing."

"He's going to be so mad at me." He hung his head.

Leela squeezed his hand. "You were trying to be supportive, a good friend. I don't need to tell you how important it is for Rahul to have friends in his corner."

Neil nodded.

"And now that you've told me, he has at least two people on his side. Listen, Neil, what you said earlier, about people making homophobic jokes in his hearing even if they were not directly addressed to him, that's bullying too. It's abusive behaviour. It's not okay."

Neil nodded again.

"Does his family know about this?"

"No. He doesn't want them to know."

"Okay, but I'm going to need to talk to Rahul, all right? And I'm going to have to talk to the whole school about bullying."

Neil's eyes went round in horror. "Oh, no, Ma, you can't! Then they'll know that Rahul complained and it will be worse for him."

"What's the option, Neil? To stay quiet and let the bullies and abusers continue with this nonsense? Or let them know that it's not on, that what they're doing is criminal? Tell me which one you'd have me do."

* * *

Leela drummed her fingers on her desk, twisting her chair back and forth. On the other side of her desk sat Rina Pant, the senior school supervisor, Anil Dikshit, vice-principal, Asha Rao, Rahul's class teacher, and Zara Kashif, the school counsellor.

"And so," Leela concluded, "they point-blank refused to give me the names of those who have been making homophobic jokes around Rahul, but I thought between us we might have an idea who these kids are."

"My money is on Prateek and Rajesh," Anil said. "They are the troublemakers of the batch. They do have a fan following, but I get the feeling the other kids are just hangers-on."

"Maybe so, but they're enabling the abuse. It has to stop."

"To be fair," said Asha, "calling it abuse is a bit extreme, no? I mean, they've only made some jokes, from what you say. And that too indirectly. It's not like they're beating him up or even calling him names to his face."

Leela turned to her, her train of thought stalled. She glanced at Rina, whose expression said that she would love to put her hands around Asha's neck and squeeze till her eyes popped out. Even Anil, inscrutable at the best of times, seemed taken aback.

It was Zara who stepped in, ever the voice of reason. "They are making him uncomfortable and making him feel unsafe. Surely no child should be made to feel this way?"

"But these are kids, they say mean things. These things will happen."

"So it's up to us to point out that this behaviour is not on and these things should not happen," Leela put in, her voice tight with suppressed anger. "And if these are the same people sending him abusive emails and messages, then there are sections of the IT Act that apply. I had a chat with the deputy inspector general of the Cyber Crimes Cell this morning. Her granddaughters are in our junior school."

"Even so, it's like a rite of passage. Rahul should toughen up a bit."

"Asha, please, you're embarrassing yourself," Rina said. She was known to be brusque when her patience ran out. "What you're saying is tantamount to victim blaming."

"No, no, you're misunderstanding me. I'm not saying it's Rahul's fault. Just that the way of the world is such that we have to adapt and behave in certain ways. Surely Rahul has to realise that at some point in his life and start acting more like a boy." Asha turned to Leela and spread her hands, like she was entreating her to understand. "You know what I mean, right?"

"No, I don't actually," Leela replied. "Could you elaborate, please?"

"Er, just that, at one level, we are making a mountain out of a molehill. Boys, after all, they are always getting into trouble. It's just the way it is."

"The school policy is very clear on bullying—zero tolerance," Anil pointed out.

"That's what I mean, there's been no bullying really. It's only messages and emails. No one has touched him."

"Bullying isn't always physical," Rina said.

"Aren't we too soft these days? When we were young, the kind of things that happened. We all learnt to cope."

"When we were kids, no one gave a second thought to making homophobic and casteist jokes and all other kinds of nonsense. Things have changed. As they should."

"This is nothing. You want to see real bullying, you should see some of the bigger schools. Do you have any idea the kind of stuff that goes on there? If the administrations of these schools were to deal with each and every case, they wouldn't have time to do anything else."

The conversation was veering off on a ridiculous tangent. Leela had had enough. "What happens in other schools is not my concern. I have to make sure that every student in my school feels safe. So we have to stem whatever it is that's going on.

To start with, I want to address the school about bullying in general, remind them that we take a very serious stand on it. Also, Deputy Inspector General Khan has offered to come down and talk about cyberbullying." She added grimly, "I am hoping it scares the life out of the bullies, if they are the same. I also feel the senior school needs to be talked to in more specific terms, including making homophobic comments and jokes. Rina, will you organise it with all the class teachers?"

"Sure."

"And Zara, you will need to brief all the class teachers on how to speak to the students. I'd like it if you were also present to answer any questions they may not be able to deal with."

"Of course. I have another suggestion."

"Go on."

Before Zara could speak, Asha jumped in. "Do you really think we should be talking to the students about these things? The parents will be up in arms."

"What kind of things?" Anil was clearly puzzled. "About bullying?"

"No, about gays and things."

"There are LGBT students in the school, Asha." Rina's tone was curt. "They must not feel threatened."

Asha's mouth fell open. "What? Who are these students?"

"I don't know specifically who they are. I meant statistically."

"I think," Zara said before Asha could formulate a reply, "we need a mechanism to deal with this sort of thing in the school. A platform where students can come to us for help or even advice. They are not always able to talk openly about subjects like sexuality, so we need something a bit more subtle."

Leela looked around. "Any suggestions?"

"I really don't think we should encourage this sort of behaviour. The parents will not be happy," Asha said, shaking her head.

"What sort of behaviour?" Rina's tone bordered on the belligerent. Leela groaned inwardly. She hoped she wouldn't have to pull her back in line.

"Talking about these kind of adult subjects."

"Perhaps a letter box can be installed in the school, where any student can put in a note?" Anil seemed to have decided that Asha wasn't there at all and hadn't spoken. Leela appreciated the tactic. She really had no patience that morning to deal with any sort of nonsense. On second thoughts, she'd never had patience for this particular kind of rubbish. "It can be anonymous, and the matters that come up can be discussed in assembly or by class teachers."

"Or something online," Rina suggested. "A virtual letter box, where anyone can write in."

They threw around a few more ideas, and in the end agreed to go with the letter box because it could be set up immediately. Anil volunteered to take care of it. It would be installed, they decided, in a secluded passage between the library and the auditorium, so the letter writers' secrecy could be maintained if they wanted.

As the others were filing out of the office, Leela called Asha back.

"Asha, a moment, please."

"Yes, Leela Ma'am."

Leela gestured to the chairs in front of her. "Please sit down." She waited till Asha was seated. "I need you to be on board with this. One hundred per cent. The parents are hard enough to deal with, but I draw the line at having staff members who condone bullying in the name of toughening up."

Asha gazed over Leela's shoulder and out the window into the playing area behind the building. "I am uncomfortable with the idea of putting ideas into children's heads or encouraging children to be gays. It's inappropriate. It's for Rahul's own good if he toughens up."

"You do know that people are not gay because they have been encouraged or discouraged, right?"

"Come on, ma'am, I'm being realistic."

"No, *I* am being realistic."

Her eyes drifted back to Leela, a bit unsure now. "I don't understand."

"It's true that I don't know every teacher's personal beliefs, but I cannot turn a blind eye to one who is openly hostile to students who may or may not be homosexual. We have all kinds of students in the school and every one of them deserves respect and fairness. Most of all, they deserve to feel safe."

"What about the other children? Those who feel uncomfortable with the behaviour of certain students?"

"Then they must be made to realise what living in a diverse and pluralistic society means."

"Are you saying if I don't share your personal beliefs and back this encouraging of your gay agenda, you will sack me?"

"There is no agenda, Asha. I just need you to be a decent human being." It wasn't even ten o'clock and Leela was already exhausted. "You must decide whether you're with me on this."

"And if not?"

"Then you must consider if Hanssen is the right place for you."

Asha stood up, palms on the table, eyes blazing. "How dare you!" she said through gritted teeth. "I have been teaching for twenty-five years. You think you know more about the children, spending all your day in your cushy office? You namby-pamby bleeding-heart liberals have no clue how to deal with children in real life. Also, I'll tell you this, you didn't hire me, the board did. So you can threaten me all you like, but I'm not going anywhere."

"Then, you're welcome to speak to the board about this." Leela also stood and went to the door. She held it open and waited for Asha to leave. "And after that, you can let me know if you are with me on this or if you would rather hand in your resignation."

PART III

JANUARY–MARCH 2018

Nandini waved a hand in a don't-mention-it gesture. "You look frozen. Come right in and park yourself next to the heater."

Nandini guided her through the house, her hand lightly on Leela's elbow. Even through all her layers, the touch still left a warm imprint on Leela's arm. Nandini's familiar perfume wafted towards her. Suddenly, she wasn't feeling so cold after all.

She was shown into a large living-cum-dining space, big enough for a proper sitting area, a reading nook in an alcove, and an eight-seater dining table. The kitchen was visible just off the dining area, all gleaming countertops and polished knobs. The furniture was the kind of simple that hinted at the expensive, with low-level monochrome sofas, leather recliners, a glass-top dining table with a wrought iron frame, plain wooden bookshelves, and an L-shaped bar cabinet with high stools. There were cotton rugs on the floor, artworks that Leela recognised as fractal art and handicrafts on the walls, and LED tube lights that bathed everything in a warm glow.

"Wow." The reaction popped out of her mouth before she could stop herself. "Your place is fantastic. So much open space."

"Thank you." Nandini led her towards the sofas. "Though I have to admit it hasn't come through honest toil. My parents had this place, and they gave it to me some five or six years ago. It is nice, I admit. I'll give you a tour later, if you want."

"Are they still in the jewellery business?" Leela sank down into one of the sofas. It was softer than she had anticipated, and she had the momentary sensation of being swallowed whole by a spongy monster. A snazzy black-and-grey portable radiator next to the sofa ensconced her in a warm embrace. She shrugged out of her shawl.

A copy of the *Indian Express* lay on the coffee table before her, weighed down by a thick Val McDermid novel. Nandini's reading glasses lay on top of the book. An empty mug rested on a coaster beside it, which Nandini picked up and carried to the kitchen, turning her head around to reply.

"Oh, no. Retired. My father sold off his share to his nephews since neither Abhinav nor I were interested."

CHAPTER SIXTEEN

Leela pressed the doorbell outside Nandini's front door. As a musical chime sounded deep inside the house, she pulled the edges of her shawl around her and hugged herself tightly. Her breath came out in tiny white puffs. Of course, Delhi was always going to be cold in the first week of January, but this added bonus of not being able to feel her nose or fingertips had been a nasty surprise.

As she waited, she took a longer look around the exterior of Nandini's home, a thousand-square-foot bungalow in the upmarket Mayfair Garden. The small, elevated lawn, bordered with flowerbeds, ended in a porch with a sitting area that seemed to lead into the living room in the front of the house. Leela could see lights twinkling from the gaps in the curtains. An underground garage was placed below the lawn.

The dark, polished wooden door swung open and light spilled out, framing Nandini. Her face broke into a smile when she spotted Leela. "Hello, there. Come on in."

Leela stepped into the hall with relief, still chilly, but not as much as it was outside. "Hi. Thanks for having me over."

Nandini's father and uncle had owned one of the largest gold and diamond jewellery stores in Kolkata in the 1990s, a shop that had been set up by their grandfather decades before that. When Nandini's brother, who was older than her by at least fifteen years, had shown no interest in it—he was a civil engineer, from what Leela recalled—their father had been quite gutted. He had harboured a last-ditch hope that at least his daughter might go into the family business, but it turned out not to be.

"And they are still in Calcutta?" Leela asked Nandini when she came back.

"Yes, they are. They're both getting on—my father's almost ninety."

"Do you visit often?"

"I go when I can, at least two, three times a year."

"I can't imagine what it's like being so far from one's parents. Though sometimes I wish I didn't live in their pocket."

"Abhinav's right there, so I don't really have to worry. Guess I'm lucky in that regard." Nandini sat in the recliner opposite Leela. "So, how's your conference going?"

Leela wrinkled her nose. "Like conferences usually do. But I don't mind. It's been a good break—the last two weeks have been hectic. There was an ugly bullying incident in school, and Christmas is always stressful, you know, with so many relatives and so many different ways to inadvertently offend someone."

Nandini smiled, the skin along the sides of her eyes crinkling. "Looks like a tedious conference is exactly what you needed."

"Absolutely. I even managed to sneak in some sightseeing yesterday."

A portly man in his fifties darted into the living room with a glass of water on a tray. He gave Leela a big grin as he offered it to her. "You are Nandini-Didi's college friend?" he asked in Hindi.

"This is Nandu," Nandini said, also in Hindi. "He has made all the delicious dishes you are soon going to eat. Nandu and his wife look after me, and the house and the garden. They live upstairs."

Leela smiled politely at Nandu and told him in her serviceable Hindi that she was indeed Nandini's college friend. Nandu hung around, peppering Leela with questions. He seemed to be in no hurry to go back into the kitchen.

"Um, Nandu, do you think we could have some snacks now please?" Nandini asked him.

"Oho." He slapped his forehead. "I'm so forgetful," he muttered, retreating.

Leela grinned. "Seriously? Nandu?" she whispered to Nandini, switching back to English in relief. That had been Nandini's nickname in college.

Nandini narrowed her eyes at Leela in mock admonition. "Now, don't you start. Especially because I just saved you from speaking more Hindi."

"Don't make fun of my Hindi," Leela said in her best principal voice. "How's your Konkani and your Kannada, may I ask?"

"Hmm, about as good as your Sindhi and Bengali, I would say."

Leela raised both hands in surrender, laughing. "All right, all right. You win."

"Damn right, I do!" Nandini got up and went towards the bar. "Drink?"

"Sure. What do you have?"

Nandini had a very well-stocked bar, and when she offered to make her a "surprise" cocktail, Leela agreed. Nandini mixed various ingredients with careful attention. Her hands moved like those of an experienced bartender used to whipping up delicious cocktails in a matter of seconds. So what if she knocked over the ice bucket in the process?

Leela swept her gaze around Nandini's living room. Back in college, as twenty-year-old students who usually had to scrounge for cash for movies and eating out, Nandini had never seemed to have money problems. Leela hadn't considered the implications of having a family that owned a gold jewellery business at that time, but she suspected now that that could have been one of the reasons her parents had notched a black mark against Nandini: they thought the rich, spoilt, "north Indian" brat was going to put ideas into her head. It was a little hypocritical of her parents, of course, considering they hadn't exactly been strapped for cash either.

She accepted the drink that Nandini handed her, and they clinked glasses.

"Well?" Nandini said, watching as Leela took a sip.

"It's…interesting," Leela replied.

Nandini tilted her chin upwards, her eyes narrowing. "What are you saying? This is my highly acclaimed special secret recipe, certified to win an award if I enter it in any competition."

"What can I say? I'm a woman with particular tastes."

For a beat, Nandini rolled her tongue inside her cheek. "Don't I know it," she said with a twinkle in her eye.

Leela played that interaction back in her head. *Oh my God. Did I just flirt with her? I just flirted with her!*

Nandini cleared her throat. "Er, you want me to fix it? A little more lime juice perhaps?" Her question was directed at the drink rather than at Leela herself.

"Um, sure." Leela's ears were on fire.

Thankfully, Nandu appeared just then with a collection of nibbles—flavoured chips, salted peanuts with chopped onions in them, and some sort of dried fruit. While Nandini tinkered around with the drink, Leela took a few deep breaths to regain her composure.

"This isn't your first time in Delhi, is it?" Nandini handed her drink back and settled into one of the recliners.

"No, but they've usually been whirlwind trips," Leela said, grateful that the conversation was back on safer grounds. "Like the last time, railway station to airport."

"Ah, the Amrudpur trip?" Nandini smiled into her drink.

Oops. Leela leaned across to help herself to some chips, looking down the whole time. "Never really spent time here, if that's what you mean. It just seems huge to me."

"It does to me, too, after more than ten years living here."

Nandini spooned some peanuts into her hand and then transferred them to her mouth. Even casually dressed in loose trousers and a linen shirt, she was impeccably put together. Leela thought about her own clothes—jeans and a thick sweater. With a shawl thrown on because the cold had taken her by surprise. She could've tried wearing something a little less drab.

"Does ten years in the city make you immune to the cold?" she asked, looking pointedly at Nandini's shirt.

"Ah no." Nandini grinned. "It just makes you invest in a wide variety of thermal inner wear."

A vision of Nandini looking stylish and sophisticated in inner wear that hugged her in all the right places flashed through Leela's mind. A fresh flush of heat suffused her body. She cleared her throat. "So, how's work?"

"Good. We've got another school that we're setting up in, right here in Noida. They're very keen on having some augmented reality modules. So we have our hands full. Vikrant is our AR expert, so I suppose it means I'll have to take on a larger role in the other projects and make more trips to Bangalore."

"Wonderful." Leela hoped her smile was casual enough. Much as the thought of seeing Nandini more often was delightful, it was laced with some degree of apprehension. She took a long sip of her drink. That spark they had alluded to all those weeks ago in her office in Bangalore didn't seem to be showing any sign of abating, and she wondered if proximity to Nandini was the best thing for her sanity.

The doorbell chimed. Nandu shuffled out of the kitchen to answer it, and there was indistinct conversation. Soon there were footsteps, and someone came into view around her side.

"Hi, sorry, I forgot you were entertaining today," a breathless voice called out.

Nandini's eyes widened in surprise even as she smiled. "Oh, hey. It's all right. Come on in."

A small, slender, and androgynous, not to mention very pretty, woman appeared. A few inches shorter than Leela's five foot five, her willowy frame and pixie-cut hair gave the impression of being very young. Upon a closer look, though, Leela pegged her at early thirties.

"Hello. I'm Mita."

"Leela. Hi. Nice to meet you."

"Likewise." She smiled. "Nandini has been talking about you nonstop."

Leela raised her eyebrows at Nandini. "Oh dear, whatever has she been saying?"

Nandini dropped her gaze. Leela was sure there was a hint of colour on her cheeks.

Mita tittered. "It's all good, don't worry." She gestured with both hands, pointing behind her. "I just came to pick up my stuff and I'll be out of your way. Sorry to interrupt, I was just passing and thought…"

"Stay," Nandini said. To Leela, she asked, "You don't mind, do you?"

"Of course not."

"Can't stay for dinner," Mita said, "but maybe a drink. Excuse me a minute."

She went off through one of the doors down a passage next to the kitchen.

Leela leaned back into her sofa.

"Refill?" Nandini pointed to her glass.

"I'm fine, thank you."

"So, you were saying, you don't really know much of Delhi?"

"Not as much as I'd like to. I finally got to see Qutub Minar and India Gate yesterday."

"When are you going back?"

"Tomorrow night. I'll have the day to myself after lunch. Any thoughts on what to do?"

Nandini laughed. "There's plenty to do, it depends on what you want. Eat, explore, laze."

"Hmm, all three? Perhaps some place where it isn't crowded."

"Ha! Not crowded? In this city?"

Mita came back, carrying an iPad along with its charging cable, which she dumped on the coffee table. "Found it. Phew. Got any beer, N?"

"Of course." Nandini started to get up. "I'll get it."

"No, no, that's fine." Mita reached out and patted Nandini's arm. "I can get it myself. Fridge, right?"

"Yup," Nandini said, and Mita went off to get her drink.

"Do you two work together?" Leela asked when Mita came back, popping a can of beer.

"No, no," Nandini replied. "Mita works at an advertising firm."

"We met through work, though." Mita shrugged out of her coat, dropping it on the arm of the sofa perpendicular to the one Leela was sitting on. She bounced down into the seat.

Leela studied her from the corner of her eyes. This was the first chance she'd had to catch a glimpse of Nandini's life—her city, her home, her friends. And she had to admit, she was intrigued.

"Oh, right. You designed our first logo for us, didn't you?"

"How kind of you to remember." Given Mita's playful smile, that was a joke. She kicked off her shoes, ankle-length boots lined with fake fur at the top, and tucked her legs under her. "You're a school principal, I hear," she said to Leela.

"I am."

Mita seemed pleasant, but there was something that Leela couldn't quite put a finger on.

"I feel I should be afraid of you, I don't know why. You don't look scary at all."

Leela had to smile at the way she said it. "Were you always in trouble when you were a kid?"

Nandini laughed. "I bet you were."

Mita leaned across and slapped Nandini's thigh with the back of her hand. "Mean!" She added, a bit sheepish, to Leela, "I was, actually."

"There you go, then," Leela said, grinning. "You're conditioned to be afraid of all school principals."

Mita had a natural charm that Leela couldn't help admiring. A bit of a chatterbox, but she had a sense of humour and didn't talk about herself, both of which were big checkmarks in her favour. Within minutes they were all chatting like they were old friends. Leela was particularly amused by Mita and Nandini's back-and-forth banter. There was clearly an age gap, but the two of them seemed to have an easy camaraderie. And yet, there was something…

Hang on. Back up a minute.

And then, in an excruciating slow-motion second, it all clicked together. All that easy familiarity with Nandini's house, the casual touches, the personal items left behind—something squeezed Leela's insides. They weren't *just* friends.

Leela pressed back into the sofa, feeling like the biggest idiot in the world. And then she noticed that they were both looking at her.

"Well?" Mita asked.

"Uh…pardon? Sorry, I…I missed that."

"Oh, let it go, Mita," Nandini cut in. "You're boring Leela to death."

"No, no, not at all." Leela laughed, her voice sounding hollow and forced to her own ears.

"I was just asking if you also thought the film was sexist," Mita enquired.

Leela blinked at her. She had no idea which film Mita was referring to and was pretty sure she couldn't care less. She was still trying to process her recent…should she call it a discovery?

Fortunately, Nandu came in just then. He went over to Nandini, leaned close to her ear, and announced in a sibilant whisper that dinner was ready and could be served whenever she wanted.

"In ten minutes," Nandini told him. "That okay with you, Leela?"

"Perfect." Leela stared into her drink, uncertain what she was feeling.

Mita stood up. "That's my cue to leave."

"Sure you won't stay?" Nandini asked.

"No, yaar, I have a big day tomorrow." Mita was already pulling her coat back on. "Bye, Leela. It was nice to meet you."

"Likewise," Leela said, managing to smile back.

Nandini went to see Mita off, a hand on her back guiding her forward. She gave her a hug at the door and laughed at something she said. Mita put her hand on Nandini's shoulder and gave it a little rub with just her thumb. "So tomorrow, then?" she said. Nandini nodded in confirmation and waved as Mita disappeared through the front door.

"Want that refill now?" Nandini asked as she came back into the living area.

"Sure." Leela held out her glass. "So, er, that shirt Mita was wearing. Is it the same one you picked up in Bangalore?"

"Mm-hmm."

Leela glanced up to see Nandini watching her, her hands poised over Leela's glass. Leela shifted in the sofa. Could Nandini see through her? But what was it that she was feeling? Should she be feeling anything at all?

"Mita and I, we're sort of seeing each other." The corner of Nandini's mouth twitched.

Leela gave her a half smile. "I was wondering about that."

Nandini made them their drinks and reclaimed her seat on the recliner. "How's Neil?" she asked.

"Oh, he's fine," Leela said.

"And your parents?"

"All good." She struggled to elaborate—or come up with anything new to say.

Nandini played with the stirrer in her drink. The air between them felt strained now.

Once again, Nandu came along to save the day, announcing that dinner was on the table. He had made dal makhni and palak paneer, with soft, fluffy naans. For Leela, there was also butter chicken, one of her favourite dishes at the best of times, but tonight it tasted of rubber.

The evening of warmth and easy camaraderie was gone. Even when Nandu brought out a bowl of steaming homemade carrot halwa, she couldn't rustle up the enthusiasm for more than one helping.

CHAPTER SEVENTEEN

"Where are we going?" Leela asked, unable to keep her curiosity in check as Nandini led her through the narrow, twisting lanes.

"It's a surprise, I told you." She glanced at Leela, her face shining with enthusiasm. "You said you wanted to visit somewhere not crowded, right? I assume you meant some place historical?"

When Nandini had texted earlier that morning suggesting a sightseeing plan for later in the day, Leela had wasted no time in agreeing. Given the awkward end to last night, for which Leela still harboured a tinge of embarrassment, she was glad that Nandini wasn't holding it against her. Perhaps it was too much to hope that Nandini hadn't noticed anything untoward in her behaviour in the first place.

"Ye-es." Leela looked around. It was the furthest thing from *not crowded* that she could imagine. The narrow lanes were abuzz with activity, buildings slotted tightly together, shops and homes jostling for space. And in between rows of concrete structures, there was traffic—pedestrians, bicycles, auto-rickshaws, and even the odd car. Wherever there was a large stretch of free land, rows of carts had lined up selling fresh vegetables and fruit.

The vendors called out to the two women as they walked past, and Leela couldn't help admiring the bright red tomatoes, carrots in bright orange and purplish black, verdant bunches of an assortment of leafy vegetables, plump yellow lemons, lush white cauliflowers, glistening green beans, and more—everything arranged in carts with such precision that each item seemed to have been individually placed.

A bunch of boys played with tops at the corner of a small, dusty park, tightly crowded together in concentration. Women congregated near open doorways of houses wherever there was a patch of sunlight, knitting and chatting. Young men and women, students, given the books they were carrying, scurried past as they crossed the entrance to a reading room—"24 hours open," it said. They passed another small park, this one occupied by a group of men, each wrapped up in a shawl or blanket with only their noses visible, sitting in a circle on another blanket, playing cards. A notebook with neat, small handwriting lay next to them. "The local top-secret gambling circle," Nandini said, nodding towards them.

Leela and Nandini attracted some glances as they walked past, but nobody seemed to have the time to stand and stare. It was the kind of bustling activity, even if that activity appeared to be leisure, that made Leela feel guilty for not really knowing what she was doing.

"We're almost there," Nandini said, as if sensing her impatience. They turned a corner into a lane just wide enough for maybe two bicycles to pass. One side was lined with shops—a grocery shop, a tailor, a "men's haircutting saloon," and a toy shop—the other just a plain, high wall plastered with posters about coaching classes for various exams. "I came here once many years ago," Nandini went on. "I'd forgotten about it. Here we are."

Leela stared in surprise at a vast monument that rose up before her. It was bound by a black iron fence, with an open gate and ziggurat-style steps leading up towards the wide, arched entrance. Just inside the gate, a crooked white-on-blue notice from the Archaeological Survey of India claimed that this was a "protected monument." The lack of any sort of other signage and tourist crowd, however, was a testament to neglect. Nevertheless, to Leela the monument looked in pretty good shape. Apart from a group of little children running in and out of the arch above the rectangular flight of steps leading inside, the place seemed empty. She felt a pang of envy towards Delhi—oh to have a gem like this hidden bang in the middle of a crowded residential colony.

"Welcome to Begumpur Mosque." Nandini's voice cut into Leela's ruminations. "A forgotten remnant of Delhi's exciting past."

"This is fantastic," Leela exclaimed as she followed Nandini up the steps. "This is from the Tughluq era, right?"

"I think so. But don't ask me who built it. It must be, what, three, four hundred years old?"

"If this is from the Tughluq times, it must have been made in the fourteenth century. Mosque, you said?"

"Mm-hmm. I think this was the biggest mosque in Delhi till the Jama Masjid was built. Have you seen that?"

"No. I really wanted to."

"It's lovely. It's still a functioning mosque as well. Well, next time, then. Come on, let's explore this."

Leela followed Nandini through the entrance and out into a huge courtyard. She stopped, putting up a hand to keep the pale winter sun away from her eyes as she took in the expanse of the mosque. A gigantic off-white structure caught her eye right across the courtyard—Leela estimated at least a hundred metres between the two ends—flanked with twin minarets. All around them were arched cloisters, with rows of windows along the ones on the left and right. There was a series of low domes along the top of the cloisters and most probably a larger dome in the centre that Leela couldn't see from her vantage point. The courtyard was paved with stone, bits of grass sprouting here and there.

It was deserted, except what appeared to be a young courting couple up on the roof towards the left. Leela squinted, tried to imagine the place packed with people gathered for prayers, but it was hard given how empty and desolate it was.

They made a slow promenade around the courtyard and along the covered passageway, marvelling at the old structure and how it had endured. Leela pointed out what she could identify from the Tughluq-style architecture. "This is stunning," Leela told Nandini. "Why is there no one here?"

"I have absolutely no idea."

"Neil would say it's 'awesome,' if he were here."

They explored the prayer halls along the main hall of the mosque, and the mihrab, the niche that indicated the direction of Mecca. On the other side, the roof had caved in, so there wasn't much to see.

"Come on," Nandini said. "Time to go upstairs."

"Upstairs?" asked Leela, intrigued.

Nandini led her to a narrow opening in a wall and Leela saw a dark, dingy staircase inside it. Nandini disappeared confidently up it, leaving Leela to follow gingerly in her wake.

It was very narrow, perhaps two feet wide at best, and quite dark. It turned slightly at the top, and when Nandini's hand reached down towards her to help her out onto the roof, she took it gratefully.

Leela emerged into warm winter sunlight and was immediately treated to a bird's-eye view of the surrounding neighbourhood—a vast park filled with multiple cricket and football matches in progress, and a patchwork of rooftops with clothes billowing in the gentle breeze and people sunning themselves.

"Isn't it lovely?"

Nandini's voice once again tugged Leela back to reality. "It is," she said, smiling at the almost childlike happiness in Nandini's face. The wind rose in that instant, whipping Nandini's loose hair around her face. She tossed her head to get the hair out of her eyes, the sunlight catching in her eyes and shining in her hair.

For a second or two, Leela was spellbound. She couldn't look away. Then Nandini's eyes alighted on hers, the light in them charged with an intensity that gave Leela a sense of being pulled into an unknown abyss. With a shock, Leela realised she was still holding Nandini's hand. She dropped it like she had suddenly discovered it was a piece of burning coal, breaking the contact between them, and the spell.

Nandini looked down at the floor and Leela saw her rubbing her hands along the sides of her jeans. Her face seemed flushed, matching the heat that had risen in Leela's.

Turning away, Leela walked along the sides of the domes. They passed the two youngsters, who were no longer holding hands, standing by one of the domes and pretending to look at their phones.

They strolled in silence, Nandini just behind Leela. They went up another short set of steps and then, feeling adventurous, Leela led the way through another impossibly narrow and dark staircase that curved up and opened out to the top of the mosque's central hall.

The view from here was stunning—and a bit dizzying. In silent agreement, they sat along the broad parapet.

"Thank you for bringing me here," Leela said.

"You're very welcome."

"Just that, the thought of climbing all the way down is a bit daunting." She smiled and risked a glance at Nandini.

She was looking away, over the treetops, and pointing her mobile phone at the view.

"So. You and Mita." Leela cleared her throat. "How long have you two been together?"

Nandini lowered her phone and examined the photograph she had just taken before replying. "A few weeks, but we've...it's not our first time."

"What do you mean?"

She gave Leela a crooked smile. "We have an on-off thing going. It's in an 'off' phase right now."

"So...not serious?" The idea brought a little excited flutter to Leela's insides that she ignored.

Nandini's shoulders rose and fell in a shrug. "If you mean whether we're in it for the long haul, then no." She turned towards Leela, one knee up on the parapet, and glanced down at the stone cobbles of the courtyard. "The thing is, I don't do relationships. I like being on my own, I like my independence. I'm not closed off to the possibility, of course, but I can't see myself 'settling' at the moment, if you know what I mean. Mita gets that, and we seek each other out when we…well, sometimes."

Leela nodded. "And she knows about…me, I mean about us."

"Do you mean the recent history or the ancient history?" Nandini asked, her mouth curling up in a smile.

"Both."

"Yes, she knows."

"Then, I take it she's not the jealous type."

Nandini shook her head. "That's not the kind of relationship we have."

"What do you mean?"

"Just that there's no commitment, no expectations."

"You're quite fond of each other, though. I could see that."

"We are good friends, yes."

"So…that means, you're…"

"Friends with benefits?" She grinned. "Yes. That about covers it."

Leela nodded. "I see." And she did. Then a thought struck. "Er, so…when we were in Amrudpur…were you two on or off?"

Nandini pursed her lips. "Yes, that was another of our 'on' phases."

"I see," Leela said again.

"Does that bother you?"

"No, of course not."

"Okay, good." After a couple of seconds, she said, "Can I ask you something?"

"Sure."

"Since…Kiran, have you been involved with anyone?"

Leela surveyed the row of domes lined up along the roof. Some of them had fallen in, some others were smeared with graffiti. Someone had scratched "GAY" across one of them in giant letters. "Just the one," she said, then made a face. "Though not for want of my parents trying. His name was Alok. He was a friend of a family friend. It didn't last very long, just a couple of months."

"What happened?"

It was Leela's turn to shrug. "I'm not really sure. I think it's what you said—I had just started to like my independence, I didn't want a commitment. Alok was in a hurry to get married."

"So it's just been men for you, then?"

Leela laughed. Her face warmed. "Oh, no. There...there was..." She scratched her ear. "Nothing happened, of course. But..."

Nandini leaned closer, a curious grin on her face. "Go on, don't stop now!"

Nandini's expression was of rapt interest. She shaded her face from the sun with one hand, and her lips were slightly parted. Only inches separated them. If only Leela just leaned forward, she could close the gap between them—

The thought startled her with its suddenness. As did the overwhelming sensation of wanting to kiss Nandini, *needing* it. Leela jerked backwards and jumped as Nandini's hand circled her arm, gripping her hard.

"Careful!" Nandini said, her eyes wide with concern. Then her voice dropped to a gentler tone. "It's a long way down."

"I...yes...sorry." Leela pulled away and stood. Her heart hammered, blood rushing to her head. Her limbs felt leaden. What was wrong with her? Why was she behaving like a lovelorn teenager—and what if she had actually fallen? It was at least eighty feet down, and those stone cobbles were not going to be a soft landing.

"Are you okay?" Nandini stood as well.

"Y-yes, I just...I think we should be heading back."

"Sure." She studied Leela curiously. "Did I...Are you sure you're all right?"

Leela forced a smile. "Yes, of course. I just need to pack and…you know."

"Of course."

CHAPTER EIGHTEEN

Leela loved her son, but right at this moment, standing in her parents' living room, she wanted nothing more than to turn around, march back home, and ground him for the rest of his life.

This ire had blossomed when he had sauntered home and in all casualness relayed the message that his grandfather had summoned her. On further probing, her guilty-faced offspring had confessed that he had told Joseph all about his upcoming "job" at Rahul's sister's birthday party.

And so here Leela was, staring circumspectly at her father and wondering what level of firefighting she'd have to do this time. Joseph was sat in his wooden armchair in the far corner of the living room that had been turned into a study, ostensibly immersed in the pages of a thick, leather-bound book. His furrowed brow and set jaw, however, told Leela that he had noticed her presence and that he was furious. A sense of unease engulfed her like an old habit. How many times had she stood in the exact same place during her growing-up years awaiting a reprimand from him? She shook off the unwanted memories and approached him.

"Dad," she said. "You wanted to speak to me?"

As expected, Joseph didn't react immediately. Then, with deliberate moves, he shut his book and placed it on the desk, which was already stacked with neat bundles of papers and journals held down by paperweights. Two pen holders placed on each end of the mahogany desk overflowed with pens, pencils, scissors, a torch, a couple of screwdrivers, and numerous other unidentifiable long cylindrical objects that could fit inside a pen holder. An empty spectacles case lay next to a coffee mug, which Joseph now picked up. He took off his glasses, placed them inside the case, shut the case, and finally met Leela's gaze.

"What is this I'm hearing, Leela?" The iciness of his tone gave away another clue to the degree of his anger.

"What, Dad?"

"Neil is going to a party to draw pictures. For money? And you're letting him?"

"Yes, I thought it would be a good experience for him considerin—"

"Absolutely not." Joseph got up from his chair and walked towards the bookshelf on the other side of the table, pulled out another leather-bound book, and opened it. It was almost as if he hadn't heard her.

"But, Dad—"

"You know I don't like all this," he said as he flipped a page.

"I told him it was okay." The matter-of-fact quality of her own tone impressed her.

"You can now tell him that it's not."

"It's just a small party, Dad. And Neil has been looking forward to it for months."

"No grandson of mine will be a performing monkey at some party. He shouldn't be wasting his time on these frivolous things. He needs to focus on his future."

"This *is* his future. You know he wants to study art," Leela said, ignoring the slight.

Joseph shut the book with a bang. "Rubbish! What type of a career can he have with that? At this rate, he'll be painting people's houses. And what kind of a mother are you? You should be encouraging him to become a doctor or an engineer, or to go into the teaching profession like the rest of our family. Instead, you're sending him to birthday parties with a begging bowl."

Leela clenched her fists. But a yelling match wasn't going to solve anything. She unclenched them.

"We have discussed this before. Neil is preparing to apply to the top design institutes in the country—you know that. A lot of famous people have studied in these colleges and gone on to do brilliantly in their careers all over the world. It's not like the old days when there were no career opportunities in the creative field. A lot has changed since then."

"Enough! I don't want to listen to any of this. I have made my decision."

Leela closed her eyes for a few seconds and took a deep breath.

"I can't do this to him, Dad. He'll be very disappointed. Besides, I've already told him he can go, and I don't see any reason he shouldn't."

"I see. And what about our feelings? Have you thought about that? I never thought I would live to see a day when my own daughter would talk to me in this manner."

And here we go again.

"You think now that you are the head of a rich foreign school your status is higher than your parents?" Joseph continued. "You don't need to listen to us or take our advice?"

Leela looked up at the ceiling and then back at her father. "Dad—"

"You have no respect for me or your mother or what we want. He's our grandson."

"Let's not—"

"I have nothing more to say to you, Leela. This conversation is over." Joseph strode into his bedroom and banged the door shut.

Leela stood looking at the door for a few seconds. *Great. Just great.* She turned to find Elsie standing at the threshold of the kitchen. Was that disapproval on her mother's face or sympathy?

Too irritated to care, Leela walked out of the house and shut the door behind her, resisting the juvenile impulse to slam it.

* * *

Leela laced her fingers together and stretched her arms away from her. Her hands were aching from the relentless typing. But all that was left now was a coherent conclusion to sum up her report, and she would be done for the day.

It was almost five o'clock and the school was deserted. She could take the pending work home. But if she did that, the universe would conspire to make sure her mother manufactured an "emergency" for her to deal with. Best to get it over with now. Reluctantly, Leela returned to her keyboard.

The only drawback to staying late in school was that she'd have to battle rush-hour traffic on the way back. At least she wasn't driving today—she had carpooled with Davi in the morning—and a long wait for an Uber or an auto-rickshaw was much preferable to negotiating the bumper-to-bumper crawl herself.

It had been a busy week at school, with pre-board examinations for classes ten and twelve. She and the other senior staff members were also keeping a close eye on the senior school in the aftermath of Rahul's bullying. They were still none the wiser as to who had been sending the abusive messages. However, after D.I.G. Khan had given her very impressive—and rather alarming—talk, the backseat bullying had eased up, from what Leela and the others could tell. Neil also reported that some of the students from their batch had formed a protective cordon around Rahul, making sure he was never anywhere by himself.

For Leela, that was what made what she did worth it—she'd reached the good kids, the ones who knew right from wrong and weren't afraid to stand up for themselves and their friends. Even though they sometimes needed a prod in the right direction. But that was fine, because what mattered was that they were willing to listen, learn, and act.

It didn't stop her from wishing, though, that she could provide a safe environment for kids like Rahul so they wouldn't need a posse of bodyguards in the first place.

The knock at the door startled Leela. She clucked her tongue when she realised her palm had been resting on the spacebar and she had ended up with half a page of blank space in the middle of a sentence.

The door opened and Nandini's head peered around it. Leela's eyebrows shot up. Had she fallen asleep at her desk? Was she dreaming?

Nandini had occupied quite a bit of her waking moments, too, in the past three or four weeks since her return from Delhi. Now that some time had passed, Leela could look back on what had happened a little more objectively. No doubt she was still attracted to Nandini, and it seemed that attraction had intensified in Delhi. *Something about the air in North India has that effect on me!*

Perhaps it was because she had been away from her usual environment, just like she had been in Amrudpur, where her actions did not impact her well-ordered life in Bangalore. Or perhaps Nandini's revelations about the nature of her relationship with Mita had something to do with it, which had opened up possibilities Leela hadn't considered in the past. If she had been a different person, living a different life, she might have even considered them.

But now that she was back on her own turf, and had had the benefit of hindsight, she was glad she hadn't been foolhardy and done anything she would've regretted.

"Hey, I heard you were still in," Nandini said. "Though, from the look on your face, it seems like you've seen a ghost."

"To be honest, I thought I was dreaming," Leela responded.

"So you do dream about me." Nandini's grin was huge.

Leela opened her mouth to say something, but no words came out. *Why can't I stop flirting with her?* She randomly shuffled some papers on her desk to give herself a few moments. Then she plastered the biggest grin she could muster on her face and met Nandini's gaze.

"No, seriously, what *are* you doing here? You weren't scheduled to be here this time around, were you? Or have I completely lost it?"

"You haven't. Vikrant was supposed to be here, but he's just had a premature baby, so I had to step in."

"Oh. Hope everything is okay."

"The doctors are saying the baby's doing well, so fingers crossed."

"That's good. Did you just get in?"

"About an hour ago. Thought I'd get the software upgrade done before the session tomorrow. If I'd known you were still here, I would have looked in before." She nodded towards Leela's desk. "But you seem busy."

"I am, but I'll be done in about half an hour." She paused. "Join me for some coffee?"

"Sure, I'll be done by then too. Want to come over to my guest house? They do great snacks. It's just round the corner."

Leela hesitated. Would that be a good idea? Then she brushed her misgivings aside. Anything that she didn't want to happen wouldn't happen. And all she wanted was to get to know Nandini again—as a friend.

"Sounds like a plan."

CHAPTER NINETEEN

Large drops of rain pelted them as Nandini's hired car dropped them off in the driveway of the guest house.

"Lovely," Leela said as they dashed for cover. "As if rush hour wasn't bad enough, now there's rain. I'll never get any transport at this rate."

"You could always wait here till it lets up," Nandini offered as she fished in her bag for her room key. "Or my car can drop you back."

"First, let's have the coffee you promised."

"Sounds good to me."

Leela followed Nandini into her room. She was surprised to find herself in a suite with a small sitting room. A door on her right stood half open, showing a neatly made bed.

Typing out a message to Neil, she pressed the send button on her phone. She tried to quell the disquiet that was starting up inside her thinking of her parents' reaction not only at her returning home late, but also about not delivering her father's fortnightly issue of *Frontline* on time. Come hell or high water, he had to have the new issue in his hand every time on the day of its release to read with his evening coffee.

"I just love that wonderful south Indian coffee you guys are always drinking," Nandini said. "Do you want some pakoras as well?"

"Filter coffee, you mean," Leela said, parking herself on one end of the broad wicker sofa with her legs folded under her. "And yes, pakoras are perfect on a rainy evening."

Nandini ordered the coffees and snacks, and sat at the other end of the sofa. "You were telling me about Rahul in the car."

"Ah, yes, he is much better now, almost back to his old self. He's started coming over more often, too, and seems to be more regular in school."

"Poor kid. I hope the bullies have permanently laid off."

"I hope so too."

"I really don't envy you having to deal with hundreds of kids every day and their complex interactions."

"Between you and me, the kids are okay, it's the adults who drive me up the wall."

"How do you mean?"

"There are a handful of parents who are complaining about sexuality education. Which I'm used to—happens all the time. But more worrying is this particular teacher who seems to be blatantly homophobic and is very resistant to keeping an open mind."

"Oh wow. What are you going to do?"

"I've spoken to her—let's see."

There was a knock on the door.

"That must be the coffee. That was quick." Nandini got up to open it. "How's Neil, by the way?"

A young man walked in with a tray and placed it on the glass top of the matching wicker centre table.

"He's fine," Leela replied. "He was quite upset with me for bringing up the bullying issue in school, but it looks like he's finally decided to forgive me."

Nandini laughed as she thanked the man and closed the door after him.

"Speaking of Neil, I have something for him." She went inside the bedroom and came back a few seconds later with two thick volumes. She placed them on the table in front of Leela.

"A couple of books on fractal art. I hope that's okay."

"Oh, he's going to love these. That's very sweet of you, thank you."

"You're welcome." Nandini smiled.

They helped themselves to the coffee, adding sugar from the jar on the tray in turn. Nandini sat back down on the sofa. Leela took a sip of the hot coffee and almost sighed as the warm liquid travelled down her throat.

"Just what I needed." She set the mug down on the table. "I never thought to ask you this before, have you ever wanted kids?"

"Nah, not really. I've always liked kids, enjoyed their company, but I've never had the desire to raise one myself. If someone told me they'd turn out like Neil, however," she said, holding up a playful finger, "I might change my mind."

"I'm sure he'll be happy to run away with you, too, far far away from me."

"Somehow I doubt that."

There was a pause as they both bit into pakoras. The green chilli stuffed with spicy masalas tickled Leela's nose. She took another sip of coffee, enjoying the sensation of her mouth being on fire.

"So, how's Mita?" Leela tried to keep her voice neutral, looking down at her coffee, like talking about Nandini's friend-with-benefits didn't make her self-conscious. Like she hadn't been wanting to ask that question since they drove out of the school.

Nandini exhaled loudly through her teeth. "Remember how I said we have a drift-in, drift-out kind of arrangement?"

"Mm-hmm."

"Well, at the moment it's still in a drift-out phase."

Leela glanced at her. "Out of curiosity, how exactly does this drifting in and out thing work? I mean…um…I don't know…" Leela bit the corner of her lip.

Nandini grinned. "Do you mean rules and regulations and that kind of thing?"

"I suppose…" Leela winced.

Nandini leaned her head back on the sofa and laughed. "You don't have to be embarrassed. It's okay to ask."

"All right, then. So how does one figure out when it's on and when it's off?"

"Well…" Nandini tilted her head towards the ceiling and then turned to Leela. "You simply ask. And if both are available and willing, it's on. It goes on till as long as you want, and stops when you or the other person wants it to stop." She paused, then added in a softer voice, "Just like it happened with us after Amrudpur."

Leela felt the colour rising in her cheeks. "I see. And, er, have you done thi…I mean, had this sort of arrangement before?"

"I have, yes. Once before." Nandini studied her coffee mug. "Why do you ask?" She looked up again at Leela, the question continuing to linger in her expression.

Leela wanted to look away, but an invisible force riveted her in place. The hammering of her heart reverberated through her body. "I…just…" Beads of sweat trickled down Leela's back. The room seemed to be getting smaller and stuffier.

She got up, turning away from the sofa and Nandini. The relentless drumbeat of her heart drowned out every other sound, every other thought. Her hands were clammy, and it felt like all the air had been sucked out of her lungs. She took a few steps away from where she had been sitting.

Moments passed in silence. Leela sensed Nandini get up and come nearer. Every nerve ending in Leela's back stood at attention.

"Leela," Nandini whispered. The silky lilt with which she said her name spread like warm honey through Leela's veins.

Nandini trailed a finger up Leela's arm. Leela didn't move. Nandini's hand stopped at Leela's shoulder and she bent down to brush her lips against the side of Leela's neck. A fire rushed through Leela, and she bent her head away to give Nandini more access.

"Tell me to stop," Nandini whispered as she dropped featherlight kisses up Leela's neck. The pounding in Leela's chest increased. All thought flew out of her head.

"Leela?" Nandini said again as she continued to plant tiny kisses along the side of Leela's face. A shiver ran down Leela's spine. She closed her eyes.

"Hmm?" Leela wasn't sure if she had actually uttered a sound.

Nandini held her shoulders and gently turned her around. She pressed her forehead to Leela's while her hands came to rest on Leela's waist. "Tell me to stop, please."

"I can't," Leela said, her voice husky as she let her lips brush Nandini's throat. Nandini groaned.

"I don't want you to regret it afterwards." Nandini's voice was hoarse too. It seemed her control was slipping as fast as Leela's.

"No, I won't." Leela kissed the hollow of Nandini's throat.

"Are you sure?"

Leela put her hand behind Nandini's head and pulled her closer. "Yes."

Their lips met with a fervour, and Leela felt a deep hunger inside her belly. Her tentativeness from just a few seconds ago was gone. What was left in its place was a desire to devour Nandini and wanting to be consumed by her. With frantic but sure movements, they started to pull each other's clothes off.

"The bed?" Nandini asked, panting.

"The bed," Leela confirmed, equally out of breath as she let Nandini grab her hand and lead her towards the bedroom.

* * *

From the righteous tilt of her mother's head and her stiff-backed walk away from the front door, Leela knew her parents were sulking. And sure enough, her father was perched on his usual armchair by the balcony door, seemingly intent on that morning's edition of *The Economic Times*, as usual oblivious to the doorbell or her presence.

Her mother went off to the kitchen without saying a word, not even asking if she'd like a glass of water. Leela could smell masalas being fried for dinner. The rain drummed steadily on the canopy over the balcony outside the net door. It was dark outside.

Her father continued to ignore her, though waves of pique emanated from him. Usually, her annoyance would be tarred with just a bit of guilt for not having been able to keep her end of the bargain, but today she seemed to have acquired a new, impenetrable armour. All this playacting merely amused her.

She tossed the slightly rain-splattered copy of *Frontline* on the coffee table and said, "Here you are, Dad. You seem busy, so I'll be off."

She turned to go and had mentally only just counted to three before Joseph Saldana's self-control gave way.

"Where were you?"

"With a friend." She waited for her ears to burn with shame at that admission, but it didn't happen. In fact, a surge of happiness filled her, a sense of joyous abandon. She suppressed a giggle. "I told Neil I would wait out the rain. Didn't he give you the message?" She knew he had, of course.

"Neil is all alone."

"He's just three floors up. Also, he's old enough to spend an evening alone."

"You didn't take your car today." Elsie approached, wiping her hands on a tea towel.

"I went with Davi."

"You should take your own car."

"When I do, you say I shouldn't drive so much in the traffic," Leela pointed out.

"Uff. So argumentative, this girl!"

Leela laughed. She touched her mother lightly on the shoulder. "Ma, sometimes you still think I'm thirteen years old."

Her father slammed his newspaper down on the table. "You are irresponsible, Leela," he thundered. "Not taking your car on a rainy day, coming home late, leaving your son alone at home."

Once again, like water on a duck's back, the jabs just rolled off her. "Dad, I know you're upset you didn't get your magazine on time and I know you don't really think I'm irresponsible. But I'm late and I don't have time to stand here and argue with you. So I'll say goodnight."

Before either of her parents could manage to gather their jaws off the floor, Leela beat a hasty retreat. She jogged up the stairs, a smile on her face and an image in her head of Nandini coming undone at her hands.

CHAPTER TWENTY

"You missed a spot," Leela said, pointing to a brownish smudge at the corner of the ceiling fan.

Neil grasped the blade with one hand and scrubbed at it. His tongue stuck out from the corner of his mouth as the fan wobbled under his ministrations.

"Careful, don't break it," Leela called out.

"I know, I know."

"All right, sorry."

"I don't know why you have to make him do all this," Elsie grumbled from the background. "Poor boy."

Leela wished with all her heart she would go back downstairs instead of standing around making unhelpful remarks.

"Can I come down now?" Neil called.

"Yes." Leela took the dirty rags he handed her and held the ladder steady as he climbed down. She had to say, cleaning the fans had become much easier since Neil had got taller than her. "That was the last one, so rejoice."

Elsie made disapproving noises and disappeared into the tiny utility area just off the kitchen.

"I hate fan-cleaning season," Neil grumbled as he folded up the ladder.

"The feeling is mutual." Leela didn't add that she didn't hate it so much anymore. "Go get cleaned up." She lowered her voice. "We can go and get some pizza."

"Pizza?" Neil's eyebrows went up as he grinned. "Is that your guilty conscience speaking for using me as child labour?"

"I have no guilt for making my lazy offspring help clean his living space. Are you coming, or do I have to eat all that pizza by myself? Oh, and don't tell your grandma…"

Elsie reappeared just then with a broom and a dustpan, looking extremely put-upon. Leela resisted rolling her eyes and took them from her. "Thanks for your help, Ma." Not that she had done anything remotely helpful. "Why don't you go downstairs and rest now?"

"What are you going to do for lunch? I didn't see any food in the kitchen. Didn't Eeshwaramma come today?"

"No, she didn't. We'll figure something out, don't worry."

After she got rid of Elsie, swept up the stray dust bunnies, and washed up, she and Neil walked down to the market, to a pizza place that had just opened.

"How was Preethi's birthday party yesterday?" Leela asked as they strolled along the quiet tree-shaded lanes. She'd meant to ask him last night, but her parents had been around.

"Oh, it was good. And I almost forgot." Neil put his hand into his pocket and pulled something out. "Here."

Leela looked at the bank notes he handed her. "What is this?"

"The money you loaned me for materials."

"Oh, right. So I take it you made a profit?"

"Yes. Prabha Aunty gave me two thousand rupees."

"Hmm. Not bad for some three hours' work." She handed the notes back to him. "I think the pizza is on you."

"But it is really your money."

"Fine." Leela plucked the notes neatly out of his hand and put them in her pocket. "The pizza is still on you."

"Aw!"

She laughed at his expression. "So what are you going to do with the cash?"

He didn't reply immediately, so Leela turned her head towards him. He caught her eye, and she was sure he blushed. Her antennae went up immediately. "Well?"

"I…um, I thought I'd go out…with, um, friends."

Somehow, Leela knew that wasn't quite the whole story. "All right. Which friends?"

"Um…you know."

"Rahul?"

"No…yes…I mean…"

"I'm starting to think you're up to something, Neil."

He rubbed his hand over the top of his head and exhaled loudly. "Okay, if I tell you something, do you promise not to freak out?"

Leela narrowed her eyes. "Certainly not, especially since you think I have a very high freak-out threshold. It will depend on what that something is."

Neil rolled his eyes. "It's just…" He stuffed his hands in his pockets and shuffled along, awkwardness spilling from every pore of his body. "There's kind of…I want to ask someone out."

This time, Leela's eyes widened. "Oh? Who is this person? Is it someone I know?"

"We-ell…"

Leela suddenly found that her heart was racing a bit faster than their brisk walk warranted. True, she'd had a question about Neil's sexuality for a while, and she was certainly curious. But it wasn't as though not knowing bothered her. The only thing she worried about was having the right reaction when—if—Neil told her anything.

"So…you remember Aadya?" he continued.

"Huh? Yes, of course." She studied him, a frown on her face. "That's who you're seeing?"

"Ew! Ma! How can you say that? She's my *friend*! And she's in Bhopal anyway. It's her cousin, Radha. She's in our school."

"What?" Leela wished her brain wasn't two steps behind the rest of her. "So, you have a girlfriend."

Neil rolled his eyes again. "No, Ma. You don't listen to anything I say! Aadya told me—"

"How did Aadya tell you all this if she's in Bhopal?"

"Oho. On WhatsApp. Do you want to know or not?"

"Yes, yes, go on."

"She said that Radha likes me. And I like her too. So, I thought I'd, um, take her out or something. Like a movie, maybe. I don't know."

"Take her out as in, you pay for everything?"

"Yeah. I don't know." He appeared uncertain. "Is that okay? I mean, should I pay for everything, or should we split? Are boys *supposed* to pay for everything these days?"

Leela laughed. "Oh, Neil, I have absolutely no idea what the protocol is in the teenage dating department. Usually, the person who extends the invitation foots the bill. But in this case, since it's a date, I think you should just ask her."

"Okay…" He glanced at her. "You're not mad or anything?"

"Why should I be mad?"

"Um…nothing."

Leela glanced at him fondly. So he wasn't gay. Or maybe he was. Perhaps he was fluid. She was surprised at how little it mattered. Even though he might have tricked her out of getting to be the coolest mother in the world.

"Later on, we shall have a conversation, okay?" she said. "About respect and consent and boundaries."

"Oh, Jesus Christ!" Neil's face was a beetroot purple.

Leela laughed.

CHAPTER TWENTY-ONE

For a change, it wasn't raining. That said, Leela much preferred the rustle of raindrops on the trees outside Nandini's window instead of the sounds of traffic.

She sat up, winding her loose hair into a bun before lying back down, propping herself on an elbow, watching Nandini watching her. "Penny for your thoughts?"

Nandini's arms were crossed behind her head, her hair messed up and her look thoughtful. Leela found this pose of hers quite enchanting. Post-coital Nandini had a sort of fluidity to her expression, a softness and depth that was quite alien to the professional, and even the friendly, face that she had on otherwise.

"I was thinking, I suppose we can say goodbye to keeping it *professional*," she said, a tiny smile at the corner of her mouth.

Leela grimaced. "I think that ship has well and truly sailed."

After their first time at the guest house, something inside Leela had shifted. The heady feeling that had stayed with her since then had not just been about having let go of whatever had been holding her back. It had also been about allowing that tiny crack in the carapace of her tidy existence to let a little bit of chaos in. Who would have thought that could be so liberating?

Sleeping with Nandini had been a spontaneous act, but even so, she had made the decision fully aware of what she was starting. And knowing that she could do so in a way that wasn't going to affect anything outside of itself.

This was the third time in less than a week that they'd met up like this. On the days that Nandini didn't have an after-school workshop, Leela had been coming over to her guest house. Her parents were not happy about the amount of "extra work" she was doing, though Neil seemed quite pleased with the alone time. It gave him bonus time on the computer to "explore fractal art," which Leela was well aware translated to "Skyping with Radha" now that she'd agreed to go out with him.

"So how do we define this not-quite-professional fling we have going?"

"You tell me, since you're the expert," Leela proffered. "What's wrong with friends with benefits?"

Nandini made a face. "It sounds so…transactional."

"Is that a bad thing?"

"No. Just not…enough."

"How do you mean?"

Nandini trailed the tips of her fingers along Leela's side, running down into the dip of her waist and then up the curve of her hip. Goose bumps rose along her body, making her draw her breath in sharply. She had to struggle to keep her mind on the conversation.

"Friends with benefits sounds like an arrangement of convenience. But we have too much history for it to be that simple."

"It is simple, though, isn't it? It's ancient history—us, I mean. Not one of those Bollywood movies in which lovers meet after twenty years and realise they're still not over each other, or they unearth some old, unresolved, deep-seated grudge that drives a wedge between them."

Nandini smiled. "No, I guess not. It's been too long to want to pick up from where we left off. Wherever that was. I don't even remember now."

"Me neither. Except that…"

"Except?"

"I hated you when you left."

Nandini's eyes went wide. "Wow. Why?"

"I thought you cared more about going abroad to study than about me. Which"—Leela held up a hand to forestall Nandini—"was extremely sensible of you, I know. But I was only twenty-one and I felt rejected."

Nandini sat up, arranging herself cross-legged, facing Leela. It was an extremely disconcerting pose. How Nandini expected her to continue to use her brain if she sat like that was beyond Leela.

"Wow," Nandini said again. "I'm so sorry, I don't even remember and…"

"Oh dear, no, no. Please don't apologise." Leela sat up too. She wanted to laugh at Nandini's contrite expression. "What I'm trying to say is that we were silly little kids then, and we are mature, forty-two-year-old women now. At least, one hopes."

"So, no leftover, deep-seated grudges, then?" asked Nandini carefully.

"What do you think? Here I am, in your bed, completely naked."

"Okay, you have a point."

"And if there were any old, leftover grudges, I'm afraid my memory is just not what it used to be." Leela reached for Nandini's hand and kissed the tips of her fingers. "The one thing I do remember is this…" She pulled Nandini in for a slow, lingering kiss, drawing their bodies close together once again.

"I'll say," Nandini mumbled against her mouth.

Leela pulled away after a few seconds, reluctantly. "Just to be clear, we're…this…it's still no strings attached, right?"

"Absolutely."

"Can you imagine what sort of turmoil it will throw my life into if it were anything else?"

"Yeah, I can picture your dad's face."

"Please, can you not bring up my father right now!"

Nandini laughed. "Sorry, sorry."

"This time you'd better be." Leela leaned across to the bedside table for her phone. "Oh, look at the time. Best be off. Remind me again, when are you going back to Delhi?"

"Tomorrow night, after the session."

"And when will you be back?"

"I don't know yet. Soon, I hope."

"I hope so too. I'm going to miss…this."

They may not be looking for a serious relationship, but Leela couldn't recall when the sex had been better, and she was loath to let that go. Not knowing the next time she would see Nandini—see her like *this*, that is—was disappointing.

Nandini had a knowing twinkle in her eye. "I read somewhere that women have the best sex of their lives in their forties. Think they were right?"

"Fishing for compliments?" Leela asked in a playful voice as she reached for her clothes.

"Think I might have just snared one."

"Dream on."

* * *

Nandini held the door open for Leela. "So tomorrow, then, in our professional avatars?"

"Yep. Straight-faced and straight-laced."

Nandini laughed, and the wantonness of it made Leela smile.

She stepped out of Nandini's suite, adjusted her bag more comfortably on her shoulder, and turned to wave at her. The door directly opposite her opened and a young woman emerged, talking on the phone.

"Leela, what a surprise. What are you doing here? Oh, hi, Nandini."

For a horrible moment or two, Leela went rigid like a deer caught in headlights. She sneaked a look at Nandini, who seemed equally stumped. Through her daze, Leela heard Maia

Hanssen-Hussain bid farewell to the caller on the other end of the phone line.

"Hey, Maia." Leela even managed a smile. "Wh…what are you doing here?"

"I'm here for the Discover-E meeting tomorrow, of course." Maia seemed puzzled at the question.

"Oh, of course."

Maia and her father lived in Chennai now. Leela remembered—a little late—that Nandini had been recommended this particular guest house by the school itself because it was where Maia and Raza also stayed. She kicked herself for not making the connection and not being more careful.

"And as it happens," Maia continued, "I've also been deputed to attend a wedding reception on behalf of my father."

Leela's heart still beat wildly and she only half listened to Maia's enthusiastic telling of how her—rather distant—cousin had met her husband-to-be. Behind her Nandini seemed rooted to the spot, but Leela didn't dare turn around to check. Maia suddenly stopped, as if she'd remembered something. "Look at me going on and on. How come you're here, Leela?"

"Oh, er…"

Then Maia's face brightened. "Of course, silly me. I keep forgetting you two are childhood pals."

"Yes, um…of course. Just catching up," Nandini said from behind Leela.

"Right." Leela nodded several times. *Keep it simple and as close to the truth as you can.* "Catching up. Yes, catching up." *Shut up now.*

A pregnant pause ensued. Nandini cleared her throat. "Er, Leela, I'll see you tomorrow then?"

Leela jumped and pointed to the exit. "Oh, yes. I must run. See you tomorrow, Nandini. You too, Maia."

"Yes, of course. Bye," Maia replied.

Without a backwards glance, Leela escaped. *It wasn't a close call. It's perfectly normal to visit old friends in their guest house rooms.* She kept repeating that to herself like a mantra. And yet, it was only when she got into the car that her heartbeat deigned to slow down.

She took out her phone and texted Nandini: *Phew!*

I'm still holding my head in my hands. Nandini's reply came almost immediately.

Okay, back to real life now. But there was a smile on her face as she reversed out onto the road. So many things could go wrong in their secret fling. Yet the thought of the risk did nothing but send a frisson of thrill down her body.

CHAPTER TWENTY-TWO

Davi's light grey Santro i10 drew up by the kerb and stopped. Leela opened the rear door to put her things in the back and then let herself into the passenger seat. "Morning," she said.

"Hello, stranger," Davi replied, giving her a long look up and down. "Nice to meet up with you after all this while."

"Yes, well, it's been that kind of week," Leela said with not even one iota of shame. She did have to bite her lip to keep from breaking out into a wide grin.

Davi put the car into gear and they were off. "If I were the dramatic kind, I would say you were avoiding me."

"Avoiding you? Why would I be doing that?"

"I don't know. You tell me."

"I'm not avoiding you, Davi."

"Fine. Then what are you not telling me?"

Leela glanced sideways at Davi, who drummed her fingers on the steering wheel, waiting for the light to turn green. A part of Leela was dying to tell Davi about Nandini, but another part wanted to hold it close to her heart, like a delicious secret that would lose its charm if she shared it.

It was early morning, so the roads were relatively empty. Leela always loved the morning commute to work—the cool breeze, scores of schoolchildren on the footpaths, flower sellers on the street, morning walkers, the smell of a fresh new day. It was a different world from when she came back home. That was all honking and traffic, and usually also rain.

She reached for the car radio and turned it on to one of the FM channels. It was still early for too many advertisements, and she found a channel playing Hindi film songs from the 1990s. She smiled. It reminded her of the time when she was in college, of those awkward years of breakdance, friendship bands, *Friends*, and baggy fashion. And that, inevitably, brought back flashes of memories of the previous evening with Nandini. Memories of the way their bodies touched and moulded into each other, of Nandini's fingers inside her, of her mouth on her naked skin. They accompanied an aching hunger deep inside Leela. And yet the longing was a pleasant one, knowing that there would be a next time.

"You're smiling." Davi's voice interrupted her thoughts.

"What?"

"You're smiling."

"Oh. I like this song. It reminds me of my youth."

Davi shuddered. "Me too. It makes me cringe when I think of those two actors doing their synchronised dance moves on top of a mountain in Shimla, looking like a couple of epileptic morons."

Leela laughed out loud, as much at Davi's explanation as how accurate her description was.

By the time they pulled into the school's car park, Leela had made a decision.

"Davi, there's something I want to tell you."

Davi, who was reaching towards the back seat for her bag, stopped. "Ah, so there is something."

Leela took a deep breath. "Do you remember I told you that when I was in college, I had a relationship with another girl?"

"Uh-huh." There was an anticipatory frown on Davi's face. "And that you do occasionally get attracted to women as well. Yeah, I know all that."

"That girl was Nandini."

Leela was staring at the gearstick as she spoke, but when Davi didn't reply for many long seconds, she was forced to look up. Her friend was staring back at her like she hadn't heard her.

"Say something," Leela said.

Davi stirred herself. "Nandini. As in…" She nodded towards the school.

"Yes."

Davi exhaled. "Well. I—I don't know what to say." She studied Leela, her eyes narrow. "Are you okay? Has it been awkward?"

Leela shook her head. "No, yes, I mean, well, it was a very long time ago, so, you know. But yeah, it's been a bit awkward now and again—"

"You two seem to get along great." Davi seemed puzzled. "I'd never have guessed there was anything between you."

"We do get along great," Leela said. "It has been easy to reconnect. But the thing is…" She took a deep breath. "When we met in Amrudpur, we, um, we hooked up."

Davi's perfectly shaped eyebrows rose northwards. "And by that, you mean…"

"We slept together, yes."

"Wow." Davi exhaled again. "And…was it a one-time thing?"

"Technically, a two-night stand. We decided to keep it clean while we were working together, but…" Leela paused and cleared her throat. "It seems like we didn't really succeed."

"What do you…You mean, you and Nandini Mirchandani…"

Leela pursed her lips. "Yes."

"Oh my God." Davi stared out through the windscreen of the car. She seemed to be studying the back of the school building with undue attention. It was a good few seconds before she spoke again. "And?"

"And what? There's nothing more."

"Don't be stupid. Is it serious?"

"No, of course not. You know my life, Davi. How could I start something serious? That too with her."

"How long has it been going on?"

"Not long. Since she's been in Bangalore this time—about a week."

Davi turned back towards Leela. It disconcerted her that she couldn't read Davi's expression or tell what she was feeling.

"So, what? You two are only...It's just sex?"

"Pretty much."

"But you have history. Aren't you concerned that it can get complicated?"

"Is that all you have to say?" Leela felt a burn of resentment. Why couldn't Davi be happy for her? "Do you have a problem that she's a woman?"

Davi's lip curled. "If I had a problem with that, I wouldn't have been your friend for twenty years. I can't believe you just asked me that." She snatched her bag out of the back seat and got out of the car, banging the door shut. Leela extricated herself from the seat belt, got her things, and exited. Davi pressed the remote to lock up the car.

Neither of them said anything as they walked towards the school building.

"I know you think you are in control," Davi said when they came to the turn at the corridor where they would part ways. "But with old friends, it's never that simple. Think about it."

Leela stared at Davi's retreating back with a sense of disquiet. Her words, she knew they were well-meant, but they sounded portentous. Worse, the uneasiness bled into her. It felt like the happy bubble she had ensconced herself in this past week had been poked.

* * *

Leela hummed to herself as she put the hairbrush down on her dressing table. Then, she twisted her hair expertly into a bun and inserted the carved wooden pin that would keep it in place.

"Neil? Are you ready?" she called out as she checked herself from head to toe to make sure she looked her usual principal-y self. "The bus will be here very soon."

She reached for her reading glasses from the bedside table and rummaged around for her phone under the newspaper that lay on the bed. She tutted at being so forgetful. Of course, earlier in the morning she'd plugged it in the hall to charge, all the juice drained from it after her midnight chat with Nandini. She grinned at the memory of Nandini's inappropriate suggestions about how her office could be put to more diverse uses. She popped her glasses into their case and then inside her bag, and checked her laptop and the papers she'd need for the day.

Stepping out of her room, towards the table where her phone was charging, she wondered what Eeshwaramma had prepared for breakfast.

She froze. Neil was standing before the little hall table, and, to her horror, holding her mobile phone in his hand. He tapped and scrolled expertly with one hand while the other shovelled a piece of French toast into his mouth. Her heart leapt to her mouth. Nandini's chat messages!

"Neil! What do you think you're doing?"

Neil jumped, the phone almost falling out of his hand. He turned to her, his eyes wide in shock. "I...I..."

"What have I told you about phones being private?" Blood rushed to her head; she could feel the veins throbbing. It was all she could do not to rush over and snatch the phone out of his hand.

Neil swallowed his mouthful. "I...I just...wanted to send myself those photos you took at Victor Uncle's place the other day." His voice was mouse-like.

"Put that down," she barked. She knew she was sounding on the verge of hysterical, but the fear coursing through her was overpowering.

"Sorry...I...only..." He put the phone back on the table, looking like a five-year-old.

Eeshwaramma came out of the kitchen with a plate of French toast for Leela, her face creased in concern. "What happened, Akka? Everything all right?"

Leela forced herself to take a deep breath. Neil continued to stare at her, looking only slightly less petrified than he had a moment before.

"Yes, everything is fine." She took another calming breath. "Would I ever pick up your phone and look at it without your permission?" she asked Neil a lot more evenly.

He dropped his eyes to the floor. "No."

"Then, I'd appreciate it if you extended the same courtesy to me."

"Sorry."

"All right. Apology accepted." She paused for another moment to gather the last few threads of her sanity. "Are you done with breakfast? It's time for the bus."

"Yeah."

Leela studied him as he laced up his shoes. She trusted him, but he could have seen something accidentally. *Had he?* Perhaps tearing into him hadn't been the best reaction she could have had.

"Neil?" she said to his retreating back as he opened the door.

"Yeah?" He turned around but didn't catch her eye.

Oh shit! He's seen something!

"I'm sorry I yelled at you."

He looked up at her at that, his face full of anguish. "I don't know why you had to freak out like that. I've used your phone before. It's not like..."

Phew. He hasn't seen anything.

Despite wanting to sink into the floor with relief, Leela silenced him with The Look.

"All right, all right." He held up his free hand in supplication. "I won't touch your phone ever again."

"And I'll send you the photos."

"Now?"

"No, Neil, not now. I'm going to have my breakfast now."

"But—"

"I'm sure the world won't end." Leela forestalled any argument and continued towards the dining table. "Now go catch your bus or you'll have to travel in the car with me."

Eeshwaramma shook her head as Neil left the house. "Children." She sighed.

Leela agreed wholeheartedly. She was certain Neil had shortened her lifespan by at least a decade with that scare.

About time she put in a password on her phone.

Yet she had to suppress a grin as she sat down to breakfast. Nandini had been saying to her just last night that they should start making a list of their close calls. This would definitely go at the top.

CHAPTER TWENTY-THREE

Those who knew Davi in passing thought her to be aloof and grim. Her straight-talking tendencies tended to put people's back up when they got on the wrong side of her. But to her friends, Davi was someone who could always be relied upon to speak her mind. Even though it wasn't always what you wanted to hear.

No doubt Leela's confession to Davi had been badly timed. The very next day Davi had to leave town to attend a family wedding, which meant that exactly a week had gone by since they had last spoken. Somehow talking on the phone hadn't seemed like a good option since Leela wanted to be in a better position to gauge her reaction.

Davi was not a sulker—she was far too sensible for that—but after twenty minutes of a not-quite-comfortable silence in the car, Leela wondered if her revelation had brought about a personality shift in her friend.

But the silence was killing Leela. "So," she said when it had bubbled over the unbearable mark. "Looks like we have an elephant in the room."

"Four months!" Davi slapped the steering wheel. "You have a one-night stand with your ex and you don't tell me for four fucking months!"

Leela stared at her, dumbfounded. "What? *That's* what you're upset about?"

"What else would I be upset about? The most exciting thing to happen in your life in a bloody decade and…" She pursed her lips and addressed the ugly bobble-head pug on her dashboard. "No, of course, she doesn't tell me, because, you know, why would she? After all, I'm more or less her only friend in this whole wide world."

"I'm sorry," Leela said, hoping she sounded contrite enough. "And technically, it was two nights."

"And then she goes and turns the *two*-night stand into a full-fledged fling and *still* doesn't tell me." Davi continued to address the dog, which nodded as if it couldn't agree more with what she was saying. Leela glared at it, and then turned back to Davi.

"I'm really sorry, Davi. I wanted to tell you, but…"

"But what? Thought I would ram into a lamppost because you're sleeping with a woman?"

Leela wanted to smile at that image but chose not to. It was probably wise.

"No, just…"

"What? Go on?"

Leela glanced at her. "I thought you'd disapprove."

"Disapprove? Of what?"

"You know…that I was sleeping around."

"Oh, you should be so lucky! When was the last time you had any action in that department?" She waved a hand in the direction of Leela's lap. "Sleeping around, indeed. Ha!"

"Ouch," Leela said.

"What was that guy's name? The fellow with the sexy beard—Alex? Anil?"

"Anil is our vice-principal, Davi. You mean Alok?"

"Yes, him. That's been *years*. Have you had any action since then?"

"Will you please stop saying 'action'?"

"Fine. But just so you know, I don't disapprove. It's just that I think, given that you have history with Nandini, it's easy for things to get complex. I overreacted that day because I was huffy you didn't tell me earlier. I just want you to be careful."

"Noted." Leela looked out of the window. This bringing up of her and Nandini's history was beginning to annoy her. "And this history you talk about, you make it sound like that's the most important thing between us. It isn't. We may have had a relationship, but it's been more than twenty years. We moved on, built lives. We've been happy. And we didn't—don't—carry any leftover baggage. We've reconnected anew."

"Yes, but you did love her once, didn't you?"

"I loved the nineteen-year-old Nandini. She was skinny and fidgety and a complete klutz."

"What? That doesn't sound like the Nandini I met."

"Exactly. This dignified businesswoman is nothing like her. Well, except for the klutz bit."

"Listen, Leela, you're a big girl, I know. I just don't want you to get hurt."

"Don't worry, I won't."

They rode in silence the rest of the way. When they were pulling into the car park, Davi asked, "You are happy, right?"

"Yes, of course."

"Good, because I want you to stay that way. Happy and uncomplicated."

"Oh, Davi, my life is already very complicated. Elsie and Joseph Saldana make sure it stays that way."

Davi snorted with laughter.

"What?"

"I'm just trying to imagine what would happen if your parents found out."

Leela shook her head, this time unable to hide her smile. "Uff, what is it with you people all wanting to scandalise my parents?" She paused before adding, "They'd probably have me un-baptised, if they could."

* * *

Leela picked up the phone lying on her bedside table. It was 11:00 p.m. She should've been asleep by now, but she just couldn't get herself to settle down. This was all Nandini's fault, of course, for getting her used to all the attention that her body was now craving. And her partner-in-crime who could have shared her predicament and done something about it—on the phone if she wasn't in town—was absconding. The single grey tick next to the text she had sent Nandini screamed at her once again that it hadn't been delivered yet.

Where *was* she? When they had spoken yesterday, she hadn't mentioned anything about her plans to travel tonight.

She reread her text.

Hey, what are you up to?

And she sighed. Might as well try to get a full night's sleep then—for a change. As her finger moved towards the sleep button, a second tick appeared next to the first one and both immediately turned blue. In the next instant, her phone pinged:

Nothing much.

Reaching the guest house in about 5 min.

Leela sat up on her bed and texted back:

You're here in B'lore? You told me you wouldn't be back till next month?

Sudden change in plans.

Have a new client meeting here tmrw.

Was going to text you.

But thought I'd surprise you instead.

Come over!

What?

To your house?

Now?

Don't know how to answer the first one. But yes and yes to the second and third.

What about Neil?

He's a teenager. Sleeps like a log.

You sure?

Absolutely.

Okay. Just dropping off my bag.
And then I'm on my way.

Oh shit! The roads would be empty and Nandini would be there in ten minutes. Leela had to get out of her ratty T-shirt and pyjamas, wash her face, comb her hair...

"Oh shit! Oh shit!" Leela muttered as she scrambled out of her bed.

Fifteen minutes later, Leela's phone pinged again, and she switched on the torch on her phone and tiptoed to the door. Her pulse quickened as she opened the door. Holding Nandini's hand, she led her towards her bedroom. No words were exchanged.

A couple of steps inside, Nandini's foot caught on the leg of the rocking chair. The chair screeched as it was pulled from its place on the old terrazzo floor. Leela instinctively grabbed its arm before it crashed into the small coffee table next to it. For a moment or two, both of them froze.

But there was silence from the rest of the house. Except for the low hum of the fridge, nothing else stirred. Leela breathed again, and the two of them continued towards the bedroom without further incident. Leela breathed a sigh of relief as she latched the door.

"That was clo—" Leela began, turning towards Nandini. Bathed in the soft glow of the bedside lamp, Nandini stood with a slight smile playing on her lips. Leela forgot how she had been intending to finish that sentence. As Nandini's eyes travelled down Leela's body, the low purr of desire that had been thrumming rose to a crescendo.

"So, care to tell me why I've been summoned to your home in the dead of the night?" Nandini's voice was low. She had a glint in her eye as she crossed her arms in front of her chest.

Leela mirrored her action. "I'll give you one guess."

"Hmm…" Nandini tilted her head up as if she were pondering a very difficult problem. "If I were to guess, I'd say I'm your booty call."

"And I'd say you're very sharp."

With a silent assent, they moved closer.

"Do you have a problem with that?" Leela asked.

"Do you see me complaining?"

Leela hooked her hand around Nandini's elbow and pulled her closer. "You know, there is one important rule in a booty call. There's either no talk…" She brought her lips closer to Nandini's ear, blowing hot air into it with her whispered words. "Or there is very dirty talk."

Nandini shivered and her hands squeezed Leela's waist. Her voice was thick when she spoke. "And which one are we going with tonight?"

"How about you choose," Leela whispered as she let her mouth trail at an excruciating pace from Nandini's ear towards her mouth.

* * *

Leela turned, more asleep than awake, shifting back slightly to rearrange herself in a more comfortable position. Something warm and heavy lay across her middle. She smiled—Nandini's arm, of course. She grasped the hand and pulled it up close to her chest as she snuggled back into Nandini's softness, waiting for sleep to reclaim her. She could get used to—

Her eyes flew open. Nandini was still here!

It was dark outside, so it couldn't be very late, Leela reassured herself. She reached for her phone on the bedside table. It was 4:57 a.m.

Oh shit!

She jumped out of bed. "Nandini!" she said in a loud whisper, almost pushing Nandini off the bed as she shook her. "Get up. You have to go. Eeshwaramma will be here any minute. And my dad's going to step outside for his morning walk."

A bleary-eyed Nandini glanced up at her. "Huh? What?"

"Come on. Hurry up. There's no time." Leela twisted her hair into a loose bun. Gathering their clothes off the floor at lightning speed, she threw Nandini's at her. Then she pulled her own T-shirt over her head and grabbed her pyjamas.

Nandini sat up groggily and started getting into her underclothes. "We forgot to set an alarm," she said, a little more lucid as she pulled up her jeans and buttoned them.

"I see you're feeling very bright this morning," Leela said as she fiddled with her phone.

Nandini's response was a grunt.

"I've got you an Uber. It'll be here in one minute."

"Thanks."

"Hang on. Let me check if the coast is clear." Leela strode towards her bedroom door.

"Hey," Nandini said. When Leela turned, she had picked up her handbag and was now looking at Leela with a question in her eyes. Leela walked back to her, cupped her face, and gave her a quick kiss.

"I'll see you in the evening?"

Nandini nodded.

With Nandini safely seen off, Leela sagged against her front door in relief.

That was…fun!

Who would've thought that Leela Saldana, the epitome of responsibility, could abandon all care in the world for a night of pleasure? Just two months ago it would've been laughable. But here she was, living out a delicious secret life for herself. This new version of herself both exhilarated and terrified her.

The door shook behind her, as if nudging her, and Leela stepped back hurriedly. The rattle of a key in the lock, followed by the door swinging open revealed Eeshwaramma.

Her hand flew to her ample chest. "Akka, you scared me!"

"I…was just checking if the—"

"Newspaper?" Eeshwaramma held up a neatly folded copy of *The Times of India*.

"Ah, thank you." Leela took it from her and with it reclaimed her equanimity.

"So, what do you want me to make today?" Eeshwaramma asked, heading towards the kitchen.

"The fish should have defrosted by now. And maybe scrambled eggs for breakfast?"

PART IV

APRIL–MAY 2018

CHAPTER TWENTY-FOUR

Leela adjusted the soft cotton material over her hips, letting it fall to her knees. She ran a hand lightly over the kurta, turning slightly to examine it from the side. She congratulated herself on her impromptu shopping stop at Anokhi. This shade of blue did suit her, even if she said so herself.

She studied herself in the mirror, marvelling at the way the material draped her body. The cut of the kurta was perfect, almost as though it had been tailored for her. It hugged her body in a delicate, understated manner, turning her into the very picture of dignity and authority. And, for a certain Ms. Mirchandani, laced with a whisper of sensuality. If all went well, later today she would have the pleasure of taking it off Leela.

Leela picked up her phone—now suitably secured with a password—to check if Nandini had texted back about their plans for the evening. She hadn't.

Oh well, at least they would be meeting in school. Leela couldn't wait to see how Nandini could possibly keep her eyes away. It would be fun to see her try. A smile split her face as she combed her hair.

Neil sat hunched over the table when Leela walked into the dining area. He was shovelling *poha* into his mouth with the sort of aggression that seemed unwarranted towards breakfast.

"What's the matter with you?" Leela asked as she twisted open the lid of the insulated dish and served herself.

"Nothing."

Leela raised her eyebrows and studied her son. He looked like he had his own personal thundercloud residing above his head. But she knew better than to probe.

He finished eating without another word. No second helping, which indicated something was definitely wrong. By the time he deposited his plate in the kitchen and was putting on his shoes near the front door, Leela was trying to concentrate on an opinion piece on the demonetisation drive having wrecked the economy, and the long and difficult road to recovery that the nation had to look forward to.

"Bye," Neil said shortly as he pulled the door open.

"See you," Leela responded. "Do you want a ride with me?"

"No." The front door banged.

Leela hadn't expected him to say yes—he had always resolutely insisted that she pay his bus fees so he wouldn't have to live down commuting to school with his mother, the principal.

He had been generally subdued these past few days, and Leela couldn't figure out why. For a horrible few moments, she wondered if he had seen Nandini sneak in or out of the house the other day.

"Stop overthinking it," Leela said aloud as she got up to clear away her breakfast. Another ten minutes to finish her coffee and then it would be time to leave and get on with her day. Hopefully, whatever it was with Neil would sort itself out. Otherwise, if it was serious enough, she would know whenever he was ready.

* * *

The moment she had received an urgent summons from her office to the senior school quadrangle, Leela's sixth sense had gone into overdrive, making her stomach churn. She'd had an inkling that her day was going to go downhill from here. That said, never in her wildest dreams would she have come up with this particular scenario.

A gaggle of students were pressed restlessly towards one side. A handful of teachers bustled about, trying to maintain a semblance of order. In the middle of the quadrangle stood Neil, his collar torn, trousers scuffed, and ugly scratches on his face, his chest rising and falling rapidly. Beside him was Prateek, kneeling on the ground, hunched over, equally dishevelled, and a hand held over his mouth, blood seeping between his fingers.

It was as though someone had planned an elaborate and impossible tableau just to mock Leela. Putting together the bits and pieces before her, at first it made absolutely no sense, and then, when she'd had a moment to think about it, it was a nightmare come true.

"Where's the nurse?" Leela barked. The sound of her own voice, commanding, steady, and brusque, came as a surprise.

Scurrying footsteps sounded from the corridor behind her even before she had finished speaking. The school nurse appeared with her first-aid box, accompanied by a girl from the twelfth who had obviously been sent to fetch her. The nurse knelt by Prateek and proceeded to examine him.

Leela looked around at the onlookers, who were all staring at her in anticipation of her next move. Irritation prickled her, especially at the undisguised glee with which the students watched the drama unfold. Where there had been silence when she had first appeared on the scene just seconds ago, there was now a hum of conversation. Even the teachers seemed uncertain.

"Go back to your classes," Leela called out, as much to the students as the teachers. When nobody moved, she added, "Right *now*!"

That sent the entire lot scrambling and within seconds the quadrangle was empty, except for herself, the nurse, Neil, and Prateek.

First things first. "Will he need a doctor?" Leela asked the nurse.

"No, ma'am, it's just a cut on the lip," the nurse said, standing up and hauling Prateek up with her. "We'll go to the sickbay." She gave Neil the once-over. "Are you hurt too?"

Neil shook his head. He had been rooted to the spot since Leela had got there.

"Clean yourself up and see me in my office," Leela said, turning to him. "On the double."

"Yes, ma'am." His voice was a joyless whisper and he didn't meet her eyes.

"And you too—in my office, when you're done in the sickbay," she said to Prateek.

He nodded back and wouldn't meet her eyes either. That afforded Leela a semblance of relief, because it meant that whatever had happened, he had been at fault too. She turned and walked away, resisting the impulse to clench her fists. She would have liked to murder Neil but told herself that that wasn't very principal-y of her—or very maternal, for that matter.

* * *

Leela glanced from one silent, sullen boy to the other. Prateek's lip had swollen on one side, making him look like a cartoon villain. But apart from that, he seemed unscathed. Neil had discarded his ruined shirt for his sports T-shirt, which seemed none too clean either. The scratches on his face had evolved into angry red welts.

"We don't have all day," Leela told them. "The sooner you tell me what happened, the faster we can decide what to do and get back to work."

Silence. Leela exchanged a look with Rina Pant and Asha Rao, also present in the room. Rina shrugged at her. Asha didn't look at her, kept staring at the two boys.

The mobile phone that lay in two pieces on her table wasn't Neil's, at least she knew that much.

"Does this phone belong to you, Prateek?"

He nodded.

"Do you know that phones are not allowed in the school?"

He nodded again.

"How did it break?"

Silence.

"Neil?"

Silence.

"Neil, I asked you a question. Do you know how it broke?"

"I broke it." Neil's tone was harsh, almost challenging. He looked up then, straight at Leela. His eyes were hard as stone. "And I hit him."

Leela gripped her knees, glad they were out of sight from the others. "Why?" she asked, and when Neil didn't reply, she asked again. "Why did you break his phone and hit him?"

She wanted to take him by the shoulders and shake him till this determined, pugnacious silence that he had embraced shattered. Call her biased, but this was definitely unlike Neil. And given that Prateek, too, seemed resolved to not breathe a word, her instincts were now screaming that whatever the circumstances, Neil had been severely provoked.

Not that it made things any easier.

"Did you hit Neil back, Prateek?"

The other boy shook his head.

"Neil, do you confirm that?"

Neil nodded.

Leela pressed her lips together. "Did anyone see what happened?"

It was Rina who spoke. "Apparently most of the elevenths and twelfths witnessed the fight. I spoke to them, but nobody is willing to say anything."

"You do realise, don't you," Leela said, addressing the two boys again, "that if neither of you speaks up, I will have to take action based on what I think happened?" Not surprisingly, neither of them responded. "Now, the two of you can step outside for a couple of minutes."

It did only take a couple of minutes for Leela to confer with her colleagues and the boys were back standing in front of her again.

"Prateek, I've called your parents. They feel that since it's a minor injury, there is no reason for you to go home. You can rest in the sickbay for the rest of the period and then you can go back to class."

Then Leela turned to Neil. "As for you, you are suspended with immediate effect. Your grandfather will come and pick you up."

Neil's sharp intake of breath was audible in the silent room. He looked up at her, his face a mask of disbelief.

"You know the rules of the school. Hitting another student is immediate suspension."

"But…"

"Yes?"

As Leela spoke, Prateek's head whipped around to Neil's. *Aha. So there is something there.*

Neil dropped his eyes to the floor. "Nothing."

"Don't think this is the end of it," Leela reminded both of them. "We will look into the matter in further detail. So if there's anything you want to say, you should say it now." She waited. "Nothing? Fine, if that's how you both want to play it. Prateek, you may go. Neil, you can wait in the lobby, but you're not allowed anywhere else in the school. Rina Ma'am will go with you to collect your things from your class."

"Fine," Neil said, teeth clenched.

Leela's patience, already in very low supply, plummeted to zero in an instant. "Excuse me?"

"Yes, ma'am," he said in more contrite tones.

"And why are you still here?" Leela asked Prateek, who was fidgeting before her.

"Ma'am, m…my phone?"

"Hereby confiscated."

She held her head in her hands when she finally had her office to herself. What the hell was the matter with Neil?

She picked up her phone and messaged Nandini.

Crisis in school. Have to cancel this evening. Hope you don't mind.

Nandini's reply came in a couple of minutes:

No prob.

Everything ok?

Leela stared at her phone, wondering what to say. Then she typed:

Long story. Will tell you when we meet.

CHAPTER TWENTY-FIVE

"Hi, Vidya," Leela greeted her parents' cook, who had answered the door.

Vidya waved her in and scurried back to the kitchen. The first thing Leela saw was Neil lounging in front of the TV. His shoulders tensed when she entered the room, an indication that he had noted her presence even though he didn't acknowledge her. The remains of a milkshake and a plate with cake crumbs lay on the table before him.

Her annoyance spiked. Treating her son to homemade cake after he had been sent home from school in disgrace was just the opposite of how she would have liked the situation handled.

"Oh, there you are." Joseph looked up from his armchair, folding the newspaper he had been reading and putting it down on the table. He didn't even wait for her to reply before he ploughed on. "I don't see why you had to suspend him. Boys sometimes get into fights. It's natural."

Leela gripped her bag so tight that she was surprised the handle didn't disintegrate into dust. She bit down the urge to snap at her father.

"Upstairs," she said to Neil. "Now." She turned to her father, raising her eyebrows at him like she was noticing him for the first time. "Hello, Dad. Talk to you later. I have to deal with you-know-who right now." And she turned around and walked out of the room, not giving Joseph a chance to open his mouth.

"Leelu?"

Leela groaned—she had almost escaped. Her mother appeared from the bedroom, brows furrowed.

"I hear Neil got into a fight? You *suspended* him?"

"It's the school's policy, Ma. I can hardly make an exception for him."

"Yes, but still. Your father was saying—"

"Sorry, Ma. I have to go."

Neil's truculent silence grated on Leela's nerves. Leaving him stewing for a bit longer, she took a shower. When she went to confront him, he was in his room, lying in bed, curled up, face towards the far wall. The quick rise and fall of his back indicated he wasn't asleep. He hadn't even changed out of his grubby school uniform.

She pulled out the chair from under his desk, turned it around, and sat down. "Talk," she said. "I don't care about the whys and the wherefores, I just want to know the truth. Take your time. I'm not going anywhere."

Neil sat up with a lurch, taking Leela aback. She hadn't expected him to capitulate quite so early. His face was contorted in anger and there were dirty tear tracks on his cheeks. Leela kept her expression and posture neutral, afraid to even breathe in case she sent him springing back into his shell.

"It's your fault, it's all your fault!" he said in a shaky voice and started to cry afresh.

He pulled his legs up and buried his face on his knees, shoulders shaking in silent grief. Leela's heart broke. She wanted to wrap her arms around him and tell him everything was all right. But she needed to get to the bottom of the matter. She sighed inwardly and went to sit next to him, putting an arm around his shoulders and hugging him.

She let him cry for a few minutes, then shook him gently. "What happened, Neil? Come on, tell me."

He wiped his face with the back of his hands and reached for his school bag, a ratty rucksack that he was inordinately fond of, and rummaged in the well. He pulled out a crumpled paper bundle and handed it to Leela. She unwrapped it and stared at a handful of pills.

"What is this?" She picked up one of the small white tablets and squinted at it, but the embossed text was too tiny to read. Where were her specs when she needed them?

"I found them in Rahul's bag."

Comprehension wrapped its cold fingers around Leela's heart. Her first instinct was to fume at Neil and ask why he had waited so long, but the voice of reason intervened. The pills were here, Rahul was okay. For now. And she needed to hear the rest of the story, though now it was more or less clear where it was headed.

"It was Prateek, it's been him all along," Neil went on. "We all knew it was him and we did what we could to stay between him and Rahul, but then Asha Ma'am paired them for bio practicals—"

"She did *what*?" Leela burst out. Prateek had been one of the pupils who had been flagged for the bullying against Rahul, and the teachers had been instructed not to put the two of them together. Leela felt like she would spontaneously combust from rage.

"Well, she did, and I'm not in science so I don't know what happened exactly, but Rahul said he was making life difficult for him in class. This was after that special assembly and the talk about bullying. See, I told you not to do anything."

"And what, Neil? Let Rahul continue to get bullied?"

"But it only got worse, don't you see? At first the mails and texts stopped, but they got partnered in bio and Prateek started saying things to him. Then things started happening on social media. A fake Snapchat account in Rahul's name started sending photos to the other students, photos like...you know, Photoshopped dirty photos...morphed...you know?"

Leela nodded.

"There's this other thing we use called Sarahah where again he started getting messages. Sarahah is all anonymous anyway, so you don't know the sender. Rahul was getting more and more upset, and I kept telling him that we needed to speak to somebody, but he wouldn't agree. Some of us even threatened Prateek that we'd report him, but he just kept saying, 'Where's the proof?'

"Then, this morning, I found the pills in Rahul's bag and I lost it. I knew Prateek was doing it, so when he went for games period, I searched his bag and found his phone...and I found the fake account and the images..."

Neil's voice had changed to a deadpan monotone and tears started rolling down his cheeks again.

"I'm so stupid...I should have just taken the phone to Zara Ma'am. Or you...I'm sorry, I just...couldn't..."

Leela hugged him tight and rubbed his back. "Shh. Don't be sorry. You were looking out for your friend."

How the hell had all this been happening—and for months—with nobody being any the wiser? And to think that they'd all been congratulating themselves on having handled the situation. Rage coursed through Leela, most of it at herself. There were no two ways about it—she had failed Rahul.

"I shouldn't have hit him."

"No, you shouldn't have. Violence is never the answer, and in future you will remember that. Yes?"

Neil nodded.

"Now come on, go and wash your face. Your work is not done yet."

"What do you mean?"

"You still have to be Rahul's friend and stand by him. Get ready. We're going to his house. I need to hear the story from him."

Neil sniffed and dragged himself out of bed. "Ma, am I still suspended?"

"Oh yes, you are."

* * *

Pranav Gupta's face flushed to an unhealthy red. A vein throbbed in his forehead.

"How dare you!" he thundered, slapping his hands on his thigh. "Do you know who I am? Do you know how many times I have contributed to the building fund of this school? And this is how you repay me? By expelling my son? Just when he's about to go into the twelfth? This is bloody nonsense!"

The boy cowering at the corner of the sofa flinched every time his father's voice rose. Having been deserted by his usual bravado, he seemed like an overgrown child rather than the hairy, thuggish wannabe criminal that Leela had pegged him as. Deep down somewhere, she felt sorry for him.

"Mr. Gupta, as I've explained to you, your son was responsible for cyberbullying a fellow student to the point of driving him to the brink of suicide. This isn't something we can ignore or simply punish with a rap on the knuckles. This is criminal behaviour, and we cannot compromise on the safety of the other students."

"These are children, Ms. Saldana. This is just childish games that have gone a bit too far. I have heard that your own son was involved in this. He punched my son. Is that not criminal behaviour? Are you expelling him as well?"

"He has been suspended, in keeping with school policy."

"This is partiality!" Pranav's voice started to rise again. "I—"

"Mr. Gupta." Leela raised her voice too. "Perhaps you are not understanding the seriousness of the situation. Prateek is over eighteen years old and if Rahul's parents choose to file a complaint, he will be charged as an adult. There is evidence on his phone—the pictures, the prepaid SIM card from where the messages came, the fake Snapchat account. I have been told this by Deputy Inspector General Khan, who heads the cybercrime unit of Bangalore Police." She paused, but not long enough for him to get a word in. "Her granddaughters study in this school."

She waited to see how long it would take for the penny to drop. Fury suffused his face as understanding dawned. Leela sat back in her chair and pushed a thick envelope with the school's logo towards him. "Prateek's papers are ready. You can take him away immediately."

With lips pressed so hard together that his mouth was reduced to a thin line, Pranav snatched the envelope and stood up. With a glare at Leela, he reached down and yanked Prateek up by his ear.

"Useless, good-for-nothing fellow!" he snarled as he marched the whimpering boy out.

Leela took in a deep breath and let it out slowly. Her hands were shaking. This was the first time she'd had to expel a student and hoped it would be the last time.

She ran her hands over her face. Things could have been much, much worse. It didn't bear thinking about. This part of her job—the dealing with people, the juggling of tricky situations—had always filled her with vigour. It was what made her want to get out of bed every morning. Not today. Right now, the thought of dealing with messed-up kids like Prateek and clueless adults like Asha who messed them up even more filled her with a wearying sense of hopelessness.

But most of all, she was consumed by an acute sense of guilt for failing a vulnerable youngster like Rahul who had been caught in the crossfire.

She shook herself and picked up her phone, her difficult day far from over.

"Gulshan, is Asha Rao in yet? Okay, send her in in five minutes." Today was also going to be Asha's last day in Hanssen.

CHAPTER TWENTY-SIX

"When you said you had the perfect idea on how to kill an hour or so," Nandini said as she and Leela claimed a bench along the promenade of Sankey Tank. "I had no idea this is what you were thinking of."

"What did you think I meant?"

Nandini only smiled.

"You have a one-track mind, did you know that?"

"Would you have me reform?"

"Hmm, I'll get back to you on that one," Leela responded in her best schoolteacher voice, making Nandini laugh. Two elderly women out for their early evening constitutional turned their heads in their direction as they went past.

The lake—officially a tank meant to supplement the drinking water of Bangalore in the late nineteenth century—was now a park, with a walkway that went almost all the way around, generous landscaped areas with flowerbeds and canopies, plenty of benches for visitors to sit on, a play area, and even an outdoor gym for seniors.

The bench Leela and Nandini sat on was set back from the water's edge, so they could watch the walkers walking and the children playing. It was about a quarter past four in the afternoon, the park having just reopened for the evening but already filling up. The sun had disappeared behind heavy clouds and there was a slight damp chill in the air.

Leela hugged herself. "I love this weather. It reminds me of my childhood, back when Bangalore used to be cool all year round and it rained almost every day."

"Really? I thought you said you hate it when it rains because it clogs up the traffic."

"But right now, I don't have to deal with the traffic, so let's be happy about that." She took a deep breath and leaned her head back. "I'd forgotten what fun it is to escape work early. Goodness knows I needed to get away today."

"Yeah, you've had a tough week. I've barely got to see you this time."

"A week that isn't over yet. One expulsion and one sacking today. I'm shattered."

"I don't envy you. How's Neil taking his suspension?"

"He's spending his time drawing. He's okay now that he knows I'm not angry, Rahul's okay, and also that he's something of a hero back with his classmates."

"And Rahul? He really is okay?"

Leela nodded. "I had our school psychologist speak to him. She says he's going to be fine. I just hope I can convince the parents to let him get some counselling."

"Do you know where he got the pills from?"

"Stole them from his grandfather, but it turns out they were harmless anyway."

"Still, it's not the pills themselves, it's the fact that he was thinking on those lines."

"I know." Leela closed her eyes tight and tilted her head up towards the sky. "I messed up, Nandini, I messed up so badly."

She felt Nandini's hand on her thigh. "You didn't. You sorted the mess." The tenderness in her tone made tears spring to Leela's eyes. She didn't deserve the kindness.

"I was responsible for protecting him. I feel so helpless sometimes. I feel like we keep failing kids like Rahul over and over again."

"Hey, these kids are lucky to have you." Nandini squeezed Leela's thigh briefly and let go. "It can't be an easy job that you do, but at least you care about them and not about some bottom line, which is what most schools are about these days."

"I do love my job most of the time," Leela admitted. "But on days—weeks—like these, I want to quit and move to the hills."

"You know, I don't know anything about kids; you're the expert there. But I do know what it's like to be a teenager trying to come to terms with her sexuality. Back then I would've given an arm and leg to have someone in my corner. To hold my hand and tell me that there was nothing wrong with me, that I was normal. Rahul has that. He has you and Neil and the entire school machinery behind him. I don't think you should underestimate the value of that for Rahul and all your other kids."

Leela nodded.

"And of course there are the holidays," Nandini continued.

Leela frowned at her, puzzled.

"Your job. You get to have many more of them."

Leela laughed. "True. Can't scoff at holidays."

Nandini reclined back on the bench, staring out at the lake. "I like this place. And lounging in the middle of a workday does feel good. Very decadent."

"Speaking of decadent, I should resume my morning walks."

"You? I never had you down as a morning walk type of person."

"Hey!" Leela put her hands on her hips, the best she could in a sitting position. "What's that supposed to mean?"

"It means that I bet you snooze your alarm at least three times every morning."

"I do not. I bet you get up at nine o'clock."

"On a working day, yes," Nandini said with a straight face. "On weekends, eleven is more like it."

"Now *that* is decadent. Actually, you're right, I used to love to sleep in, but Kiran was an annoying early morning person.

He was the one who got me used to a morning jog. There was a time we even ran a half marathon."

"A half marathon? That's, what, twenty kilometres?"

"Twenty-one."

"Wow. But you don't run anymore?"

"No. It was something we did together."

They sat in silence for a few moments. It was companionable. Nandini said, "Tell me about Kiran."

Leela turned to her in surprise.

"If you want to, that is," Nandini added. "I mean, I'm just curious. He was an important part of your life and…"

Leela shook her head. "It's okay. I was just surprised because no one asks. Quite the opposite—everyone feels it's a subject they have to tiptoe around."

"Why?"

"Because he died and left me…bereft, I suppose."

"I'm sure he didn't do it on purpose."

That made Leela smile. "No, he didn't. He wouldn't—he was such a stickler for detail that the idea of unfinished business would make him extremely antsy."

"Was he funny?"

"No, he was quite a serious guy. But he did have a sense of humour. Neil is so much like him."

"So, was he artsy, then?"

"Oh, God no!" Leela laughed. "The most artistic thing Kiran ever did was match his socks. We often wondered where Neil got his artistic genes from." She paused. How could she describe her late husband to someone who had never met him? "He was a very quiet, retiring type of person. He hated the limelight. I always thought he was a bit shy. You know what they say about the quiet types having a temper?"

Nandini nodded.

"It was completely untrue in Kiran's case. He could be so infuriatingly calm. It used to drive me insane."

"Must be annoying to have a fight with him."

"Extremely. He would just sit there, unruffled and rational, and I would be going stir crazy with anger and indignation." Leela fell silent.

"You must miss him." Nandini's voice was quiet.

Leela sighed softly. "You know, it's a funny thing. I do and I don't. Is that a terrible thing to say? When he died, I was, well, I felt adrift, like I didn't know what I was doing, where I was going. I couldn't see one step ahead of me, forget the next day. But then, somehow, I healed, at least as much as I could, and I got used to not having him around. It's almost like I got used to missing him. It just became regular." She looked at Nandini. "That makes me sound like a cold, unfeeling person, doesn't it?"

"No. It makes you having come to terms with losing your partner."

They were quiet for a while. "You know, you take it so much for granted, that your partner is going to be by your side forever."

Nandini's hand slipped into hers. Their fingers intertwined and the silence stretched till Nandini spoke again. "And what was he like with Neil?"

"They were quite inseparable. Neil had a rough time afterwards."

"He must have been very small when Kiran died, right?"

"He was six. No age to lose your father."

"No, definitely not. Still, you've done a fantastic job with him. He's the only teenager I know who doesn't make me want to strangle him. My niece and nephew—such whiny selfish brats they used to be."

Leela laughed. "Thanks. Neil thinks you're quite the cat's whiskers too."

CHAPTER TWENTY-SEVEN

Three cups of coffee lay untouched on the table. Leela itched to reach for hers, but it somehow seemed disrespectful in the circumstances.

Sridhar and Prabha, Rahul's parents, sat in a huddle of disbelief on the sofa in Leela's office. Leela herself was on the single-seater at right angles to it. As they appeared to grapple with the details of what she had told them so far, she wondered how two such ordinary-looking people could have produced a striking human being like Rahul. She looked down for a beat to dismiss that uncharitable thought.

"So you had no idea that he was being bullied in school?" Leela asked, breaking the silence that had begun to stretch uncomfortably.

Prabha shook her head, making the thick plait that lay over her shoulder undulate. "No idea at all." She glanced at her husband. "Rahul is such a quiet boy, we just thought…"

How could they have "just thought" whatever it was they had, and never considered trying to find out anything more?

Surely they couldn't have failed to notice the drastic change in their son? Rage seethed in her veins, directed not just towards them but also towards herself. She was in no position to point fingers at anyone else, after all.

"I am truly sorry we didn't find out what was happening sooner and stop it. I want to assure you that we take all instances of bullying very seriously, and we have put measures into place to make sure that this sort of thing doesn't happen again. Rahul is safe here—you have my personal guarantee. But I will not put any sort of pressure on you if you feel that he isn't and that he'll be safer somewhere else."

"You want us to remove Rahul from the school?" Prabha asked. She had been doing all of the talking so far, Sridhar silent as a gravestone beside her.

"No, no, that isn't what I meant at all," Leela hastened to reassure her. "What I wanted to say was that it is up to you and up to Rahul. He has to feel safe. Everything else is secondary."

"We thought that things would be different here, you know." Sridhar finally spoke. His voice had an uncharacteristically high pitch to it, not at all his usual manner.

"Sorry, what would be different?"

Prabha was the one who answered. "He was also bullied in his last school. It was bad, but not like this. He was so unhappy there. So we decided to try Hanssen Academy. And Rahul really liked it here. Then he made friends with Neil and everything was going so well…" Her voice faltered.

Leela leaned forward, frowning. "He was bullied in his last school? And yet you didn't realise…" She forced herself to stop. She had no right to berate the parents for not noticing anything amiss.

"We had such high hopes." Deep frown lines etched Sridhar's forehead. His eyes were focused on the floor.

His distress played out on his face, and when he didn't speak again, Leela looked down at her hands. "I know my word may not mean much to you, but—"

"This is not enough!" Sridhar's outburst startled Leela. "It is not enough for you to assure us that this will not happen again, that he is safe. We had high hopes of this school, we thought…"

Big tears rolled down his face. He folded his hands together and looked up at Leela. "Please, I beg you, I will fall at your feet. Please, ma'am, fix our son."

The seconds ticked by as Leela stared at his anguished face, at a loss for words. This was not what she had bargained for. Then Prabha, her head bent into her chest, her hands tightly clasped together, spoke in a small voice. "Please, we'll do anything you say. Just make him normal."

"What do you mean?" Leela asked her.

"You've seen the way he is. We thought you'd be able to make him more like a regular boy."

Leela took a deep breath. "Sridhar, Prabha, please understand, there is nothing to fix about Rahul. He is a fine, perfectly normal young man, and he deserves to be who he is and express himself the way he feels most comfortable. And our job—yours and mine and all his teachers and his friends—is to make sure he's able to do that and support him."

"But you've *seen* him." Sridhar spread his hands as if to emphasise his statement. "Your own son is his best friend. We thought he would have a positive influence on Rahul."

"Actually, it is Rahul who has had a positive influence on Neil," Leela said. "Please don't assume that Rahul is weak because he is different."

"He's not a child anymore. How can we continue to indulge his behaviour? Soon he will be going to college, getting a job. How will he…cope?"

Leela stared from one parent to the other, struggling to keep the helplessness roiling inside her at bay. Would anything she could say make a difference to these two parents who saw their son as broken? Who saw him as the problem rather than the way he was treated by everyone around him?

She couldn't just do nothing and leave him at their mercy, could she? Not without fighting for him. She couldn't pretend it wasn't any of her business. She owed it to Rahul, to Neil, to everything she herself believed in.

Whatever she said next could make or break Rahul's world. The thought cut through her like a serrated knife.

"If you stand by him," she began, "he will cope with anything. But if you make him feel that he is wrong for being himself, then you will lose him."

She leaned forward, crossing her fingers mentally, hoping that her words weren't going to backfire.

"It isn't easy to be different in this world we live in. In fact, it takes exceptional courage to stand out from the herd. And I know it's easier saying all this than actually seeing your own child struggling to navigate life. I also know that we want our children to have easy lives, to be happy and safe and successful. And I understand how frustrating it can be when we see that they are making things harder for themselves. Especially when it seems it would be so easy to just be...regular. To be like everyone else. We want to tell our kids, 'Look around, everyone is doing it, why can't you?'

"Yes, of course, it's easy and convenient when our kids are just like the others, when they don't do anything to rock the boat. But when they are not, we are afraid that they will be singled out. More than that, I think we are also afraid that it will force us to change the way we think and the way we are, and we don't want to do that because we will find that we are not brave enough to be as brave as our children."

Leela paused for a moment. Both Prabha and Sridhar had their eyes on her. *They are still listening. Good.*

"I've seen a lot of kids trying valiantly to be what their family want them to be because that is the only way they will be accepted. Prabha, Sridhar—please don't give up on Rahul, please don't force him to be your imagination of what he should be. Because if you do, there will come a day when you will no longer have him in your life. Or if you do, he will be a broken, unhappy young man."

Leela stopped. Her words had tumbled over one another to get out. But she hoped and prayed that some part of it had got through.

"Y-you're saying he's unhappy because we want him to be normal?" Sridhar asked.

Leela cringed at "normal." "He needs to know that you love him just as he is, and you don't see him as damaged or someone who has to be put right. And he also needs to know that you will stand by him."

"It's easy for you to say that. What if it was Neil?" Prabha asked. "What would you do?"

Leela didn't answer immediately. "I would do whatever it took to let him be himself," she said. "At least, I hope I would have the guts to."

"We hear what you're saying, Leela Ma'am, and we respect your opinion," Sridhar said. "But you have to understand, we are a traditional, God-fearing family. These kinds of things, they're not for people like us. These things don't happen in families like ours."

"Sridhar, with all due respect, these *things* that you refer to happen everywhere. They are just very well hidden in families like ours. I do understand your apprehensions, but if you don't provide Rahul the support he needs, he will eventually go behind your back and you will no longer be part of his life. And you don't want that, do you? You don't want him to stop trusting you."

Neither of them replied, which was perhaps a good sign. "You don't have to do this all by yourselves," she said. "There are professionals who can help you—and Rahul—navigate this."

"Psychiatrists, you mean?" Sridhar's lip curled. "You think we are mental cases?"

"Of course not. You are clearly sensible and responsible parents who are concerned about their son." A stretch, but a bit of flattery wouldn't go amiss. "Don't you think it might help to talk to someone who could give you a better picture of Rahul's state of mind, and help all of you deal with everything that has happened?"

After Sridhar and Prabha had left—with the contact details of a psychologist that the school sometimes referred children to—Leela leaned back in her seat, eyes closed. The heavy stone that seemed to be set in the middle of her chest showed no sign of lifting. She fought back tears, her heart breaking for Rahul. She hoped his parents would come through.

CHAPTER TWENTY-EIGHT

Leela parked herself at the dining table, her laptop and a mug of filter coffee in front of her, settling down to sort through her notes for the annual report.

She made a face at her laptop. Working during summer holidays reminded her of holiday homework, something she had loathed as a child. She stretched as her computer booted.

I shouldn't complain. At least she was working from home, in her own bright, cheerful, and comfortable living room. *And let's not forget peaceful.* Neil was away at his paternal grandparents' place and wasn't due back till tomorrow.

The icing on the cake, however, was seated on the sofa, legs propped up on the coffee table, her brows furrowed under her black-rimmed glasses, lips pursed, furiously typing away on her MacBook.

Leela smiled to herself as Nandini bent forward to pick up her coffee mug from the table. Their eyes met.

"What do you think you're looking at?" Nandini demanded in mock aggression.

This was their third Saturday together, the third time that they had found themselves seated in exactly the same place, hammering away on their respective keyboards in companionable silence. But who was counting?

"Just taking a bet with myself to see how long before you'll spill that coffee on your computer."

Nandini narrowed her eyes, took a sip of her coffee, put the mug back on the table, and returned to her keyboard. "I'm just going to ignore you."

Leela smirked as she pulled her own laptop closer. Time to get some work done too.

"Are you hungry?" Nandini asked in a while.

Leela glanced up. Nandini's laptop was folded away and she was reading. "What time is it?"

"Almost two."

"Really?" She'd been lost in a world of budgets and board results for two whole hours?

"Yep."

Leela pointed at her laptop. "Give me five minutes to wrap this up."

"No problem. I'll place the order. Chinese okay?" Nandini asked, swiping at her phone.

"Sounds good."

Leela shut her laptop a little while later. "Done." She stretched her arms above her head, making her joints pop.

"Come here," Nandini said, putting down her book. She propped her legs on the sofa, resting her back against the armrest.

Leela got up and climbed between Nandini's legs, sitting with her back towards her. Nandini's hands moved to her shoulders and started a slow massage. Leela moaned. "This feels so good."

"You work too hard," Nandini whispered.

Leela quivered at the trail of hot breath on her ear. She tilted her head back as Nandini's fingers touched a particularly hard knot. "Pot, meet kettle."

"Pfft. I just think you could do with some pampering."

"Mmm, I could certainly get used to this." Leela's eyes closed.

"This is just the beginning. Stick with me and you'll see how multi-talented these hands are."

"I think I'm familiar enough with their talents."

"Are you?" Nandini murmured as her lips grazed the side of Leela's neck. Her hands travelled down Leela's body, caressing her breasts over her shirt.

Leela groaned as her head fell against Nandini's shoulder, Nandini's breasts pressing against her back through their clothes.

"Is this what you meant?" Nandini whispered again, her hands continuing their movement.

"Mm-hmm," was all Leela could manage.

Then Nandini's stomach gave a ferocious growl.

Leela chuckled. "Looks like the other kind of hunger is screaming for attention too."

The doorbell rang.

"Ah, perfect timing. That must be our lunch," Leela said.

"Worst timing ever is more like it," Nandini muttered under her breath as she kissed the back of Leela's neck.

Leela shivered. "You have to stop doing that if you want me to open the door."

"Okay, but you're not off the hook." Nandini waggled a finger at her. "After lunch," she added, almost making it sound like a threat.

Leela's eyes gleamed. "I can assure you I have no desire to be off the hook."

She ran her tongue across Nandini's lips and got up, walking in an exaggerated swagger towards the door. She turned once to bat her eyelids at Nandini, who let her mouth fall open in mock incredulity.

Leela opened the door, a smirk still on her lips.

"Neil!" Her smile dropped and she stepped aside to let him in. "What are you doing back today?"

"I came back." He didn't meet Leela's gaze as he dragged his feet into the house.

Leela stifled the urge to roll her eyes. "I can see that. Care to tell me why?"

He didn't. "Hi, Nandini Aunty," he said drably when he spotted her on the sofa.

"Hi, Neil," Nandini replied. Her legs were off the sofa. She was the very picture of composure.

"Neil." Leela's tone was firm.

He turned towards her, his head still bent

"Tell me what's going on."

His shoulders rose and fell. "Nothing. I just wanted to come back."

"Did you fight with your grandparents?"

"No."

Leela sighed. It was pointless trying to get anything out of him when he was in this mood. Good thing they'd ordered extra food. "Go get cleaned up. Lunch is on its way."

* * *

"Get out. Just, out." Leela put her hands on her hips.

"But   " Nandini tried to protest.

"No." Leela pointed towards the door.

"All right. Fine." Nandini threw her hands in the air and walked out of the kitchen.

"Neil, help Nandini Aunty with the cut on her finger," Leela called out.

She surveyed the burnt rice in the pressure cooker and the haphazardly cut vegetables on the blood-streaked chopping board. She should've known better than to take Nandini up on her offer to help with cooking dinner. She sighed. Now she would have to undo the damage. Maybe they should have ordered out for dinner as well.

"Okay," Neil replied.

"You should put some Dettol on it," Leela heard him say a few moments later. "Let me do that for you."

He still sounded a bit mopey. Maybe he had a fight with Radha.

"Okay, thanks," Nandini said.

"So, er, do you not cook?"

Leela suppressed a snort of laughter at Neil's tentative question.

"I do sometimes when I'm in the mood."

"Ha!" Leela yelled from the kitchen. "You burnt the rice! Who burns rice?"

"I'm a little out of practice, that's all," Nandini yelled back.

"Riiight!" Leela stretched out the word.

"Ouch!" That was Nandini.

Leela wasn't sure if her reaction was to the jibe or the sting of the Dettol.

"Do *you* cook?" Nandini asked Neil.

"Yeah."

"What kind of food?"

"All kinds. I like trying out different kinds of Indian food."

"Bet you don't know any Sindhi recipes."

"Of course, I do. When Ma told me you were Sindhi, I learnt a few dishes."

"What can you make?"

"I can make Sindhi kadhi."

"Wow. That's a tough one."

"Um, not really. It's the easiest. Seviyan is harder."

"Amazing," Nandini replied. "What's your favourite cuisine?"

"It keeps changing. It used to be Naga, but I'm totally into Gujarati food right now. I can do a full Gujarati thali. They have so much variety, the Gujaratis; I haven't managed to try everything yet. But I think I have made a serious dent in the list."

Leela could hear the smile in Neil's voice.

"I'm sure you have. Can you also make Mangalorean food?"

"Bo-o-oring."

Nandini laughed. The sound penetrated Leela's skin and warmed her all over.

"So the apple doesn't fall far from the tree, does it? Did your mum teach you?"

"A bit. But her range is a bit limited."

Leela rolled her eyes. *Ungrateful brat.* But she found herself smiling anyway.

"So when do I get to see the master chef in action?" Nandini asked.

"Ma doesn't let me cook during the week. We could do it next weekend. If you're around, that is."

"Sadly, next weekend I'm back in Delhi. How about the weekend after that?"

"Ma!" he called out. "Can I make Gujarati thali for Nandini Aunty the weekend after the next?"

"Sure, but on one condition. You have to limit the number of dishes to two," Leela replied.

"But, Ma, I won't be able to do a proper thali with just two. Please let me do at least six."

"No, Neil. That's wasteful and you know it."

"How about five then?"

"Three, and that's final."

"Okay," he said. He didn't sound too disheartened. The excitement of acquiring a new guinea pig had undoubtedly overshadowed his disappointment of not being able to lay out a spread.

Anyhow, Nandini's presence seemed to have broken Neil out of his sulk faster than usual. Who knew how long he would've stayed in his bubble of gloom otherwise. And grumpy teenagers on summer holiday could be a pain in the butt.

The volume of the television rose, and by the sounds of it, Neil was channel-hopping.

"Are you and Ma going to watch another boring drama after dinner?" Neil's voice came through the *pock-pock* of a tennis match.

"Would you like to join us?" Nandini's tone was teasing.

"Er, I have to finish a couple of sketches for my portfolio."

"What a pity. It's so much fun to watch you cringe."

Leela poked her head out of the kitchen. "Dinner's going to be ready in about twenty."

Neil was sticking his tongue out at Nandini.

CHAPTER TWENTY-NINE

Leela and Nandini sat entwined on the sofa. Neil had gone to bed a while ago. The low hum of the television was punctuated with the night guard's intermittent whistles and the thumping of his stick on the road. Now and then, a dog howled in the distance to complete the familiar nightly chorus.

She and Nandini had started out on either ends of the sofa, and she had no idea how they had ended up in a cuddle. Nandini's head rested on Leela's shoulder, her hand on Leela's knee, its gentle movement sending mild currents up Leela's leg. *Fire* was playing on the television, a film about two unhappy sisters-in-law in a traditional joint family who find love with each other.

"This takes me back," Leela said.

"Remember how excited we were when it released?"

"Yep. We skipped college—how many was it? Thrice?—to watch it."

"And the furore it caused." Leela shook her head. "Quite unusual for that time. Not like these days when everybody gets upset about every movie."

"True. In hindsight, though, it was dodgy how the director kept saying it's not a film about lesbians but about the choices one makes in life."

Leela nodded. "Yeah. Even the movie shows the women turned to each other only when they were rejected by the men."

"She is so good, though." Leela sighed as she watched the emotions flitting across Shabana Azmi's face while the actor sat on the ground behind a bamboo charpoy inclined against the wall, the shadows of the jute weaving matching her moods.

"She is," Nandini replied.

"Do you and, er, Mita do this?" Leela didn't take her eyes away from the screen.

"Huh?" Nandini turned towards her.

"Movies, you know. Do you watch them together?"

"Is that supposed to be a euphemism for something?"

"Of course not," Leela said, aiming for nonchalance and keeping her fingers crossed that she was getting there.

Nandini pressed her lips together but it didn't hide her grin. After a couple of beats, she said, "I haven't seen her in a long time."

"How come?"

Nandini shrugged. "I don't know. I suppose neither of us has felt the need to reach out."

Leela nodded.

"Besides," Nandini said, giving Leela's knee a squeeze. "Now I have you for all my desired services."

Leela laughed as a knot in her stomach released. "Yes, you do," she said, caressing the back of Nandini's neck.

A sudden clatter ripped them apart. Neil!

Leela sprang away from Nandini, her heart leaping to her mouth. Within half a second, both she and Nandini had straightened themselves and shuffled back to either ends of the sofa.

"Um, all okay, Neil?" Leela asked when he came out of his room. She clenched her clammy hands together in her lap, her heart still going at full pelt.

"Just getting some water," Neil croaked.

He picked up a bottle from the table, tilted his head up, and glugged water directly into his mouth. Then he shuffled back to his room.

Leela exchanged a look with Nandini.

* * *

At 6:57 a.m., Leela gave up on her Sunday-morning lie-in. The steady simmer of uneasiness made her stomach clench. Last night—that had been a close call. Rubbing her eyes as if it might erase the scenes replaying in her head, Leela pushed herself out of bed.

He couldn't have seen anything. But it was more wishful thought than firm reassurance.

And if he did? Another question that Leela would prefer not to have to think about.

The house was silent when she went out into the living room. Of course, Neil wouldn't be up yet. His door was ajar, though. He liked to leave it that way—the cross-ventilation from the window created a cool draught that he called "my natural air conditioner." Leela pushed the door open a little further inside. There he was, fast asleep. Like he hadn't a care in the world. And that was exactly how she wanted it.

She tiptoed closer, picking the covers that had fallen to the floor and settling them back on Neil. He looked so peaceful, his face calm, long eyelashes almost touching his cheek. Her heart clenched. She reached out to run a hand along his head but stopped at the last moment.

What had he seen? What did he know? Worse, what was he thinking?

What am I doing? The effort not to append *with Nandini* at the end of that thought made Leela draw in a sharp breath. She placed a hand over her mouth, her heart pounding.

Leela retreated, one foot behind the other, and dropped into the sofa. She squeezed her eyes shut and let her head fall into her hands.

"Stupid, so stupid," she murmured, and punched the armrest. She gave herself a shudder, as if to shake off the shell of anxiety that had cocooned her. Taking a final deep breath, she stood again.

If he *had* seen her and Nandini, then she would just have to deal with that—when she knew what she was dealing with.

As for what that meant for her and Nandini… Leela gave herself another shake. *Not now. Right now, I'm going to make pancakes for breakfast.*

Neil surfaced an hour later, shuffling out into the living room, even his crew cut looking dishevelled. Leela studied him over the Sunday newspaper from the sofa as he shambled into the kitchen, clattered about, and came back out with a steel tumbler. He paid Leela no heed.

"Good morning," she called out.

"Morning," he mumbled.

Leela's eyes narrowed. Was his grumpy phase back, or was it her worst fear? Her gaze followed him around as he made a circuit of the living room scrolling through his phone. If he was upset, he would have retreated to his room, right, and not be roaming about?

"You don't want breakfast?"

"I'm having juice."

"I made pancakes."

He looked up from the phone, as if noticing Leela for the first time. "Oh," he said. He disappeared into the kitchen, returning with a generous pile of pancakes. "Can I eat in my room?"

"No. Meals at the table—you know the rule."

He rolled his eyes. "Fine," he said, pulling out a chair and sitting down.

He worried the edge of the table mat with his free hand as he steadily shovelled honey-laced pancakes into his mouth. His complete oblivion to her tension made Leela want to scream with frustration. She took a slow, deep breath, instead.

"Got any plans for today?" she ventured.

His shoulders rose and fell in a shrug.

All right, if that's how he was going to play it, then it was time to show her trump card. "Nandini Aunty has offered to treat us to the new *Orange Triangle* movie, if you're up for it."

His head snapped up, eyes wide. "The 3D one? It just got released—impossible to get tickets."

It was Leela's turn to shrug. She shook out the newspaper with exaggerated force and turned it the other way round. "Do you want to go or not?"

Some four hours later, as they exited the movie theatre, it was a question Leela was regretting having asked. Her head throbbed, as much from the shouting and shooting in the movie as from listening to Nandini and Neil arguing about the mind-bending plot. But the sight of Neil so animated, thanking Nandini so profusely, made it worth it. Just about.

"It was *awesome*, Nandini Aunty, the seats in gold class are just *amazing*—I watched the whole movie almost lying down, and I would have, but then the snacks came. Getting food served right at the seats, wow, that has to be the greatest idea ever!" He paused for breath and turned to Leela. "Wasn't it awesome, Ma?"

"It was, thank you," Leela said to Nandini. "It must have cost you a fortune."

"You're welcome. It was well worth every paisa."

"Nandini Aunty, can I treat you to ice cream?" Neil asked.

"I can never say no to ice cream," Nandini replied. "Lead on."

Leela followed them, shaking her head and wondering if Neil had the money to cover his generosity or if she'd have to pitch in. But one thing was certain—Leela was willing to bet home and hearth on it—he hadn't seen anything last night.

CHAPTER THIRTY

"Must you go?" Nandini's voice was so low that Leela almost didn't hear it through the drumbeat of rain on the windowpane.

She glanced up from pulling on her sari blouse. Leaning back against the wicker headboard of the bed, a pillow wedged behind her neck and shoulders, Nandini watched as Leela did up the hooks on her blouse. Leela smiled, slowing down.

The light quilt was twisted around Nandini's legs. Dusk was falling, and the last of the sunlight nudged her bare outline lazily.

"You don't make it easy, do you, asking me things like that while looking like an erotic nineteenth-century painting."

"You are one to talk," Nandini murmured.

Leela bent forward to pick up the sari from the chair, giving Nandini time to run her eyes down her blouse-and-petticoat-clad body. The gaze swept over Leela like a physical touch.

She tucked one corner of the sari into her petticoat and wrapped it around herself once, tucking it into her waistband again, her movements languid. The rest of the garment pooled before her as she reached for the other end, twisting it around herself and then over her left shoulder, glancing back for half a second to adjust the length of the pallu.

She looked up again—Nandini remained rapt. Moving unhurriedly, Leela measured out pleats in the sari. She tucked the folds into her petticoat, just under her belly button. Undraping the pallu, she adjusted the sari's fall around herself and put the pallu back over her shoulder. She reached down to the bedside table and picked up her brooch in the shape of a dragonfly that she pinned to her shoulder to keep the drape in place.

Nandini let out a long breath as she caught Leela's eye.

"Had fun?" Leela asked.

In answer, a hint of a smile appeared on Nandini's mouth. She reached out towards Leela, her eyes dancing with mischief in the dying light. Leela dodged, shaking a finger at her. "Now, behave."

"But I don't want you to go."

"I don't want to go either."

"So, stay."

"You know I can't."

Nandini ran her fingers through her hair and turned her head towards the ceiling. "Yes, yes, I know." Then she gave a mock pout. "When will I see you again?"

"At school, tomorrow. You forgot?" Leela teased. She stepped up to the mirror to brush out her hair. As she reached back to twist it into a bun, she saw Nandini in the reflection, throwing off the quilt and swinging her legs off the bed.

The room was almost dark now, just the streetlights dipping in from the road to highlight Nandini's limbs. Two steps brought her just behind Leela, and she slipped her arms around Leela's middle, dropping her chin in the crook of her shoulder and neck.

"You're mean," she whispered.

Nandini's breath tickled the side of Leela's neck, making a ripple of pleasure run down her body. Her breasts pressed into Leela's back and warm fingers caressed the bare skin of Leela's midriff. She leaned back in Nandini's arms. Even standing like this, looking at each other through a mirror, felt so complete. So right. So…enough.

Another fifteen minutes wouldn't hurt, would it? She could always say it had been the traffic. She pressed her hands on Nandini's, which were clasping each other across Leela's stomach. "Suppose I tell you how difficult it is for me to leave you here like this, would you believe me?"

"Mmm, I might," Nandini murmured, leaving a line of soft kisses along the side and back of Leela's neck. "It's getting harder and harder to let you go, Leela."

Leela shivered each time Nandini's lips met the sensitive skin on the back of her neck. "That might be because of my innate irresistibility."

"That…or…" Even in the darkness, Leela could feel Nandini's eyes locked on hers through the reflection in the mirror.

She waited, but Nandini didn't continue.

"Or what?"

Nandini straightened up, letting her hands trail up to grasp Leela's shoulders. "I think I'm falling in love with you."

The words were so soft that Leela wasn't sure she had heard right. Despite the lightness in Nandini's tone, they punched into Leela and plummeted through her body, crashing at her feet.

It was a truth delivered in typical Nandini style—straight and true, seeing where that got her, and facing whatever it was that came with it with her trademark equanimity. This was a truth being revealed to Nandini in that instant.

Nandini stiffened—Leela had hesitated far too long to respond. She let Nandini turn her around, let her hands cup her face.

"Oh, Leela. I'm sorry. I didn't mean to drop it on you like that."

"I…" The fist that had squeezed Leela's heart had now eased. The warmth that had rushed into her body belied the numbness she felt in her core. Nandini's words swam around in her head in a chaotic jumble. "You just…you took me by surprise," she managed.

Nandini let her go and walked backwards towards the bed. She picked up the bathrobe lying at the foot of the bed and put it on. She sat on the edge of the bed, arms crossed before her, looking down at the floor. "I shouldn't have said it."

Leela remained rooted. "It's all right," she said. "I'm not upset or anything. It's just that, this thing we have, it wasn't supposed to be anything more than—" She gestured to herself and then to Nandini.

"I know. I didn't think about what I was saying. I just…I felt it and I said it."

"I know," Leela repeated. "But love—it changes things. You can't put it out there and then take it away." She put her hand on her chest for a moment—a ludicrous, almost Bollywoody gesture—but there it was, her heart beating furiously.

"Are you going to run?"

"Running is not exactly my style," Leela said with a half smile.

"So then?"

"I don't know."

Nandini clicked her tongue. "It's just what we didn't want—complicated. And I've gone and complicated it. Shit."

Leela stepped towards Nandini and lifted her chin with a finger. She leaned down and pressed a kiss to her forehead. "Can we talk about this later? I have to go now."

Nandini didn't look up. "Sure. See you."

Leela walked out of Nandini's suite without a backwards glance, leaving Nandini in the shroud of darkness. Her mind was blank, her body drained.

Still in a daze, she got into her car. The familiar space embraced her like an old friend. Even the synthetic jasmine of the air freshener was calming. She looked down at her hands in her lap—they were shaking; her arms, her entire body was shaking. She put her head against the headrest, closed her eyes, and waited.

She remained like that for a few—or many—moments. A door slammed somewhere, jerking Leela out of her stupor. Outside, the yellow porch light flickered and insects swarmed around it.

Nandini's words rushed back into her like a tsunami. She clenched her fists. She had no right to drop this on her, to change everything. They'd had an understanding, and now Nandini had gone and spoilt it.

Leela hit the steering wheel with the base of her palm. "Fuck!"

PART V

JUNE–JULY 2018

CHAPTER THIRTY-ONE

Leela stared at the damp patch in her ceiling, but it wasn't Kiran she was thinking of this morning. She had slept fitfully, troubled by bizarre dreams—mixed-up versions of what had happened with Nandini and the various dire consequences that Leela's subconscious had raked up—but dreams that Leela couldn't fully dredge up from her memories now.

Rubbing her eyes to try to get the grittiness out of them, she reached for her phone—still another six minutes for her alarm to ring. But she was wide awake. She switched off the alarm and lay back. Today, knowing she could laze for another few minutes didn't seem like a delicious bonus snatched at the start of a new day. Rather, she was ready to give anything to keep her from getting up and facing the world. A heaviness weighed her down.

Had Davi been right? Was it impossible to have a complication-free "understanding" with someone you had a history with?

But that was a ridiculous thought. Their history was so ancient, it was half a lifetime ago. When they had met in

Amrudpur, they had done so as almost strangers, having become such different people, with different dreams and aspirations than they'd had in college. They'd even had journeys that had been impossible to imagine back then. The intervening twenty-odd years had been both good and bad, and all things considered, Leela had come through relatively unscathed. Those years had also shaped her into who she was today, and she was definitely not the same person from back then.

This is completely different. Our history is in the past!

Leela grimaced at her misguided attempt at wit. No, Davi was wrong. This wasn't one of her trashy romance novels, and she couldn't fit their philosophies into real life.

After her relationship with Nandini had ended, Leela had spent a couple of years immersing herself in academics, and then Kiran had been shoved into her path by two sets of determined parents. They had married about eighteen months later, and Leela had been happy with Kiran. Neil had been a relatively easy child, she'd got a good job, and for a while Leela had had everything she thought she would ever desire. Then Kiran had died and her perfect life had come undone. Yet she had swum through those murky waters and emerged battered but battle-hardened, definitely stronger than she had ever been.

As for Nandini, Leela didn't know the details of what she had been up to, though she did know the significant highlights. Such as the three-year relationship that had ended suddenly, and the struggle to establish her company. Nandini was strong too. It wasn't just her brilliance and poise and assurance—these things were out there for everyone to see. Her kindness and empathy were endearing, too, though you only saw them when you got to know her well. The way Nandini interacted with Neil, for instance. Leela smiled when she thought of that.

So why had that compassion and resilience suddenly deserted her now? *What the fuck is she thinking?*

They had both been so clear that it was to be casual. In fact, Nandini had been adamant about the fact that she didn't "do relationships" from even before they had begun their dalliance. What had changed now, so much so that she was considering letting herself use the L word? If the terms of the relationship had changed, how come Leela hadn't been told?

It's not fair!

How could Nandini even be thinking it? And what on earth was she imagining? With Leela settled here in Bangalore, with her work and her family obligations, and Nandini equally settled in her own life but two thousand kilometres away? What sort of arrangement could it even be when it depended on chance meetings? And then? It wasn't as if either of them could uproot themselves and run off and have a happily-ever-after, was it? No, falling in love had never been on the table.

Falling in love. Who would think that three simple words could cause such turmoil? Yet a part of Leela yearned to wrap the words around herself so tight that they became part of her. She wanted to freeze that moment from last evening—the semi-darkened room, the almost-outline of herself in the mirror with Nandini hugging her from behind, Nandini's breath on the side of her neck, the whispered words in her ear. Leela wanted to remain trapped there forever, in that single instant where she could, maybe, believe that anything was possible.

Why had she let this happen? Why had she let Nandini back into her life?

Nandini's ability to mould herself to anything life threw at her had been so contagious that Leela had found herself caught in its current. The equanimity with which Nandini had approached all that had happened between the two of them, and also in her confidence that they would be able to keep their arrangement separate from work—it had all egged Leela on. She had broken out of her carefully cocooned life, of her self-imposed boundaries, and discovered herself anew. It had been such an exhilarating ride, laced with intrigue and thrill, and Leela had enjoyed every moment of it.

What if Nandini hadn't come back into my life?

"Ma?" Leela snapped out of her reverie, surprised to find herself blinking away tears. Neil stood at her door, rubbing sleep from his eyes. "Why aren't you up? Are you feeling ill?"

Shit. Leela checked her phone again and found that it was now fifteen minutes past when her alarm would have rung. She sat up. "I'm fine," she reassured him.

As she swung her legs to the floor, the stone of unease resettled in her stomach. The truth was, she liked it when Nandini was around. She missed her when she was gone, and she looked forward to her return. It was simple, it was fun, and it worked. She wanted to keep it that way—undemanding and straightforward. Was that too much to ask?

* * *

As she pulled into her designated parking spot in school, Leela's phone rang. She fished it out from her bag on the passenger seat and peered at the display.

Nandini.

They had last spoken three days ago. When Leela had been at the guest house. With Nandini. When Nandini had said those words. Those words that had changed everything.

Despite the cool weather, a bead of sweat trickled down behind Leela's ear. Her heart strained in her chest like a wet cloth being wrung to squeeze all the water out. She shut her eyes and leaned her head against the headrest. *I can't do it. I just can't.*

She stared at Nandini's smiling face on the screen, her eyes crinkling at the corners as she looked back at Leela. The thought of that smile falling from Nandini's face even for a moment made Leela's heart ache.

But she couldn't put off talking to Nandini anymore, however much it tore at her. She took a few quick calming breaths and pressed the green button on the screen.

"Hey." Nandini's voice was only just audible.

Leela cleared her throat. "Hi."

"How are you?"

"I'm okay. You?"

"Good. Leaving for Chennai in a couple of hours."

"Yeah, I know."

"I…I just…wanted to, you know, check if you were okay after the other night."

"I'm fine."

"I know it was a lot to take in. Maybe we should find some time to talk about it?"

"There's nothing to talk about."

"No?"

"You felt something, and you said it. I heard what you said. That's it."

"Is that all you have to say?"

Leela put her head back against the headrest. The parking area, which was reserved for the school management and board and hardly ever frequented by students or teachers, was empty. Leela was glad for the privacy.

"I don't know what else you want me to say. You knew what our deal was right from the beginning. We said no strings attached."

"I know what we said."

"Didn't you say you weren't interested in a relationship? What's happened to that?"

"Things change. I've changed." Nandini paused. "I love you. I didn't intend for it to happen, but it did."

The familiar gentleness that had returned to Nandini's voice and the words she'd spoken enveloped Leela's heart like a blanket. But only for a second. She couldn't allow herself to get carried away.

She swallowed the lump in her throat. "Things haven't changed for me."

"So…what? What do you want? You want me to pretend I don't have feelings for you?"

"Yes. No. I don't know."

"Well, I do know what I want. I want more than just sneaking around."

Leela wanted to tear her hair out. Why was Nandini being so unreasonable?

She straightened in her seat. "I don't think I can give you what you want."

"You don't even want to consider making a go of it?"

What is wrong with her? Leela gripped the steering wheel hard. "There is nothing to consider! Do you even know what you're asking? What do you think? We can walk hand in hand into the sunset and have some grand future together? Just because you're footloose and fancy-free doesn't mean everyone else is too. I have huge responsibilities on my shoulders. I have parents to look after. Neil still needs me. There's also the school."

"I have responsibilities too. I have a business to run and employees who depend on me. I have friends who need me. And just because my parents live in a different city doesn't mean I don't have any responsibility towards them. As for Neil, I might not have kids, but please don't presume I am unaware of what being a parent entails."

"Exactly. We're both tied to our circumstances. How can you then even talk about giving it a go when my life is here and yours is in Delhi?"

"Because we already are making it work, Leela, don't you see? We *are* in a relationship. We might not have acknowledged it as such, but that's what it is. I don't know how or when, but at some point it stopped being just about sex for me. And I know you feel the same way. I don't know if you realise this, but there have been times I've come to Bangalore only to see you. Can you in all honesty tell me that you haven't made accommodations to your life so we could spend more time together? Can you?"

"I don't know what you're talking about."

"You can't tell me that," Nandini continued as if she hadn't heard Leela. "Because you know you've done it too, many times. All I want for you is to accept it. We have to stop lying to ourselves."

Leela closed her eyes and shook her head. "You're asking for too much, Nandini."

They sat in silence for a few moments.

"Do you love me, Leela?"

Leela banged her fist against the steering wheel. There was that word again. How could she throw it around like that?

"You think that's what's important?" Leela spat.

"Yes! It's the most important thing, don't you get it? Everything else you just said is bullshit."

"You think my worries and concerns are worthless? How dare you?"

"That's not what I said, and you know it."

Leela took a deep breath. She was tired. So tired. "I can't talk about this anymore. I have a class evaluation in ten minutes."

"Can we talk later, then?"

The hopefulness in Nandini's words tore at her insides. "I don't know if there's anything left to discuss."

"Are you saying it's over?" Nandini's voice cracked.

The question broke Leela. The word she needed to say was "yes," but every fibre of her being pulled her back from uttering it.

Instead, she said, "I have to go." And she disconnected the call.

CHAPTER THIRTY-TWO

Leela stepped into the middle-school corridor. The children milled around in flashes of blue, running, talking, laughing, pulling each other's legs, their voices blending into a restless hum that would soon settle into a different kind of low buzz when classes began. It was the long way round to her office, yet these days Leela was compelled to seek out the chaos first thing every morning.

Every time she walked into the surge, she imagined herself to be the eye of the storm, a point of calm and equilibrium as chaos reigned around her. This sensation of serenity only lasted a moment or two, though. As if on cue, one of the kids spotted her, and the bedlam morphed into order within seconds. But those few moments were enough to ground her, remind her of something tangible that she could still count upon.

"Good morning. Morning. Yes, good morning." She returned the students' greetings, and once she turned the corner, she paid no heed to the steadily rising decibel levels. The bell hadn't rung yet; they were allowed a few more moments of abandon.

If time was the great healer, then Leela found herself dissatisfied with its services. Day eight and the memory of her last conversation with Nandini remained a wound refusing to heal. And today, even clipping her way through the high-spirited middle-schoolers had done nothing for her composure.

Was anything going to calm her down today? She doubted it. Not until she walked into the Discover-E status meeting later that afternoon and made sure it wasn't Nandini she would be facing. Her life was going to intersect with Nandini's for the first time since their parting of ways, and she couldn't stop thinking about it. Her. So much for keeping business and pleasure at arm's length.

Gulshan rushed towards her as Leela neared her office.

"Leela Ma'am, there's no water anywhere in the school except in the senior wing! A pipe has burst near Mantri Mall."

Great. Leela stared at her distraught secretary. "Have you called the administrator to arrange for backup?"

Gulshan at least had the grace to look abashed. "Er, no, ma'am."

"Honestly, Gulshan." Leela shook her head as she walked into her office.

By the time afternoon rolled around, Leela had battled the water crisis (and a missing administrator), sat in on a supervisors' meeting about the new curriculum, congratulated the school quiz team for winning the regionals, and taken two classes to fill in for absent teachers. All this apart from her other principal duties, that is. She hadn't even had the time for a proper lunch break.

An uneasy knot remained lodged in her stomach, however. The last bell rang and the knot uncoiled into full-blown nerves.

Oh, stop it! Nandini won't be here, she scolded herself as she paused outside the meeting room, clutching her diary so hard that her fingertips hurt. Giving herself a mental smack for being silly, Leela pushed the door open. And there was Vikrant Sinha, sitting at the table, scribbling on a sheet of paper.

The knot eased. To be replaced by a twinge of disappointment. "Hello, Vikrant," she called out.

Vikrant looked up and smiled. "Hello."

They were so similar in many ways, he and Nandini, that it tugged at Leela's insides. He had the same casual grace and the impeccably put-together appearance, from the tips of his polished leather shoes and knife-like crease of his shirt cuffs to his perfect posture.

Leela took a deep breath to steady herself. This was her chance, with the peons still setting up the projector and screen, and the other teachers yet to come in. Sure, it was going to hurt like hell, but not doing it was going to drive her crazy. Especially when one of Nandini's closest friends was sitting barely three feet away from her.

Leela's throat was dry as she set her diary and phone down near the head of the table. She turned towards Vikrant and opened her mouth to speak to him. Her phone started to vibrate, the screen lit up with her mother's image.

Leela wanted to fling the handset out of the window. Instead, she grabbed it, muttered an "excuse me," and stumbled out into the corridor.

"Yes, Ma, what is it?"

"Your pearl necklace, the one I was going to wear for the reception tonight. The clasp broke."

Leela kneaded her forehead. "I'm sorry, Ma, I…" *Wait, why am I apologising? She broke my necklace.* Leela gave herself a shake. "Look, I'm about to go into a meeting. Can't you just wear something else?"

"But it goes so well with my black silk. I can't wear that gold necklace, I wore it last time."

"Oho, Ma, just go upstairs and get something else from my locker."

"Okay, I'll do that. We'll be late tonight, so don't worry."

Leela sighed. "I won't worry. Now I have to—"

The door to the meeting room swung open as Bopanna and his companion came out. Leela could already spot some of the other teachers heading towards the room. She had lost her chance to talk to Vikrant. Now she'd have to wait for the meeting to end.

"Neil will also have left by the time you come home," her mother went on, relentless. "Shall I heat some food and leave it for you in a casserole?"

"Yes, thank you. Sorry, I have to go now. The meeting is starting."

When she stepped back inside, most of the seats were filled and Vikrant was ready to begin. Leela sat down and kicked off the meeting with a brief introduction.

She sat back in her chair and tried to listen to Vikrant. He was a good speaker, erudite and professional, though without Nandini's easy charm. But he was such a strong reminder of Nandini that it hurt to even look at him. Many a time Leela had to drop her gaze and close her eyes to allow the pain to subside before she could focus again.

By the time the meeting ended, Leela wanted to pick up her diary and run back into her office. Instead, she forced herself to wait till the gaggle of teachers that had surrounded Vikrant dispersed, and then went up to him. Her heart thudded, and she clasped her diary in a death grip once again to steel herself.

"Thank you, that was a great status report," she told him.

"You're welcome. Your teachers are a keen lot. It's been great working with them."

"The feeling is mutual. You must be the first people we've worked with who will have finished their project more or less on the date they promised they would."

Vikrant tilted his head. "Thank you."

"Your cheque is ready, by the way. I was going to courier it, but since you're here, you could pick it up."

"Of course." He picked up his briefcase and followed Leela out. "And, I must tell you, you are one of those rare clients who pays us before we have to ask."

In her office, Leela handed him the envelope with the cheque. He thanked her again and turned to leave. It was now or never.

"How's Nandini?" The words came out in a rush.

Vikrant stopped. He turned around, his eyebrows slightly raised. He was usually quite inscrutable.

"I mean, she's the one usually handling the project and she's…I thought I'd…" Leela's face burned. Overexplaining was as bad as staying quiet. Worse.

Vikrant looked down at his shoes, the shiny leather now coated with a thin sheen of dust. "She's…tied up at the office."

"Oh." Leela's heart fluttered.

She looked away and, as the seconds stretched, struggled for something to fill the silence.

"She'll be all right." Leela's head snapped back up. Vikrant was watching her. "Are *you* doing okay?" he added.

There was only kindness in his voice.

"I…yeah…I mean…I'm fine, yes. Thank you," she replied, swallowing down the lump in her throat.

He nodded, and like a switch being flicked, his distant, professional mask was back in place. "See you, then."

And he was gone, splintering Leela's last connection with Nandini, leaving her more alone than ever.

CHAPTER THIRTY-THREE

Leela took off her glasses and put them on her desk. Rubbing her eyes, she checked the clock on her computer—nine thirty. Everyone would've left by now, except of course the night shift guards.

Leela rested her head against the chair and shut her eyes. She should be heading home too. These two days a month when Neil was away at Kiran's parents' were normally a welcome break for her. And though she loved her son to pieces, to not be responsible for another human being was, in a sense, liberating. She could wake up as late as she wanted, watch television the whole day, eat instant noodles if she didn't feel like cooking, listen to eighties pop as loudly as she liked, and be a slob without worrying about setting a good example. More recently, there had been Nandini to share that time with. A two-day respite from their crazy lives and the nonstop sneaking around.

But this time there would be no Nandini—no laughing about silly movies, or serious discussions about life and politics; no teasing Nandini about her klutziness in the kitchen while they cooked; no catching up on each other's lives over dinner; no languorous lovemaking afterwards; no post-coital cuddle; no whispered conversations late into the night; and no burnt omelettes as witness to Nandini's attempts to serve breakfast in bed.

A lump formed in Leela's throat. The only thing she had to look forward to in the next two days was an empty, cold house and more sleepless nights. She wanted to dial back time and return to the more carefree days of just a bit more than a week ago. To forget what had transpired in the guest house that day.

But that was not an option. Nandini had changed the rules of their game and Leela had had no choice but to stop playing it.

* * *

Leela's watch told her it was eleven as she climbed the stairs to her apartment. That walk around Hanssen's premises and then through the quiet green residential area where the school was located had been a sad attempt at avoiding going home. Not that she had admitted it to herself in the moment. But the concerned frown on the security guard's face when she had passed the school gates for the third time told her that her time was up.

As she turned the lock on her front door, exhaustion hit her like a tonne of bricks. All she wanted to do was fall into bed and try once again to get the much-needed sleep that had been steadfastly eluding her this whole week. In the semi-darkness, she dumped her bag and keys on a chair and traipsed to the dining table to get a drink of water. As she reached out to pick up the bottle, a shadow moved at the other end of the dining table. Leela gasped.

"Ma, you scared me!" She clutched the table to steady herself. "What are you doing here so late? Where's Dad? Is he—"

"He's fine. He was tired after the wedding, so he's gone to sleep," Elsie said in a tone that filled Leela with a sense of foreboding. She pulled up one of the chairs around the table and sat down.

"Why are you sitting in the dark? What's wrong?"
Elsie was silent.
"Ma? You're worrying me now."
"What's the meaning of this?"
"Of what?"

Elsie didn't look at Leela. In fact she hadn't looked at her in all this time. She had been resolutely staring at the table. Leela's eyes had started to adjust to the darkness, and the pale yellow light streaming in from the balcony windows was enough to illuminate the small jewellery box sitting in the middle of the table that Elsie stared at.

Leela bristled. *What the hell?* It was almost the middle of the night, she was on her last legs, and her mother had chosen this moment to talk jewellery with her? And that too with so much drama!

Leela opened her mouth to give Elsie a piece of her mind, but the words stuck in her throat. Her eyes went back to the jewellery box. It was an oval shape made of clay with a floral carving on one side of the lid. She knew this box. It contained the silver bracelet Nandini had gifted her a month ago.

A sudden chill engulfed Leela, beads of sweat formed on her upper lip, and her hands felt clammy. *Oh my God! The note!* She'd forgotten all about the note in the box.

Leela,

Remember this? It's the exact copy of the one I gave you for your 20th (at least, that's what I was going for). I still remember hiding it in your bag, waiting and waiting till you found it. The smile on your face lit up my life for days. So did the kiss afterwards. Your wrists are still sexy, so I hope you'll like it again. Wish I was there to put it around you like last time…and collect my reward. Happy 42nd.

Yours,
Nandini

Despair hit Leela like an eighteen-wheel truck. She pressed her eyes shut. She looked up to see her mother's mouth moving and hear the sound of her voice, but the words didn't make any sense.

"What?" Leela asked. Her own voice sounded like it was someone else's.

"I said, what is the meaning of…" Elsie's face scrunched in undisguised repugnance as she nodded towards the card on the table. "This? Please explain it to me, Leela, because I can't—"

"Why were you rummaging in my cupboard?"

"I wasn't rummaging in your cupboard. *You* said I could get something suitable from your locker. And then I found *this*. Leelu, tell me honestly, what does this mean? Is it…did you— chhee! These dirty, disgusting words! I can't even bring myself to ask!"

Leela rubbed her eyelids with her fingers. "Ma, please, I'm very, very tired—"

"Answer my question." Elsie's voice rose, shaking with anger. "Did you or did you not have *relations* with this girl."

A bubble of laughter erupted from Leela. She was still sitting there, like an errant child before her mother, eyes still closed and hands pressed to them. And Elsie referring to Nandini as a girl and her delicate euphemism for sex utterly ridiculous. Was her exhaustion crossing into hysteria—or insanity?

"Oh God, I can't believe what I'm hearing!" Elsie burst out.

You aren't hearing anything because I haven't said anything.

Elsie's voice had risen to a high-pitched cry. "How could you? How? We have raised you so well. We have given you everything. And yet, you go and do something like this? Do you know how abhorrent and despicable this is? You will go to hell for this!"

I feel like I'm already there.

"I knew that girl was trouble the moment I set eyes on her all those years ago," Elsie continued. "That's why she's not married, isn't it? What kind of a man would marry a girl like her? That deviant! Look how she's led my daughter astray!"

Her mother's words jarred Leela out of her silent rebuttals.

"Will you please stop referring to her as a girl?"

Elsie's eyes widened. For a second, it seemed her mother had run out of steam. But clearly, her outrage was more than a match for Leela's exhaustion, for it took Elsie only a few moments to regroup. Her face contorted into a mask of revulsion.

"How dare you?" she began, her voice now low and dripping with disgust. "How dare you dishonour us in this way? Does all this mean nothing to you?" She waved around her. "Your life, your family, your son? Us? Everything we have done for you, is this how you repay us? Don't you owe your son anything? You are a widow. A mother. What are people going to say? Don't you have *any* respect? For *any*thing?"

"Ma, please—"

"No, stop!" Elsie stood up, her hands shooting out towards Leela, palms outwards, like she was staving off an attack. "I don't want to listen to anything. I don't want to listen to you justify your abhorrent, sinful, disgusting behaviour or to defend that shameless, vulgar girl…woman, if that's what you want. I want you to promise me that this was a mistake, that it will never happen again, that you will repent. I don't want to have to tell your father—how can I even tell him? I don't have the words to express the disgusting things you have done."

Leela flinched again at the word "disgusting," but there was no energy left in her to put up a fight. In any case, Elsie wasn't about to let her get a word in edgeways.

"Promise me you won't see her again. You won't even talk to her. You won't even think about her. Promise me that you will repent. Promise me."

Leela stared in front of her, her eyes unfocused and unseeing. Her world was falling apart around her and she couldn't do anything about it. She was broken, physically and mentally, and incapable of putting even one logical thought in front of the other. Perhaps her mother finding out was a sign that it indeed had been time to end things with Nandini.

"It's already over." As the words came out of her, listless and defeated, the last vestiges of her energy seemed to seep out with them. She turned around and willed her leaden legs to lead her into the bedroom. She climbed into her bed, not bothering to remove the bedcover, and curled up into a ball.

Hugging herself tightly, Leela shivered. Whether it was from the cold, rain-heavy breeze from the open window or from the utter desolation she felt from deep within, she couldn't say. It didn't feel unfamiliar, though. The emptiness sucked her into its vortex like it had after Kiran was gone. She shut her eyes tight against the whirl, hoping against hope it wouldn't be as devastating as before. Her gasp for breath turned into a deep sob. The dam inside her broke, and the tears rushed out.

CHAPTER THIRTY-FOUR

Leela's intercom buzzed. She picked it up. "Yes, Gulshan."

"Raza Sir called. He's on his way here."

Leela frowned. "Now? Is he in town? Did I have an appointment with him today?"

"You don't. He said it couldn't wait. Shall I send your class eight group to the library?"

"Yes, Gulshan. Thanks."

Fifteen minutes later Raza Hussain was seated across the table from Leela, sipping the coffee that Bopanna had brought in, his demeanour quiet and sombre. Not that he was talkative otherwise, but this level of preoccupation was new.

Leela cleared her throat. "To what do I owe this sudden visit?"

Raza studied her in silence.

"Raza, is something wrong?" she tried again, shifting in her seat.

"Not wrong, no. But a bit worrisome."

"What is it?"

Raza took out his phone, swiped and tapped it a few times, and held it out towards Leela.

"I received this email last night."

Leela took the phone from him and read the email.

Dear Mr. Hussain,

I would like to make you aware of an unfavourable situation in the Bangalore branch of the Hanssen Academy. You should know that the principal of the school, Ms. Leela Saldana, is a lesbian and is having relations with other women. It is abhorrent that young innocent children are being exposed to such perverted and deviant behaviour. I as a concerned citizen will not stand by and allow this to happen. Therefore, I would like to urge you to dismiss Leela Ma'am from the school. If she is not gone by the end of this month, I will be forced to leak this information to the press, which could cause irreparable damage to the reputation of the school as well as to you.

Yours truly,

Well-wisher

Leela's eyes widened as she looked up at Raza and then back at the phone. A jumble of questions raced through her mind.

"Who sent this to you?"

"I don't know. As you can see, the email address is just a bunch of letters and numbers."

Leela couldn't breathe. How could anyone know about her and Nandini? They had always been so careful.

"Raza, I—" she began.

"You don't have to explain, Leela. Your personal life is neither my concern nor the school's."

Leela sagged with relief. In the next instant, she frowned. Had she been about to deny the allegation the blackmailer was making? Had she been about to lie? Raza had let her off the hook. But the questions were disturbing.

"You are too valuable to the school," he continued. "You are an educator in the true sense of the word and have made Hanssen a trailblazer in many respects. I would like you to continue doing good things here. So there is no way I'm going to ask you to leave. There's also the fact that I don't appreciate being blackmailed.

"Having said that, I am concerned that if this spreads, it will have serious repercussions for you and, let's face it, also for the school. Much as I'm inclined to ignore this email, I can't. Therefore, we have to figure out what to do about it."

A deep fatigue settled within Leela. It was as if she was standing on a cliff and each gust of wind was pushing her closer to the edge. She dropped her head into her hands. *How am I supposed to deal with this too?*

"Leela?" She heard Raza's voice calling her from somewhere very far away. "Are you all right?"

Lifting her head took everything out of Leela. "I'm sorry, Raza. Could you please give me some time to think about this?"

"Of course," he said, getting up. "I want you to know that the board and I will support you in whatever you decide. Needless to say, we want you to stay."

Leela nodded and put her head back in her hands. She didn't see Raza leave the room.

CHAPTER THIRTY-FIVE

Leela loved Davi's balcony. It wasn't very big, but Davi had turned it into a cosy nook, with a handmade wooden swing and her collection of potted plants lined along three walls. The wall facing the swing had a bamboo trellis to support the creepers. A picket fence was laid out above the parapet to block the view from the flats directly opposite and provide privacy. Being here was a respite from the disaster that was her life these days.

The swing bobbed gently as Leela adjusted her position, its familiar creaks providing comfort. The creak became a screech as Davi joined Leela on it, handing her a cup of tea.

"Thank you." Leela set the cup down carefully on the little table before them.

"So who do you think sent it?" Davi jumped right in.

Leela shrugged and shook her head. "I haven't the foggiest."

"Who would want to do such a thing? And why?"

"It's probably someone who has a score to settle with me."

"Hmm. You said that the email refers to you as 'Leela Ma'am.' It could be a student or a teacher at the school." Davi paused. "Oh, Leela, it could be Prateek."

She took a long sip of her tea—too sweet as usual, the way Davi liked it—before she replied.

"The thought did cross my mind when Raza showed me the mail on Tuesday. It does appear to be Prateek's modus operandi, doesn't it? What I don't understand is how he or anyone else could know about Nandini and me. We have...had been so bloody careful."

"Hmm." Davi pursed her lips. "You know what I think? That this is just a shot in the dark, a very lucky coincidence for this guy. I think he just went for the lesbian scenario because you busted him for homophobic bullying. Because over these months, I have seen Nandini and you together in many social and professional situations, and if I didn't already know, I wouldn't suspect a thing. You guys haven't put a step out of line, and the mail doesn't mention Nandini at all. In fact, it suggests you are involved with more than one woman."

Leela sighed and rubbed her forehead. "Well, all of this doesn't matter now. It's not like finding out who's behind this and how much they know is going to solve my problem."

"Why not?"

Leela didn't respond.

"What are you going to do?" Davi prodded.

Leela fingered the rim of her teacup, tracing the golden trim along the edge. This, too, she had given some thought to. "Davi...I...I think I'm going to have to resign."

Davi set her cup down on the table with a clatter. "*What?*" The swing wobbled with the vehemence of her words. "You can't be serious!"

Leela flicked tea droplets from her sleeve as she put her own cup down. "This information can't come out. I don't see—"

"Mummyyyy—" Divya, Davi's seven-year-old daughter, wailed from inside. The sound of running footsteps was followed by Divya sticking her head out into the balcony. "Bhaiya won't let me watch *SpongeBob*. He keeps switching the channel to *Doctor Who*."

"Go and get him," Davi instructed, mouthing a "sorry" at Leela.

"Okay, Mummy." Divya turned around. "Bhaiya!" she screamed from her spot. "Mummy wants to speak to you!"

Leela winced.

"Ouch," Davi said. "I said bring him here, not blow our eardrums out."

Davi's son, Sikander, dragged himself outside. "Whaaat?" he drawled.

"Sikander, please let your sister watch what she wants."

"But, Mummy, I missed this episode when it aired."

"It will air again. Or you can record it and watch it later."

"But, Mummy—"

"You know it's Divya's TV time. Either you watch what she's watching or you find something else to do."

Sikander muttered something to Divya as he turned away.

"Mummy, he's saying 'I'll get you!'" Divya protested.

"Sikander, behave." Davi's voice took on a stern edge. "Divya, go watch your programme *quietly*. Leela Aunty and I are discussing something important and don't want to be disturbed. Is that understood?"

"Yeah," the kids chorused, giving each other murderous looks. Davi sighed as they trotted back inside, then narrowed her eyes trying to gather her thoughts.

"Where were we? Yes, resigning. Leela, I think you're wrong. You can't resign. That's letting the a-hole win. I suggest we go to the police. Let's try and find this fu..." She glanced inside the house. "I mean, this deviant idiot."

"I can't believe you're saying this. Do you realise how risky that is? It's like poking a beehive."

"It's blackmail."

"But this *deviant idiot* is definitely going to talk if I go to the police. And I don't have to explain to you what the consequences of that will be."

"Explain them to me."

"Don't be silly."

"No, seriously. Humour me. Talk me through them."

"Okay. For starters, my career in education is going to be over. No one is going to hire me in this field ever again. My family and I will become subjects of malicious gossip. My parents will be devastated if the church finds out. Not to mention the ridicule Neil will be subjected to. People will say all sorts of things about him and me. He might even end up in hostile and dangerous situations. I can't expose him to that, Davi. Which parent would?"

"You're right. Of course you are. You can't expose yourself and your family to all of that. But if your leaving Hanssen could prevent it, I would be the first one asking you to resign. I don't think it will, though. This guy, whoever he is, has a personal grudge against you. He is not going to just give up after he's got his way."

"What do you mean?"

"Think about it. If you resign, it will be a shot in the arm for him. It might even make him ask for more. There is nothing stopping him from going public even after you do resign. If he's feeling particularly vengeful, he might even come after you in your next workplace and the one after that. Isn't that how blackmailers work anyway, by escalating their demands?"

Davi's words opened up a pit in front of Leela. She imagined it gaping wider and wider till it swallowed her. "I guess I'll have to take that risk."

"So you're going to give up? Just like that?"

"It's not like I have any other choice."

Davi shook her head. "This is not the Leela I know."

"Davi, you don't understand." She could hear the desperation in her own voice. "I can't handle this anymore. I feel like my life is on a high-speed downward spiral and there's nothing I can do to stop it. I don't have any fight left in me. I just need this one thing to at least go away."

Leela braced herself for Davi to argue back, but she didn't. Instead, silence stretched. Then, Davi spoke again. "Why did you call it off with Nandini?"

"What?" Leela frowned at the change in subject.

"You love her. Why did you call it off?"

Leela's heart hammered in her chest. "I…" What was wrong with Davi?

"This spiral that you're on," Davi went on when Leela couldn't. "Don't mind me saying this, but one part of it is completely self-inflicted."

Leela stared at her, incredulous. Davi, even if she noticed it, pretended like she hadn't and continued.

"It's not just this email business that's getting you down. You've been looking like your world has come to an end since you called it off with Nandini."

"Rubbish! I…" Leela cast about in desperation. "I was referring to my mother finding out about Nandini and the pall of gloom that has enveloped our house since then."

Davi lifted an eyebrow.

"Okay, fine," Leela conceded. Lying to Davi was pointless— she knew her too well. "Even if we go with your theory for a second that I…" She swallowed. She couldn't say it. "About Nandini. Did I not just explain to you what would happen to my life if I get into a relationship with her?"

"No. You told me what would happen if a blackmailer spreads malicious gossip about you. When you have no control over it. But when a part of your life is only yours to share, then you decide who you share it with and how much. I'm not denying that there is some amount of risk involved even in that, but isn't finding love again worth it?"

"Neil is my priority," Leela said, steeling herself against the anguish that threatened to overpower her.

"I don't think you give that boy enough credit. Have a little more faith in him, and in the values you've raised him with. Tell him what's going on in your life instead of waiting for him to be blindsided by rumours and gossip. Get him on your side and equip him to protect himself. He's seventeen. He's not a child."

"You are talking like we live in some la-la land, Davi."

"It's certainly better than the black hole you've allowed yourself to get sucked into. I saw you rise from the ashes after Kiran passed away. I saw how you took control of your life, bit by bit, and regained your independence. How you charted out your career path. And how you gave Neil the upbringing and love he needed and deserved. Fight for your happiness, Leela.

You've always done it. Don't stop now when there is so much at stake."

"Mummy! Look at Bhaiya!" Divya shouted from inside.

Davi sighed and got up. "Give me a minute while I figure out which one of them deserves to become an only child."

Leela looked up at the white clouds dotting the deep blue sky, which were a reflection of her own scattered thoughts. Was she overthinking it? It couldn't be as straightforward as her friend was making it out to be. Could it?

CHAPTER THIRTY-SIX

"Leela!"

Leela turned. Anil was walking down the corridor towards her.

"Headed to the conference room?" he asked as he fell into step beside her.

"Yes. Ganapathy just texted to say that they've wrapped up the Q and A and the snacks are being laid out."

"Yeah, he messaged me too. Not bad for the first phase, right?"

"No, not at all."

He opened the door to the conference room and voices and laughter drifted out. "After you."

"Thanks." Leela stepped inside and stopped dead. There was Nandini, at the far end of the room. In that same instant that Leela stepped inside, Nandini turned around and her eyes found Leela too. Other voices faded away and everything slowed down. Leela ran towards Nandini in slow-motion Bollywood style, and took her in her arms while the whole room cheered.

"Leela?" The happy vision shattered at Anil's voice. Its remnants turned into a sharp pain that eddied through her heart.

In a blink of an eye, Leela regained her stride. With Anil by her side, she walked towards Nandini, who was talking to Ganapathy, the biology teacher. With each step, Leela's heart thundered. She forced a smile as she reached them.

"Nandini, how nice to see you," Anil said.

After thirty-five days, added Leela.

"Hi, Anil, Leela, nice to see you too." Nandini smiled. The crinkling of the eyes that usually accompanied that smile was missing.

"It's good that you're here," Leela said. She sounded like her usual professional self, as though their months together had meant nothing.

"Couldn't let the first phase of the project wrap up without me."

"Vikrant was supposed to be here, but his son is undergoing surgery as we speak. Nandini had to step in at the last moment," Ganapathy piped in.

"Oh." Leela looked at Nandini. "Nothing serious, I hope."

"The baby's lungs were not functioning properly because he was premature. So they're trying to fix that."

"Poor thing," Anil said, shaking his head.

Leela turned on her phone's screen, staring at it absently as the conversation continued. She swiped the screen a couple of times as if checking something, then slid away from the group. She turned her back to them and scanned the room surreptitiously, hoping for a distraction to slow down her heart.

Coffee and snacks were laid out on two tables in the middle of the room, and the teachers were standing with their backs to them, appearing to not be interested. She studied each one of them. The blackmailer could be in this room right now, keeping an eye on Nandini and her. Who could it be? Could it be Rudhir? He had taken an instant dislike to her when she'd joined. Or was it Yamini, the biggest gossip in the school? Leela had always thought she was harmless, but perhaps she did have a malicious streak to her. But when and how would either of them have seen her and Nandini together to conclude they weren't just friends? They had always been careful, so careful. All the close calls notwithstanding.

Anil came up to her. "Should we begin the proceedings?"

"Yes, let's get on with it," Leela said.

Anil gathered all the teachers around, and Leela made a short speech thanking Nandini, Vikrant, and Discover-E for successfully taking them through this phase of the project, and the teachers for their participation. She ended her speech expressing hope that there would be a second phase in the near future.

The minute the speech ended, everyone flocked to the snacks table. Leela picked up a cup of coffee, and a few of the teachers came over to talk to her. She nodded and smiled in all the right places, but her eyes raked the room inch by inch. Could the blackmailer see through her when she had been talking to Nandini just then or following her with her eyes? Could they see that her senses homed in on Nandini's every movement? That even when she wasn't looking at her, every cell in Leela's body could feel her in the room?

Pain diced through Leela's heart. She found it difficult to breathe.

"Excuse me. I'll just get some more coffee," she said to the teachers surrounding her, and extricated herself from the group. She replaced her empty cup with a full one at the table and took a quick look around. No one was paying any attention to her, so she quietly slipped out into the deserted corridor. She took a deep breath as she came to the end of the corridor that led to the main gate.

The guard at the gate came running and stopped in front of her.

"Madam, do you need something?"

"No, thank you." Leela waved him off. Perhaps her office was a better refuge.

Leela shut the door to her office, put her cup down on the table, and sank into the sofa. She sat still, hands on her lap, and stared out in front of her at her bookshelf.

An image of Nandini talking and smiling next door formed in her mind's eye. This was it. She was never going to see her again. The idea was like a stake driven anew into Leela's chest. Distance and time were supposed to have mended the hole Nandini's departure had left. Then what was this hollow feeling in her chest that was tearing her apart?

To be away from Nandini, back to her ordered life, leaving the disarray behind, however fantastic it had been, is what Leela had wanted. Then why couldn't she stop thinking about her and wishing for all the world that this wasn't where they'd ended up? That somehow they could have had a happy ending?

But where would this happy ending come from? Even her job was such a mess. Was she really going to resign because of this blackmailing business? Perhaps she could take up that supervisory role Raza had hinted at some months ago. Or she could go back to teaching full time. There would be less money in it, of course, but it might be less stressful.

Maybe a change wouldn't be so bad. But was that why she would do it? Because she was ready for a change?

She wasn't; she knew that. This was about self-preservation. Surely it was okay to compromise if it was to save her butt and to keep Neil safe. Neil was, after all, her priority.

The thoughts in Leela's head were like a thousand horses galloping in different directions. Her body felt trampled on. She lay back against the sofa. *Am I ever going to catch a break?*

There was a soft knock on the door, and it opened. Nandini glanced in. Leela's heart pounded.

"I was"—Nandini gestured behind herself—"just going to take off."

"Oh." Leela stood, her legs feeling like wilting stems. "You… you're going back to Delhi tonight?"

"Oh no. I'm around for a few days, meeting someone tomorrow and so on."

Meeting someone. A pang of jealousy ripped through her. *It's probably work*, she told herself. In any case, she had no right over Nandini, not in that way. She'd never had it, had she?

"So this is goodbye, then?" The words felt like they had to be clawed out of Leela's throat. She clasped her hands tight in front of her to stop herself from grabbing Nandini by her shoulders and asking her to not go.

"I suppose it is." Nandini made another gesture with her hands. "I, um, I think I'll be handing over to Vikrant from here on, for follow-ups and so on. And the next stage, if there's one."

"Yeah. Of course." She stared at the floor, feeling as awkward as a teenager before her first kiss. "Nandini...I...I'm sorry about...everything. How things turned out."

"I know. Me too."

Leela didn't dare to look up at Nandini. "But...we're good, right? I mean, I know it's complicated, but..."

From the corner of her vision, it seemed like Nandini's eyes were on the floor as well. "Yes, it is complicated. But it'll be okay. Eventually."

Leela nodded. There was no way to say for sure if anything would be okay, but it was just one of those things one said. "Because...despite how things turned out, I want you to know that meeting you, this past year—us—it was...it...I'm glad we met."

She braved a glance at Nandini. She was nodding too, looking down at her hands. She gave a small laugh. "Yes, I'm glad too. It was...quite something."

Leela smiled, despite bits of her heart chipping away and scattering on the floor. "Quite something" didn't even begin to describe it.

Nandini's eyes met hers and her pain was reflected in them. Leela wanted to tear her gaze away, but their connection was like a never-ending chasm that she couldn't stop falling into.

Finally, Nandini looked away, glancing at her watch. "Well, I'll be off soon." She looked up at Leela and spread her hands, as if in a question. "Do I get a goodbye hug, for old time's sake?"

Leela stepped forward into the circle of Nandini's arms. Her perfume filled Leela's nose, and it was all she could do to not melt into the embrace. She closed her eyes. The familiar, comfortable curves of Nandini's body tugged at her right from the middle of her bones. There was nothing timid or tentative about the hug. It felt like a homecoming after a rough journey, a shore of a turbulent sea, a balm to an aching limb. Leela didn't want to let go.

Before she could resist the urge to turn her face to Nandini's, look into her stormy, dark eyes and tell her to stay, Leela stepped back, silently smashing whatever was left of her heart to smithereens. Nandini's image was a blur.

"Take care of yourself." Leela's voice was thick with suppressed emotion as she wrenched those words out.

Nandini pointed a finger at Leela in a you-too gesture. She seemed to be having trouble speaking as well. She turned to leave, then stopped, her hand on the door handle. "And you... never stop changing the world, okay?" Her voice shook, her eyes bright.

Then she opened the door and was gone.

Leela's legs gave way and she sank into the sofa, alone and abandoned. She longed to curl up in her bed and pretend it was all a bad dream.

Picking up her car keys and her purse, she left her office and slipped out through the back door towards the staff car park.

She left the windows down as she drove, letting the cool July breeze tug at her carefully braided hair. The traffic was murder at this time of day, but Leela navigated the familiar route on autopilot, tuning out to the sights and sounds and smells.

She and Nandini had met in Amrudpur more than ten months ago, and their—what should she even call it, dalliance?—had lasted for about half a year. Now it was over. All those moments, those precious moments they'd spent together flashed in front of Leela. Nandini's face, her smile, her poise, her klutziness, her every gesture. They were like a million shooting stars all coming at Leela at once. She could still feel the hug they shared in every scrap of her soul, and Nandini's last words went round and round in her head: *Never stop changing the world.*

Changing the world—that's what Nandini had said the first day she had come to the school too.

Only, she wasn't. Not anymore. Quite the opposite—she was bending to its dictates. She was running, hiding, letting the world, and not her own heart and head, decide what she should do and who she should be.

Could she honestly preach about standing up for what one believed in, defending what one believed was right, while she was doing exactly the opposite herself?

That is not the legacy I want to leave Neil.

She indicated left and pulled into a narrow side street that had been left alone by the cars and two-wheelers jostling for space on the main road. She pulled up the handbrake, unbuckled her seat belt, and stared straight ahead.

It was so obvious to her now, what she had let herself become. The well of self-pity and hopelessness she had allowed herself to spiral into, pretending there was no point fighting, stood before her as clear as the windshield of her car.

She reached for her purse on the passenger seat, pulling her phone out. She found the number she was looking for and pressed the dial button, tapping her fingers on the steering wheel.

"Ms. Khan, good evening." She was sounding high-pitched and breathless, but she didn't care. "Is this a good time?…Yes, I'm fine, thank you. You?…Ha ha, yes, true…Right, so the thing is, I need some advice. Again…"

She finished the conversation with D.I.G. Khan and immediately called Raza.

"Can I change my mind?" she asked as soon as he picked up the phone.

"I was hoping you would. So, I take it you've come up with a better plan?"

CHAPTER THIRTY-SEVEN

Leela sagged with relief as Davi's distinctive henna-orange hair bobbed into view amid the crowd. She excused herself, ignoring her mother's disapproving glower, and stepped into the throng of people whose idea of a well spent Sunday afternoon was roaming around in a church fete and buying useless things.

"There you are," she said, catching up with Davi. "Thank you for coming. I owe you."

"I'll add it to the list." She scanned the crowd, frowning. "The kids have disappeared somewhere with Neil. Any idea where they might have gone?"

"He's probably taken them to the food hall inside." Leela gestured over her shoulder, behind her. "You see that stall, the one with the lurid cupcakes?"

"Emily Pinto's Designer Cakes? Oh, your mum's sitting there. I think she's glaring at you." Davi raised her hand and waved, a wide grin on her face.

Leela suppressed a laugh. She knew Elsie would be compelled to smile and wave back. She could almost imagine that smile—tight and snarly, like someone had a sharp knife pointed at her back.

"Is this her way of keeping you away from lesbianic activities?" Davi enquired, studying the colourful stalls lined up in neat rows around them. "By volunteering you for the services of the Bangalore Konkani Catholic Association?"

"One of her ways of keeping me on a tight leash, yes. Emily Pinto of the ghastly cupcakes and Elsie Saldana are also conspiring to get her son, a recently divorced father of one, and me together. He's not so bad, Albert, and just as exasperated with his mother as I am with mine. He has, thankfully, been AWOL for a while."

"Probably took a look at you and ran a mile," Davi said, studying Leela. "You look like shit. Have you slept at all?"

"Oh, thanks." Leela rolled her eyes and patted her hair. "But I can tell you this, for some strange reason, being out here in the midst of strangers and my mother's questionable acquaintances does make me feel better."

"Come, let's find some peace and quiet." Davi took Leela's elbow and steered her through the corridor between two rows of stalls.

They passed homemade cakes and cookies—staying well away from Emily Pinto's, of course—crocheted jewellery and knickknacks, a live sketch artist, a variety of women's and baby wear, home furnishings, handmade toys, and a bizarre collection of photos of auto-rickshaws. They crossed the lawn and made their way into the hall, where caterers displayed a variety of food and drink.

"There are the kids." Leela nodded at Divya and Sikander, seated at a table with Neil, each of them demolishing a large slice of chocolate cake.

"Oh great, there goes their lunch." Davi shook her head as they lined up for coffee. "Have you heard from your cop friend, by the way?"

"No, not yet. She said it'll take some time."

"But they will find out who it is?"

"She says they may be able to find out where the email came from. I still have my money on that thug Prateek Gupta. Bloody cybercriminal in the making."

"I thought you'd scared him off cybercrime."

"I thought so, too, but you know teenagers. Think they're cleverer than the rest of us, and invincible. Here, wait, let me get that. I have coupons, perks of my mother being on the committee. Want something to eat?"

"No, I'm good." They took their tiny paper cups of coffee and went out into the lawns. "Anyway, I hope this means this is the end of your ridiculous drama about resigning."

"It is. You were right. What *was* I thinking?"

"Aa-and…" Davi stretched out the word and glanced at her. "How are you doing about…otherwise?"

She shrugged. "I guess I'll be okay. Eventually," she said, using the same words Nandini had.

Davi nodded. She put her arm around Leela's shoulder and squeezed. "You will."

"You were right, I suppose," Leela said. "I'm glad you have the decency not to say 'I told you so.'"

Davi's eyebrows rose in surprise. "What are you talking about?"

Leela grimaced. "About Nandini and me. The past making it complicated and all that."

"Oh, Leela." Davi shook her head. "This isn't about the past at all. This got complicated because of your present circumstances. Your history had nothing to do with it."

Leela drank down her tepid coffee and crumpled the cup.

"Does it have to be this way, Leela?" Davi asked softly. "Look at what you're doing to yourself."

"We've talked about this."

"I know, but I can't help thinking about it. It's what we keep telling our kids, isn't it—that you must be true to yourself, even when it seems like it's the hardest thing to do?"

"Are you calling me a hypocrite?"

"No. You know I'm not. I don't think it's that black and white, what you're going through, and I know I'm not in your shoes." She turned to her again, her frank, open gaze taking Leela in. "You're one of the strongest people I've known in my life, Leela. I know you'd fight if you could. If that's what you really wanted."

* * *

On the dot of 3:00 p.m., Leela's afternoon cup of coffee arrived.

"Thank you, Bopanna," she said, putting her glasses down on the pile of notebooks she had been checking. "You are a lifesaver."

A man of few words, Bopanna beamed as he set down the coffee and two Marie digestives.

Leela rubbed her eyes and stretched. Even her brain hurt. But she had no cause to complain—this exhaustion was self-inflicted. Her war-hardened shell of self-preservation that prevented her from going to pieces and kept her moored had deserted her. How else was she supposed to stay upright if not by moving at breakneck speed?

There was a time she used to meditate, the progressive relaxation from toe to head unknotting her body and calming her mind. Not this time, though. Her mind was such a tangle of emotions that even the thought of sitting still suffocated her.

Her psychologist years ago had told her, "You can't run from your feelings, Leela. You have to feel them." But her feelings were like a storm, and shutting all her doors and windows was the only way of not letting them pulverise her.

Deep down, Leela knew she was only postponing the inevitable. Much as she quailed at the thought of braving her personal storm and pushing through to the other side, her old shrink had been right—she had to "feel the feelings."

Not today. Maybe when I'm strong enough.

Yet she wasn't going to be strong enough until she acknowledged her turmoil.

She could go round and round like this forever.

It would be so easy to stop fighting. To let her emotions inundate her, let them take her wherever they wanted. But she couldn't. She had to hold it together—for Neil, if not for herself. She couldn't let herself fall apart like she had when Kiran died.

Leela's hand reaching for her coffee stopped midway. This gaping rift in her being, this all-consuming emptiness, this feeling like a part of herself had gone—this is what she had felt when Kiran had been taken away from her.

Her hand fell back on her lap. Memories of Nandini flooded her. Holding her hand at Sankey Tank after a difficult day; curling up on the sofa, watching *Fire*; Nandini studying her with heavy, hooded eyes as she draped her sari; Neil buying her and Nandini ice cream…

The images were savage, wrenching her insides apart. Nandini had been right—they *had* been in a relationship. Somehow, in the complex matrix between Neil, her parents, and her work, Nandini had fit right in.

Why had she not seen it before? Even Davi had seen it.

There was one difference, though, between losing Kiran and losing Nandini.

Blood roared in her head. Leela was on her feet. A film had formed over her coffee. She picked up her bag, snatched her mobile phone from her desk, and rushed out of her office.

"Ma'am," Gulshan called after her. "There's—"

"Tomorrow!"

Out of the building, Leela ran towards her car. Within minutes, she pulled up in the tiny car park in front of Nandini's guest house. Without considering what she was doing, she beeped the lock on her car and hurried inside.

In the lobby, the owner welcomed her with a smile. "Are you here to see Nandini? I don't think she's back yet."

She's still in town. She hasn't left yet. She'll be back.

Then, her rational side caught up and slammed into her body. She bit her lip. Of course, the more mature thing to have done would've been to call Nandini and fix to meet up.

But if she left now, she'd lose her nerve. She squared her shoulders. "Is it all right if I waited for her?"

"Sure. But, um, I don't know when she'll be back."

"That's all right." Leela planted herself on the florid sofa. "I'll wait."

"Would you like some coffee?"

"Coffee would be great, thank you." She reached for a magazine. Her hand shook ever so slightly.

Leela flipped through the pages of the magazine, the words and pictures swimming before her eyes. Every time a car slowed down outside or someone came into the room, Leela's insides seized up. Every time, she braced herself to come face-to-face with Nandini.

But Nandini didn't arrive. The minutes passed, turning into an hour and then more, and there was no sign of her. The coffee that Leela didn't remember drinking sat uneasily in her stomach.

Leela stared at the clock on the wall. It was 4:45 p.m., exactly an hour and twenty minutes after she had arrived. Her shoulders drooped, her heart sank. Perhaps there was nothing left to fight for. She picked up her bag and stood.

The front door opened when Leela was only halfway to it. Nandini stepped into the lobby. Her eyes locked with Leela's. She stopped, her eyebrows shooting up.

Leela's legs froze. Her mind went blank. In the span of a few seconds, the script had changed. Again.

When Leela was able to feel her body, the first thing she noticed was her heart thudding, fast and furiously. She wanted to drink Nandini in with her eyes and never stop. She wanted everything to be magically all right, with no need for words and explanations. She wanted—needed—to feel Nandini in her arms again.

"Oh, Nandini, there you are." The guest house owner bounced down the stairs.

The spell that had held Leela and Nandini together snapped.

"Your guest has been waiting and waiting," he continued.

Leela wrenched her eyes away from Nandini to the floor. "I, er, need to talk to you," she said, struggling to keep her voice steady and businesslike.

"Uh…" Nandini began. Then she nodded. "Of course. Come inside?"

"Will you be having dinner, Nandini?" the owner went on, blind to the tension in the room. "And your guest?"

"What?" Nandini blinked at him. "Dinner. Yes, sure."

CHAPTER THIRTY-EIGHT

The walk down the passage to Nandini's room seemed longer than a lifetime. Every excruciating detail dragged out in super-slow motion: Nandini feeling inside her bag for her keys; her hand shaking as she fumbled with the lock; her stepping inside and running her hands along the left wall, letting light flood into the room. Leela followed her in, shutting the door behind her and stepping back against it as Nandini turned around to face her.

The air between them was heavy and charged, their eyes holding each other in a vice-like grip. Leela pressed back against the door, willing the firmness of the wood to give her courage. There was no turning back now.

She swallowed. "Ask me again." It came out in a hoarse whisper.

"Sorry?"

"Ask me again if I love you."

Nandini remained still as a hot summer afternoon. As if Leela hadn't spoken. As if Nandini hadn't understood her.

Not even a flicker of emotion crossed Nandini's face. Leela wished she could rip the mask off and find out what was going on underneath. She didn't dare move. A dog barked in the distance, cars and buses honked and rumbled past on the main road, someone laughed, muffled footsteps crossed the corridor. And then there was silence. It seemed like the world had stopped, except for the steady whirring of the fan above them.

Nandini's bag dropped from her shoulder. It hit the floor with a clang as the buckle made contact with the mosaic tile. The silence shattered.

Nandini took a step towards her. That was all Leela needed. They melted into each other, their mouths meeting in a frenetic crush. They gripped each other with the desperation of drowning women thrown a wisp of straw.

Leela wanted to devour Nandini, fill that chasm of deprivation she had carved within herself over the past weeks. The taste and familiarity of Nandini subsumed her as Leela tightened her arms around her. No matter how close she held her, she just couldn't have enough. The physicalness of their proximity, the sheer fact of Nandini's presence, rushed in to heal the cracks in Leela's being. More than that, it brought an intangible, immeasurable sense of wholeness that had been gone from her life.

Her body felt like jelly as she clung to Nandini. Her distinctive perfume besieged Leela's senses, and the desperate desire to touch, taste, and smell her stirred up a fire deep inside her belly and between her legs. Leela bunched the satiny material of Nandini's shirt in her hands, pulling it out of the way to make contact with the warm, soft flesh underneath. The curves and contours of Nandini's back were immediately known to her, as was the pliable fullness of the breasts that pushed against her.

There was a tug on her hair and her bun came loose, hair cascading over her shoulders. The wooden pin fell to the floor with a sharp click. Something released from her shoulder—her bag, pushed to the floor by Nandini's exploring hand.

Without breaking their kiss, Nandini began popping the buttons on Leela's kurta. Her fingers were like flames on Leela's skin as they grazed along her chest, dipping inside her bra and cupping her breast, kneading and pushing, catching her hard nipple between two fingers. Leela gasped as a horde of sensations swarmed her body.

They tore off each other's tops, kicked off their shoes, and came together again in the middle of the floor. Leela guided them towards the sofa till the backs of Nandini's legs hit the cushion and she fell back against it. Leela pulled her up again as their mouths met for yet another yearning kiss while her fingers fumbled to undo Nandini's trousers and push them down over her hips. Nandini kicked them off and dropped back on the sofa, pulling Leela down with her.

Leela straddled Nandini, gripping her shoulders for balance. Nandini's hands ran down her body, along her back, her waist, her hips, stopping at her buttocks and pulling her forward, closer. Nandini felt along the waistband of her salwar and loosened Leela's drawstring.

A strangled grunt escaped Leela as Nandini's hand slipped inside the layers, fingers plunging moistly into her. Currents of pleasure wracked Leela as they started to work inside her.

Leela thrust her impatient hand down between Nandini's legs, brushing over the damp underwear, making Nandini sigh with pleasure. She pushed the fabric down, slowly edging her fingers in, past the mat of hair, letting Nandini's slippery wetness coat her fingers.

Nandini moaned as Leela's finger found her clit. She threw her head back against the backrest of the sofa, eyes closed. Her breathing picked up tempo as Leela rubbed small circles with the tips of her first two fingers. She braced a hand against the backrest of the sofa to keep her balance.

Nandini tensed under her, the muscles on her face pulling tight. She wore a slight frown, giving her a look of intense concentration, and her lips were parted. A soft gasp escaped Nandini as Leela felt her strain against her hand and then, a moment later, her shuddering release.

The finger that was inside Leela, which had stilled as Nandini's orgasm overwhelmed her, started to move again. The base of her palm rubbed against Leela's clit. A new thrill lanced through her as Nandini's dark eyes fixed on her. Nandini's hand moved faster and faster. Leela gripped the backrest of the sofa as waves of pleasure circled her, drawing closer and closer with each passing second.

She climaxed suddenly, explosively, biting down on her lip to keep from crying out as her orgasm pulsed from her centre. Her eyes remained locked to Nandini's till the last quivers had passed.

Panting and sweaty after their frenzied activity, Leela didn't have the will to move away. Nandini didn't show any inclination to shift either. Many moments later, the faint glimmer of a smile touched Nandini's mouth. Her hand caressed Leela's bare back, pulling her closer, till she buried her head between Leela's breasts.

Leela raked her fingers through Nandini's hair in gentle strokes, kissing her head. She lay her cheek on top of it and held her. Then Nandini leaned back, her eyes raised to Leela's face. Leela brushed a lock of hair behind Nandini's ear and bent down till their foreheads touched. "I love you," she whispered. "I'm broken without you."

"Stay with me."

"Always," Leela replied.

Nandini's eyelids drooped as her face turned up to kiss Leela, this time a soft, gentle touch.

CHAPTER THIRTY-NINE

Leela couldn't believe her ears. She had arrived at D.I.G. Khan's office expecting to hear that the email had been traced back to Prateek—or, best case scenario, to the Gupta household. Though, if Prateek had any brains, he would have gone to a cyber cafe—did cyber cafes still exist?—especially after being rumbled for the attack on Rahul.

"And, you're sure about this?" Leela asked, following it up with instant regret at the words that had crossed her mouth. Of course Farida Khan was sure, that's why she'd called Leela in.

The officer didn't seem put out by the question, however. "I would say the evidence is pretty clear. The IP address was easily traced back to that house, and there's someone living there who has—had—a direct connection to you, and is highly likely to have a grudge against you."

"No, sorry, I know what you're saying. It's just so… unbelievable. What a horrible, petty thing to do. She could have destroyed my career."

"I think she saw it as you having destroyed hers, so she was going to do the same to you. The only difference is, what she did was illegal. Now, if you wanted to prosecute…"

"My God, some part of me is so angry that I want to throw the book at her!"

"You'll have to officially file a report, in that case."

Leela nodded. "I'll think about it. Thank you, so very much, Ms. Khan. I've lost count of how many times you've helped me out this year."

A grin split her usually serious countenance, changing her into a female version of Santa Claus in a neat, pressed khaki uniform. "I haven't yet told you of the one other thing that I have done. I sent one of my officers—a promising youngster with an inborn ability to make people shake in their boots by just saying good morning—to have a chat with this Asha Rao. Plain clothes. All very informal, you see, since this wasn't an official investigation."

Leela leaned forward, grinning. That sounded promising. "Go on."

D.I.G. Khan paused, picking up the tiny porcelain cup of coffee on her desk with delicate fingers, taking a sip, and putting it down. "Well, she was apprised of the fact that should the school press charges, then even if she wiped her computer clean, we could still retrieve information from it, or from server logs. So she might want to think about coming clean and sending the school, and you, an unreserved apology for her misguided actions."

Leela was rendered speechless for the second time in a very short duration. "Wow. Well, I can't say the thought of scaring the pants off Asha Rao doesn't please me. I doubt she's going to own up, though."

"So do I. I think she's going to lie low, hoping it'll go away."

"Thank you—again."

"No need to thank me. Just doing my job."

"Actually, you did more than that. You did me a favour. In fact, I feel a thank-you is quite inadequate."

"Leela Ma'am, listen to me." She was at least fifteen years older than Leela but persisted in addressing her formally. "I want nothing in this life more than my granddaughters to grow up safe. And thugs on the streets don't half scare me as much as the Internet does. I like the way you handle things in your school, so you can always count on me."

* * *

Leela pulled up outside the multiplex cinema and turned off the engine.

"Okay, bye, thanks." Neil reached out to unbuckle his seat belt.

"Where's Radha?"

"She's not here yet. Says she'll be another ten minutes."

"So, then, what's the hurry?"

"You're not going to hang around?" Neil's question dripped horror.

"I think Radha might want to come over and say hello. Only polite, don't you think?"

"Yes, but…" He blinked. "I…I told you I could have come by myself."

"Well, don't get used to being chauffeured around. I'm only dropping you because it's on my way."

"Yeah, yeah, I know." He stared out of the window and then checked his phone. "She's almost here."

Leela gave him a once-over. His jeans were pressed and he had his new *Orange Triangle* T-shirt on. The peach fuzz on his cheeks had been scraped off and the scent of his aftershave was beginning to make her eyes water.

"So," she said. "It's going well with Radha, then?"

He shrugged and pulled at his sleeves. "Okay, I guess."

"You guess?"

The colour rose in his cheeks. "Why are you giving me the third degree? It's just a…fun thing. It's not like we're getting married or anything."

"I should hope not!"

He made a *tch* sound with his tongue, shaking his head. "You know what I mean."

"So, is this a date, then?"

He shrugged. "Maybe."

It was like squeezing blood from a stone, but a part of Leela was enjoying it. "Have you two figured out who pays for what?"

"Hmm? Oh, we decided we should share everything, unless it's a birthday."

"That's very sensible of you." She paused. "Neil?"

He turned to her. "Yeah?"

"You look nice." His eyes widened and his face became even redder. "I mean, it's considerate, to take the effort to look good for someone else. Shows you care. I wouldn't want you going on a maybe-date looking like a slob."

He stared at her, and then his face broke into a grin. "You look very nice yourself. Got a date too?"

Leela gave him a nudge. "Wouldn't you like to know!"

He continued to study her. "You know, you've been less grumpy lately. Is it because Nandini Aunty is back in town after ages?"

"W-what?"

"Oh come on, you've been *so* grumpy this past month!"

"Er…have I?"

"Super grumpy."

"Stop saying grumpy." She squeezed his leg. "I'm sorry if I've been grouchy. I've had a few things on my mind, but everything is okay now."

"Okay."

A shadow passed across them. Radha leaned in at the passenger window. "Hello, ma'am. Hi, Neil."

"Oh, hello, Radha." Leela waved at her as Neil extricated himself from the car. "Have a good time. You'll take an auto back, Neil?"

Neil nodded. "Bye, Ma. You have a good time too. Say hello to Nandini Aunty from me."

Leela indicated to pull back into the traffic. Wait a minute. How did he know she was going to see Nandini?

"I need to tell Neil," she said to Nandini twenty minutes later. "I don't want to keep this from him."

Nandini nodded. "All right. How do you think he'll take it?"

Leela pursed her lips. "My gut says he will be all right. I hope I'm right."

"He's a sensible fellow."

They were stretched out on deck chairs in the covered patio of the guest house. The other chairs and tables lay unoccupied. A light drizzle surrounded them. Leela swirled her lemonade, making the ice clink, and stared out at the view of lush coconut trees framing the well-trimmed lawn. The high walls beyond hid the view of the main road, and if Leela ignored the sounds of traffic she could even believe that she and Nandini were the only two people in the world. That mental picture brought with it a deep sense of contentment, and Leela sighed.

The sound of a crash was like a pin poking her pretty bubble and dumping her back to reality. She whipped her head around. Nandini was regarding her upended glass of lemonade and holding up a book with a dripping corner.

"What happened?"

"I, um, knocked my glass over." She picked it up and set it upright. It seemed unharmed and there didn't seem to have been much lemonade in it.

"It's funny—for such a butterfingers, you rarely cause any damage. Which is probably good for this place," she said gesturing at the guest house building behind her.

Nandini wrinkled her nose. "That's not funny."

She dabbed the edge of her book with a tissue. Leela smiled. It was strange, but she'd missed clumsy Nandini too.

"Stop laughing at me," Nandini grumbled.

Leela's smile widened. "That reminds me, you need to close your account here. From now on, when you're in town, you stay with me. I've already cleared a space in the cupboard for you."

"You have, have you?"

"Mm-hmm."

"Aren't you worried I'll wreck your house?"

"The things you do for love."

Nandini's eyes twinkled. "Good. I hate the food here."

Leela reached across and took Nandini's hand, weaving their fingers together. "I hope I'll get to see you more often, though. I hate missing you."

"I'm going to be here a lot, Leela," Nandini said. "A lot, lot. Also, Discover-E is being implemented in a school in Chennai. I finalised the deal a few days ago. And we have some new clients in Bangalore."

"You don't have to be the one travelling down to see me all the time. I can come to Delhi too sometimes. In any case, Raza has been trying to offer me the position of development director for some time. I have been thinking about it. It will involve spending a bit of time in Delhi."

"Is that something you want, this new profile?"

"I think so. Implementing groundbreaking, innovative programmes in schools, viewing education from a different perspective, holistic learning—that's what I enjoy doing. The only thing holding me back is Neil, and hopefully he'll be off to one of the design schools he's interested in. That's less than a year away. After that, I'm more of a free bird."

Nandini rubbed her chin. "Hmm. Does this mean I'll have to find you cupboard space too? It might be a bit of a problem in my itty-bitty house."

Leela took her hand away and swatted Nandini's arm. "Ha! Funny." She gazed at Nandini and her heart expanded till it felt too big for her body. *It's happiness, that's what it is.* "Nandini?"

"Hmm?"

"My parents…"

"Your parents what?" Nandini raised an eyebrow.

"Ma found the bracelet you gave me."

"So?"

"She also found the note you wrote with it."

Both of Nandini's eyebrows shot up. "Um, Leela, I'm calling this whole thing off. I'll just go get my stuff and catch the first flight out of here. Goodbye."

She even made to get up. Leela grabbed her arm and pulled her down.

"Nandini, stop fooling around, man. This is serious."

"Okay, okay." She sat on the edge of her chair. "Tell me."

"I promised her I wouldn't see you anymore. I need to tell her I'm not keeping that promise."

"And your dad?" Nandini's voice only held concern.

Leela ran her fingers through her thick, dark hair. "If I don't tell him, my mother will have this power over me—over us. She'll use it to manipulate me and I'll always be on tenterhooks waiting for the other shoe to drop. I'd rather tell him myself than live under my mother's thumb."

"You know this can have only one outcome, right?"

Leela looked up at the grey clouds hovering above them. Joseph Saldana was going to be blindsided when he came to know of the shenanigans going on in his wake. The repercussions were going to shake up her life, possibly irrevocably. Though the idea of her parents attempting to wrap their respectable Catholic existence around the fact that their daughter was a— pause here and say in a horrified whisper—*lesbian* was a little bit hilarious too.

On a more serious note, the denial, anger, rejection, and whatever else lay ahead was not going to be easy or pretty, and yet some part of Leela could almost sympathise with her parents. If her mother's reaction was anything to go by, they thought homosexuality was something disreputable and, therefore, happened to other people. Because they—the Saldanas—were completely reputable people. Moreover, for them, marriage was the basic tenet of social order. In their eyes, not only had Leela rejected that supreme edifice of society by having refused to consider a brand-new husband after Kiran's inconvenient death, she had more or less desecrated it by getting involved with a woman. And if that wasn't enough, she was reveling in it.

Leela sighed. "I know, yes, but this is my life and I'll be damned if I'm going to let someone else control it."

This time, Nandini reached for Leela's hand. "Would you like me to be there with you when you tell them and Neil?"

Leela squeezed back. After years, for the first time that familiar feeling of someone having her back no matter what washed over her. The knowledge that she could close her eyes and go into free fall and Nandini would be there to catch her meant the world to her. Just knowing that was enough.

"Thanks, but I think this is one fight I will have to fight on my own."

CHAPTER FORTY

Leela's palms were sweating as they approached Sankey Tank and joined the early evening walkers in their promenade around the lake. She crossed her arms, hands tucked into the opposite armpits.

How was she going to do this? So much could go wrong. Her head buzzed with all the possibilities, all the various permutations and combinations of Neil's reaction. She started to speak, but all the words slipped through her mind like water from a sieve as soon as she opened her mouth.

Neil walked his usual hunching walk beside her, hands in his pockets, face etched with worry. When he saw her looking, he burst out, "You're not going to die, are you?"

"What?" He looked so distraught that it almost broke Leela's heart. She rubbed his arm. "No, Neil, I'm not. Why would you think that?"

"You said you needed to talk to me. The last time you said that and took me for a walk, it was about Daddy."

Of course. It had been early morning, and they had gone to the park behind their apartment building. She was surprised he still remembered it. Still, it wasn't the sort of thing you forgot, was it? Even if you were only six years old.

"I am so sorry, Neil. I didn't mean to scare you."

He nodded, seeming somewhat relaxed now. Despite having scared the life out of the poor boy, she had found the perfect opening.

"I know you miss Daddy. I do too. But I think if he could see us right now, he'd be happy and proud of how well we're doing."

"Do you think it's childish that sometimes I feel he's looking at us from up there?" Neil glanced up at the sky.

"Not at all. Sometimes I do too." She pointed to an empty bench and they went over to claim it. "You know, after Daddy died, Grandma and Grandpa were after me to marry again? They even found prospective husbands for me."

"Ye-ah." He stretched the word out, then grinned, his expression dripping with mischief. "Like Harry Uncle, who used to come over all the time and bring me those horrible chocolates?"

"Yes, exactly. But you were quite young. How did you know?"

"Grandma told me once that he was going to be my new father. I cried for days, in secret."

"Oh." Leela squeezed his arm. "I'm sorry. But I think your grandmother was always more keen on him than I ever was. She especially thought he'd be good for you."

"Me?"

"As a father figure."

Neil shuddered. "I don't need a father figure. I'm doing fine. Though I preferred Alok Uncle."

Me too. But it was probably best not to confess that to your kid. "Grandma and Grandpa thought I was depriving you of a normal childhood."

"I still don't get what it's got to do with me. I'm fine."

"Yes, you're fine, you're great." She squeezed his arm again. "The thing is, Ma and Dad also thought I should marry again as I'd get lonely. So there would be someone to look after me when I'm old and decrepit. And also because I might want adult companionship."

"Are you? Lonely?" The deep furrows between his brows indicated that the idea worried him.

"Honestly, no. I've been just fine. You and I, we've taken good care of each other. As for companionship, having a partner, yes, all those things are important, but I don't believe in doing them for the sake of it."

"So you never got married to the guys paraded by the grandparents because you were happy as we are?"

Leela nodded. "And also because I didn't meet anyone I wanted to be with." She searched his face. "You know that even if I did have another partner, it wouldn't mean that I loved your father any less or that our time together wasn't important. Or that I'm going to forget about him. Nobody will ever replace your father. Nobody in either your life or mine."

"I know *that*," Neil said, rolling his eyes at the sky. "I'm not a baby."

"No, you're not. In fact, you're almost grown up. Soon, you'll be off to college and starting your own life."

"Will you be lonely when I'm gone?" He was looking worried again.

"It's not your job to worry about me. Of course I'll miss you, but I'll be happy if you're happy."

"Corny." He made a face and Leela nudged him with an elbow.

"But the thing is, I've always promised myself that I wouldn't let Grandma and Grandpa bully me, and I'd only think about a relationship if I met someone I wanted to share my life with. And someone hopefully you like too."

He smiled, but his heart was not in it. "Okay. So why are you telling me all this now?" His antennae were up. Leela couldn't dither much longer.

"Because I have met someone, someone I hope will become a bigger part of both our lives."

"Who is it?"

Leela took a deep breath. "It's Nandini Aunty."

Neil was still as stone, even his expression frozen.

"Neil...I hope you will—"

"Nandini Aunty." He almost breathed the words out. He sat back against the backrest of the bench, hands deep inside his pocket. "She's your…friend?"

It was a half question.

"Yes, she is, but she's also my partner."

"Is she going to live with us?"

"No. At least not yet. But she'll definitely be around more."

He continued to stare into space, devoid of expression. Leela felt a bead of sweat run down between her shoulder blades. "Neil, I know this might be a bit too much to take in, but if you have any questions—"

"You've never been so happy before."

"What?"

"Nandini Aunty makes you happy. I can tell."

"You…can? I mean, yes. Yes, she does."

"Do Grandma and Grandpa know?"

"Not yet." She paused. "Neil, this information— I'm only sharing it with people who matter to me and people I trust. There is no one more important to me than you, and I want you to know the truth. But this is in confidence. You understand?"

"Yeah."

Leela wanted to shake more words out of him. "Neil?"

"Hmm?"

"Are you okay?"

"Yeah." Though he seemed anything but. He glanced at Leela finally. "It just…it feels strange to know…You promise you won't forget Daddy right?"

A lump appeared in Leela's throat. She wanted to hug Neil till it hurt. "Oh, Neil, I can never forget Daddy."

He nodded. "Okay."

"And…you're all right? About Nandini Aunty?"

He shrugged. "Do I have to call her something different?"

"No, of course not."

He nodded again. A loud quacking rent the air. Two crabby ducks were having a spat on the water. Leela and Neil watched them for a few minutes.

"Anything else you want to talk about?" Leela asked.

Neil played with his hands. "No...I..."

"Neil?"

"I...it's been just the two of us for such a long time."

Leela placed her hand over his restless ones. "It will always be the two of us. Nobody and nothing will ever change that." She squeezed his hands. "Look at me. Neil?"

He looked.

"Do you think there could be anyone more important to me than you?"

He stared back at her. Then he shook his head.

"Nandini Aunty thinks you're quite the best teenage brat to walk this planet, you know."

A brief smile flitted across his face. "She's cool."

"That she is."

"So...are you...does this mean...you're a...you know...?"

Leela frowned. "Are you trying to ask if I'm a lesbian? It's not a bad word. You can say it."

The tips of his ears turned a rich red-brown. "Okay. Are you?"

"Is it necessary to put a name to it? I loved your father; I will always love him. I don't want to call myself something that might make it seem like that wasn't true." She searched his face. "Does that answer your question?"

He shrugged. "Can you marry Nandini Aunty? Can two women get married?"

"Not in this country, no."

His eyes went round. "Oh, but, Ma, what about Section 377? Could you be sent to jail?"

"No, don't worry about that. The interpretation, fortunately, leaves out relationships between women. So we are not going to be arrested. But..." She paused for emphasis. "You do understand that despite that, this information about Nandini Aunty and me has to be treated with caution?"

"Yes, of course."

"Neil?"

"Hmm?"

"Are you really okay? About all this?"

"You say not to tell anyone, but people will see you together. What will they think?"

"They'll just think whatever it is they have thought whenever they've seen us together—that we're good friends. And that's true too. Some people know, like Davi Aunty. Others can think whatever they want."

"I don't want anything bad to happen to you."

"I know." She put her arm around his shoulders. "I promise you, the worst thing that's going to happen is that your Grandpa and Grandma are going to be furious."

"They'll say you'll go to hell. Do you believe in hell?"

"I don't believe God is a bigot."

"Yeah." He laced his fingers together again and stared at them. "Ma?"

"Yes?"

"I want you to be happy too."

The lump returned to Leela's throat, this time a giant one. She took Neil's hand and squeezed, too overcome to speak.

"Oh my God, don't cry! Not here! Ma!"

Leela laughed as she wiped her eyes. "It's all right. I'm just happy because you are the most fantastic kid anyone could ask for. Want to drive to Corner House for ice cream?"

"You have to ask?"

Leela stood and hauled him up. "I will buy you the biggest Death by Chocolate possible."

"Sure. Oh, can I ask another question?"

"Of course."

"What about Jacob Uncle—wasn't he also one of the guys Grandma hooked you up with? And that one who had the crazy wig…"

Leela linked arms with him. "Enough of that! I'll tell you more when you're thirty."

* * *

"Is this about Neil?" Joseph asked.

Leela shook her head. "Just please sit down, Dad. Ma, you too."

Elsie and Joseph's faces were like question marks. Though without further ado, the two of them sat down on the recently acquired yellow sofa that made Leela's eyes smart. She took the chair opposite them, her fingers tapping her thighs all the while.

"What is it, Leelu?" Elsie asked.

Bits of her phone call with Nandini in the morning played in Leela's head: "Just rip it off like a Band-Aid."

Leela took a deep breath and cleared her throat. *Right. Let's rip it off.* "You know how after Kiran passed away the two of you have been keen that I share my life with someone again? How important companionship is and how one needs it more as one gets older?"

"Yes, yes?" Elsie leaned forward on the sofa, her eyes now sparkling.

"I…I have met someone."

"Hmm, finally," Joseph said, cocking his head in his usual supercilious way with a partial smile playing on his lips. "Can't say I'm not pleased. Who is it? Is he Catholic?"

"It's Albert Pinto, isn't it? Oh, I'm so happy, Leelu!" Elsie's smile was as broad as the ring around Saturn.

"Um, no." Leela rubbed her hands on her thighs. There was no turning back now. "It's…er…" She straightened. "It's Nandini."

Elsie gasped. Leela braced herself, but no onslaught was forthcoming. There was absolute stillness. She moved her eyes from one parent to the other.

"Is this some kind of a sick joke?" Joseph's face contorted in disbelief.

There it was. Leela shook her head, her hands now fists on her lap. "No."

"This is ridiculous!" Joseph got up from the sofa with a jerk.

Elsie covered her nose and mouth with her hand and burst into tears. "Oh, Leelu, why are you doing this to us?"

Leela looked at her mother's bent head and drooping shoulders. In one fell swoop, Leela had not only smashed all her hopes and dreams, but had also brought back her worst nightmare from barely a month ago. She cut such a pitiable figure just then that she managed to evoke a modicum of sympathy even in Leela.

Leela shook off the vestiges of her nervousness and spoke as kindly as she could. "I'm not doing this to you, Ma. I'm just trying to do what's right for me."

"You stop this. Stop talking like a crazy woman!" Joseph's eyes were spitting fire.

Leela's gaze followed her father as he paced behind the sofa. "It's the truth, Dad. Nandini and I—"

"No! I don't want to hear another word. You will go home right away and you will put a stop to whatever it is that you're doing with that woman. And we will never talk about this again."

"All right. We don't have to talk about this again. But Nandini is now an important part of my life. That's not going to change."

"That is the most vile, sickening thing I've ever heard, and I can't believe it's my daughter who's saying it." He grabbed the back of the sofa and leaned towards Leela. "Leela, Nandini's a woman and so are you."

Leela bit her lip. It would not be wise to laugh. "Yes, Dad, I realise that."

"This can't happen. It's not possible..." His words were almost pleading now.

"Oh, Leelu," Elsie cried out in the middle of her sobs. "What will our relatives think? Our friends? What about the church?"

"This is my personal life, Ma. They don't need to know anything about it. Nandini is my friend and she will always be that to them. If we don't make a big deal of it, no one else can either."

Joseph screwed up his face in apparent loathing. "Ha! You think it's that easy to fool people? They will figure out in an instant how shameless and disgusting you are. And I will not allow that. I will not let you play with my reputation or my family's name."

A dull headache began making its way up from Leela's neck. Time to shut this down. "Dad, this is not up for discussion. I wanted you to know because you're my parents and I didn't want to hide it from you. That's it."

"You're the worst kind of sinner and will rot in hell for this. God will never forgive you." Joseph's jaw quivered.

"Clearly, I pray to a different God then. Because my God will never spurn love or my happiness."

"You have lost your mind. If you do not stop this insanity right away you are no longer welcome in this house. And I will not let my grandson live under a roof that encourages deviant lifestyles either. Neil will now stay here." A coldness settled in Joseph's voice.

Leela clasped her hands together to stop them from shaking. "I'm not going anywhere, Dad. It is my responsibility to look after the two of you. I will be right here, two floors above as always. As for Neil, where he lives is not up to you."

"Have you told him?" Elsie got up from the sofa, her face all scrunched up and tears still streaming down.

"He knows what he needs to know."

"Get out of my house!" Joseph pointed his finger towards the door. "We don't have a daughter anymore. You are dead to us."

"All right, I'll go. For now." Leela swallowed a lump in her throat and got up. She turned when she reached the door. "Dad, Ma, I know this is hard, but I hope in time you'll be able to see it's not as bad as you think. And you'll be happy for me."

"Leave! Now!"

Leela stepped out and shut the door behind her. She leaned against it to support her wobbly legs.

That went well.

CHAPTER FORTY-ONE

Leela paid no attention to the whine of the ambulance. Being right on the noisy main road meant this was a common occurrence. Neil, who had been out on the balcony (on the phone with Radha, if Leela had to guess), came inside and announced, "There's an ambulance in front of the building."

Leela looked up from her crossword. "Is it DeSouza Uncle again, I wonder? I should go check." She set down her pen and stood, looking for her mobile phone.

Neil went back outside.

"Ma!"

His shriek made Leela's heart almost stop. He ran into the room, his face ashen. "It's Grandma! They're taking Grandma!"

Leela was out of the flat before Neil had finished. She didn't even stop to put on shoes. She heard the front door crash into the wall as she ran down the stairs, past her parents' closed door, and through the lobby, out to the road.

The ambulance was just pulling away and a bunch of neighbours were gathered around the front. Old Mr. DeSouza was the first to notice her.

"Leela? Where were you? Your father said—"

"What happened?" Leela cut in, panting, her heart racing and yet her extremities numb with fear.

One of the other neighbours came over and put a hand on Leela's shoulder. "She had some chest pain, Joseph said, and breathlessness. They've taken her to Apollo."

"Ma?" Neil's voice was shaky. But it was the only thing that kept Leela's legs from giving way and leaving her collapsed in a heap.

She caught his arm, as much to reassure him as to support herself. "Don't worry," she said, surprised to hear her voice so calm and steady. "We'll find out what happened. Let's go up and get some shoes and proper clothes, and we'll go to the hospital."

"Leela, do you want me to drive you?" Old Mr. DeSouza's son, Sunil, asked.

"No, I'm okay, I'll manage." Leela attempted a smile. "Thank you, though."

"Anything you want or need, just ask, okay?" Sanjana Rao from the flat opposite her parents' said.

"I will, thanks." She turned and went up the stairs with Neil, almost missing Mr. DeSouza's whispered words.

"How odd that Joseph hadn't realised Leela was at home."

When this was over—and Ma had better be okay—she was going to be livid at her father.

* * *

The reception desk at Emergency was thronged by anxious friends and relatives. Leela managed to manoeuvre her way through to the front, only to be told that no Elsie Saldana had been in. She was ready to scream, but the terrified look on Neil's face forced her to hold it together.

Calm down. Think. Maybe her mother had been directly admitted or her neighbours' information had been wrong and she was in a completely different hospital. But then there had definitely been that familiar logo on the ambulance, of a woman holding a torch.

"Come on." She took Neil's hand and they went around the hospital building to the main reception. After standing in line for another twenty minutes, she was told that yes, Elsie Saldana had indeed been admitted to the cardiac unit.

"Can you tell me how she is?" Leela asked.

"Are you a relative?"

"I'm her daughter."

"Okay." The receptionist picked up the telephone receiver, punched some numbers, and spoke to someone on the other end. He put the phone down and looked at Leela. "She's stable."

"What?" Leela gripped the edge of the desk. "What does that *mean*? What happened to her?"

"Madam, I don't have that information. You will have to find out from the doctor."

Leela wanted to reach across and strangle him, but Neil tugged at her sleeve. "Ma, look." He pointed to the list of departments on a pillar, which said that Cardiology was on the third floor. "Let's just go up and find her."

They ran towards the lifts, but all of them were up on the seventh floor.

"Stairs," she barked at Neil. They made it to the third floor and asked for Elsie Saldana at the nurses' station.

"Room three-nought-nine."

"You wait here, okay?" Leela told Neil.

She darted down the corridor, peering at the numbers on the doors. She dodged a patient shuffling past, dragging an IV stand with him. Ah, there it was, 309. That her mother was in a room and not the ICU was a good sign, right?

She pushed the door open to enter a double room, with a curtain separating the two patients. Her mother lay on the bed, her eyes closed. Leela rarely saw her look so peaceful. There was a doctor and a couple of nurses, and sitting on a chair in the far corner, her father.

Joseph Saldana seemed to have aged ten years since the last time Leela had seen him, more than a month ago. He gripped the armrests so hard that his knuckles had turned white. He leaned forward, his shoulders hunched as he watched the doctor. His eyes had sunk into his face. He looked crushed.

Leela had never seen him so vulnerable. She wanted to go to him and put her arms around him.

And yet, when his eyes met hers, they narrowed with a rage that belied his distress. He started to rise but the doctor turned before he could say anything, and Leela recognised Dr. Prakash, her father's cardiologist.

"Ah, Leela," he said, grinning at her like it was a social call. "I was just going to ask Joseph where you were."

"I…er…Is my mother okay? What happened?" Leela's voice shook.

"There's no need to worry. It was a panic attack—the symptoms are very similar to a heart attack. We're just keeping her overnight for observation."

For the second time that night, Leela wanted to sag to the floor. Dr. Prakash droned on, but she didn't hear a word he said. She went closer to her mother and put a hand on her arm. Elsie looked so calm and harmless and small.

"I'll come and see her tomorrow, and we'll discharge her," Dr. Prakash continued. He laid a hand momentarily on Leela's shoulder. "You take care and don't worry."

"Thank you, Doctor."

"You're welcome."

The moment Dr. Prakash stepped out of the room, Leela turned to her father. "Why—"

Joseph's eyes were two pieces of coal. "Get out," he said. His words, so matter-of-fact, so emotionless, hit Leela like a slap.

The nurse, who was tinkering with machines that Elsie was connected to, gasped. She gave Leela a stricken glance and then put a hand on Joseph's arm. "Uncle, you don't know what you're saying. You need your daughter at a time like this, okay?"

"I don't have a daughter," Joseph said.

Leela squeezed her eyes shut for a moment. "Dad, stop this now. Have you called anyone else? You can't seriously think you're going to do this alone."

"It's not your business anymore. Leave now. And don't contact anyone in the family."

A prickle of anger rose inside Leela. "Okay, if you want me to leave, I'll go," she said. "But she is my mother, and this is my family too. I will do whatever I feel I need to do."

She turned and left the room. She followed the signs for the restroom, shut herself in a cubicle, and only then allowed herself to break down. All the complex and contradictory emotions related to her parents jostled each other to pour out of her all at once.

It took her a couple of minutes to compose herself. Then she took her phone out of her jeans pocket, found the number she wanted, and pressed the dial button.

Her father, possibly even her mother, might harbour fanciful ideas about having disowned Leela, but she still had a job to do—even if they were the most annoying people on earth. Whatever care her mother might need, her father was never going to be able to provide it, not after having spent all his life with no clue about how to run a house or look after anyone. So if she herself couldn't be the support they needed, she would get it for them from elsewhere.

"Hello, Lesley Aunty."

* * *

Lesley pinched Neil's cheek and zipped past his gobsmacked face. She dumped her purse on the coffee table and parked herself on the sofa next to Leela.

All of this happened in less than the time it took Leela to put down her book and take off her glasses.

"Care to tell me what's going on with your parents and you?"

Lesley was younger than her sister Elsie, and unlike her sister was sprightly, ramrod straight, and blunt—and still with a penchant for trashy romance novels.

"The short version is that Dad is being completely unreasonable," Leela told her. "He has this idea that I need to live my life a certain way—his way."

Lesley clucked her tongue. "Joseph Saldana was always an opinionated idiot. Be that as it may, you can't cut yourself off, no, Leelu?"

"Try telling him that." Leela threw her hands up in the air. "This is not my fault, not what I want. Short of barging my way into their lives, I don't know what to do. He even threw me out of the hospital."

"What is it that has made him so angry?" Lesley asked. Her expression was one of genuine curiosity.

Leela sighed. "He…disapproves of me, of how I live my life."

"What is it that he doesn't like?"

"I don't want to get into that."

"And that's it?"

"More or less."

"Is Elsie blaming you for her anxiety episode for the same reason?"

"Yes."

Lesley shook her head. "People are talking, you know. Everyone knows something serious has happened between you and Elsie and Joseph."

Leela shrugged, staring at the floor. "People talk. It doesn't change anything."

"We're family, Leelu. If you tell me what the problem is, maybe I can talk to your parents. Maybe some of the others can. Maybe someone at the church…"

Leela laughed. "No, I don't think that would help much. I know your intentions are all good, but it is…I don't think talking is going to do us any good."

"So that's it? You're cutting yourself off from them?"

"I didn't say that. They can pretend I don't exist, but I'm not going anywhere."

"But, Leelu, what about Elsie's health?"

"Do you think I should let my mother emotionally blackmail me into submission?"

Lesley pursed her lips. "Elsie is somewhat given to drama, isn't she?"

That is one way of putting it.

"This thing going on between you and your parents—well, I don't know, but if whatever you're doing is important to you, if it makes you happy and if they're trying to take that away, then you shouldn't let them. I love my sister to bits, but I know how stubborn she can be."

"Stubborn enough to make herself ill. I won't let her take this away from me, Lesley Aunty." *Not Nandini.* "It's not okay."

Lesley nodded. "You're right. You deserve to be happy. You're *allowed* to be happy. And over time Elsie and Joseph will come to understand that too."

PART VI

SEPTEMBER 2018

CHAPTER FORTY-TWO

"You look nervous," Nandini said, brushing a speck of lint off Leela's dress.

"You bet I'm nervous. I'm terrified," Leela replied. "I'm going to meet all your friends, and they are going to size me up and try to decide if I'm good enough for you."

"Well, they're all going to die of jealousy because you look ravishing." She pulled Leela in for a kiss. It was long and soft and unhurried, making Leela forget her nervousness.

"Anyway, you vain creature," Nandini continued when they broke apart. "It's Vikrant's birthday, so nobody will give you a second glance."

"Wow, thanks!"

Nandini gave her a peck on her lips, winked at her, and sat down in front of the mirror. Leela checked her phone—there might be an update from Neil or, less likely, something from her mother. But there was nothing.

"Your mum still pretending I don't exist?" Nandini asked her, her fathomless eyes on Leela through the mirror.

Will I ever stop feeling like I'll drown in them?

Leela grinned. Her parents had more or less put themselves on house arrest when Nandini had visited last month. It had been a most peaceful time. "Pretty much."

"Yet you think they're thawing?"

"I think whatever Lesley Aunty said to them after my mother's anxiety episode in July made some difference."

"I want to meet this Lesley Aunty of yours."

"Oh you will, sooner or later."

"And how's Neil doing?"

"Moaning about having to go to school during holidays, what else?"

"I feel his pain." Nandini made a face. "Extra classes, ugh."

Leela looked around Nandini's giant, split-level bedroom. Her bag was lying open near the cupboard—she hadn't had a chance to unpack. She smiled as a tingle ran down her body. Well, she would have unpacked this morning if she hadn't been otherwise occupied.

"What are you smiling at?" Nandini asked.

"Thinking about the welcome you gave me."

"Ah." She twinkled at Leela. "I'm good at those."

Leela laughed. "Smug much?" She went over and stood behind Nandini, squeezing her shoulders. "I'm really looking forward to this week—just you and me. No Neil, no parents pussyfooting about, no work, no grocery shopping or worrying about what to make for dinner."

Nandini's housekeepers had accepted Leela's presence with great equanimity, and this promise of being able to lie around and do absolutely nothing—unless it involved being naked, of course—made her want to weep with joy.

"I'm also good at great ideas, aren't I?" Nandini asked, tilting her head up so she could look at Leela.

"Fantastic." She leaned down and pressed a kiss to Nandini's forehead. "Wish you had some say in the weather, though."

"Oh, you Bangaloreans. Spoilt brats when it comes to weather. Hot and humid is exactly how we Delhiites like our September, I'll have you know."

"I don't care how hot it is, we're still going to Agra to see the Taj Mahal."

"That's the spirit." Nandini stood, pulling her top straight. "Now, are we ready to leave?"

"So, um, does everyone know about me?" Leela asked on the drive to Vikrant's place. The butterflies in her stomach were at it again, refusing to settle down.

"Well, most people know that I'm about as straight as a wet noodle, so they're probably going to put two and two together. Does it bother you?"

"No…I don't know. Among my friends, it's only Davi who knows. So far. I don't know how many other people I'll tell."

"You may not need to. People will just get used to seeing us together. Some people will figure it out, some won't."

"Yes, I know."

"I should warn you, Mita is going to be there. She's Vikrant's cousin."

"What!"

Nandini glanced at her as they stopped at a traffic light. "Don't worry. It'll be fine." She threaded her fingers through Leela's and squeezed. She didn't remove her hand till she pulled up outside Vikrant's place.

Of course, it had to be Mita who opened the door to them.

"N!" she cried, giving Nandini a bear hug.

Leela raised her eyebrows.

"And Leela, there you are again. So lovely to see you two together." Leela found herself engulfed in a hug that knocked the breath out of her lungs.

Nandini squeezed her elbow as they went inside. "See, I told you it'd be okay."

The names and faces that crossed her path that evening were a blur, but Leela didn't care. She only had eyes for Nandini. Every time her eyes met Nandini's—yes, across the room, over the sea of people—her heart soared. They were together. They were making it work.

Maybe this was what changing the world was all about—living your life the way you wanted to.

"I'm glad you came," Vikrant said when he was fixing her a drink.

"Thank you for inviting me," Leela replied.

"No, no." He seemed a little tipsy. "I meant, for coming to Delhi for the holidays. You've done quite the impossible, you know? Making Nandini settle down."

"Well, I don't know, she's always seemed pretty settled to me."

"You know what I mean. I don't recall ever seeing her this happy."

The words filled Leela with a warm glow, which remained wrapped around her all evening. The food was great, the people friendly, and later that night—rather, in the early hours of the morning, as they got ready for bed—Leela could honestly say that she'd had a great time.

"Was that so bad?" Nandini asked her as she lay in bed watching Leela brush out her hair.

"No, not at all." She flashed Nandini a mischievous grin. "I can promise you that Christmas with my family is going to be a very different, very painful affair."

"What?" Nandini looked aghast. "What's that about Christmas?"

"You're spending Christmas in Bangalore. Forever. You know that, right? My parents usually have a big do. They'll have to invite me or people will talk. And if I'm going, you're going. End of story."

Nandini sighed dramatically. "I suppose that's the price one pays. So does that mean I can strong-arm you into coming to Calcutta for Diwali?"

"You could try other means of persuasion," Leela said as she plaited her hair. "You have a great bunch of friends, though. I liked them."

"Thanks. They liked you too. What is it they say, that friends are the family you choose?"

Leela crawled into bed, burrowing under the light quilt they shared to stay warm in Nandini's air-conditioned-to-twenty-two-degrees bedroom. She lay her head in the curve between Nandini's head and shoulder, her arm draped over her stomach.

"Do you realise it's been almost exactly a year since we met in Amrudpur?" Nandini said softly, laying her arm over Leela's. "I'm glad you chose me."

Leela closed her eyes, letting contentment settle over her like a warm blanket. "I'm glad you chose me too."

Bella Books, Inc.

Women. Books. Even Better Together.

P.O. Box 10543
Tallahassee, FL 32302

Phone: 800-729-4992
www.bellabooks.com